Sara K Joiner

After
the
Ashes

Holiday House
New York

Library of Congress Cataloging-in-Publication Data

Joiner, Sara, author.
After the ashes / by Sara Joiner. — First edition.
pages cm
Summary: In 1883 thirteen-year-old Katrien Courtlandt is more interested in science
and exploring the Javanese jungle for beetles with her native friend than in becoming a
young lady like her despised cousin Brigitta—but when Krakatoa erupts, the tsunami
hits, and their families are swept away, the two cousins must struggle to survive together.
Includes bibliographical references.
ISBN 978-0-8234-3441-1 (hardcover)
1. Survival—Juvenile fiction. 2. Volcanoes—Indonesia—19th century—Juvenile fiction.
3. Tsunamis—Indonesia—19th century—Juvenile fiction. 4. Cousins—Juvenile fiction.
5. Families—Indonesia—19th century—Juvenile fiction. 6. Dutch—Indonesia—19th
century—Juvenile fiction. 7. Krakatoa (Indonesia)—Eruption, 1883—Juvenile fiction.
8. Java (Indonesia)—History—19th century—Juvenile fiction. [1. Survival—Fiction.
2. Volcanoes—Fiction. 3. Tsunamis—Fiction. 4. Cousins—Fiction. 5. Families—Fiction.
6. Dutch—Indonesia—Fiction. 7. Krakatoa (Indonesia)—Eruption, 1883—Fiction.
8. Java (Indonesia)—History—19th century—Fiction. 9. Indonesia—History—19th
century—Fiction.] I. Title.
PZ7.1.J65Af 2015
813.6—dc23
[Fic]
2014044158

*To Daddy and Papaw because I promised myself
the first one would be dedicated to you.*

*To Nana because she said I could do anything
I set my mind to.*

To #1 Mom because she is #1.

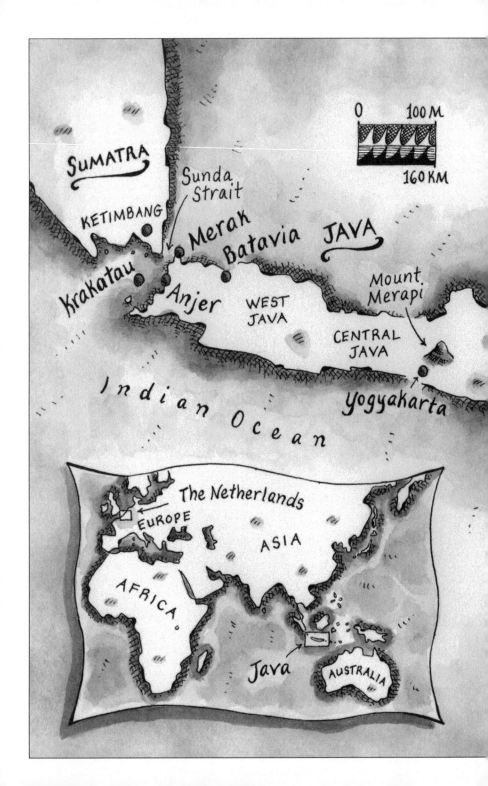

Anjer, Java, Dutch East Indies

3 NOVEMBER 1880

Dear Mr. Charles Darwin,

I recently finished reading *On the Origin of Species*, and it has opened my eyes to the world. Vader—that's my father—let me read it when I asked why the Asian paradise-flycatcher and the racket-tailed treepie both had long tails but didn't look alike.

Now I know they both evolved differently.

I see lots of beautiful birds and animals here. We live on the west coast of Java with the ocean near our front door and the jungle almost in our backyard.

I love the jungle. I explore it almost every day because I plan to prove your theory of natural selection. Did you know there are people who don't believe it's true? I'm going to do what you did and collect specimens—hundreds of them, maybe even thousands—to show how one species changes over time into a new species.

Lots of times my friend Slamet explores with me. He tells me about the plants and flowers in the jungle because I'm not very good with vegetation. I prefer animals. Slamet is native and knows all about plants. His mother is our housekeeper, but we've been friends forever. Do you think that's strange?

Some of the girls in my school think it's funny that my closest friend is a native boy, but I don't think so.

Those girls usually call us names when we go to the beach together. Slamet and I ignore them. On the beach we can see all the way to Sumatra and even the volcano on Krakatau.

Have you ever been to Krakatau? It's an island. No one lives there, but I'm sure some animals do. Birds could fly there without any trouble; it's only forty kilometers from Anjer. I long to visit, but neither Vader nor my aunt will let me. My aunt says it's too dangerous since it's a volcano. Vader said it's extinct, but he still won't let me go. It can't be that dangerous if it's extinct, can it?

Perhaps you could visit Java someday, and we could explore Krakatau together. I could be your assistant. No one could object then because you are an important scientist.

Thank you for writing *On the Origin of Species*. I loved it, and I hope one day to meet you.

Yours in admiration,
Katrien Courtlandt

Part One

Anjer, Java, Dutch East Indies

Chapter 1

I knelt down beside the giant strangler fig and reached within its latticelike trunk. There, hiding on the dying tree that was being suffocated by the surrounding fig, was a stag beetle—*Hexarthrius rhinoceros rhinoceros.*

"Careful," Slamet said. "Do not scare it."

"I won't. I've done this before," I reminded him. With gentle fingers, I plucked the insect off the trunk. It filled the palm of my hand. The enormous mandibles stretched out from its head. Some people thought they were horns. "Isn't it beautiful?"

Slamet shook his head. "I do not know why you like this."

"I'm proving a theory." I pushed up my spectacles. " *'We see the same great law in the construction of the mouths of insects.'* "

His face went blank, and I knew he didn't understand what I said. Dutch was not his first language, and Javanese wasn't mine. How could I explain about Mr. Charles Darwin and his theory of natural selection? I had read his book *On the Origin of Species* four times, but Slamet couldn't read at all.

"Never mind," I said.

He held out the funnel net, and I dropped the beetle in it with the other two I had already found, tying off the top of the net with string.

"Dank u," I said, standing up. As I did, my heel caught on my skirt and I plopped down in the mud.

"Aah!" I yelled.

With Slamet's help, I managed to get on my feet, though the brown muck stained the fabric. "My aunt won't be pleased." I tried to wipe off the filth, but it didn't do any good.

"She will punish?" Slamet asked.

"She won't be happy, but I doubt she'll do anything to me." I took the net from him.

We walked beside each other out of the jungle and toward Anjer. "You know what, Slamet?" I asked. "The capital is nothing like here." My aunt Greet, Vader and I had just returned from a three-week trip to Batavia visiting my uncle Maarten, and I was still in awe at all there was to see and do in the Dutch East Indies' capital city.

"It is far," Slamet said.

"*Ja*, but it's an easy trip by boat." Slamet had never been farther than Merak, twenty kilometers north of here.

"What do you do?"

"In Batavia?"

He nodded.

I pushed my spectacles up. "We did lots of things. We went to the zoo. I think Oom Maarten enjoyed that even more than I did. Lots of the animals there are ones I've seen here in the jungle. Though they did have some animals from Africa—a lion and a zebra."

"Zee-bruh?" He furrowed his brow.

"It's like a horse, and it has black and white stripes. Quite beautiful."

"You like Batavia?"

I thought about that for a minute. Like Anjer, Batavia was on the ocean, but the capital was much larger than my town. I couldn't hear the waves from Oom Maarten's little house. He lived miles away from the docks, which pleased Tante Greet. "There are undesirables at the docks, Katrien," she said to me. I wasn't sure what she meant by that. I only knew that not being able to hear the waves meant I didn't sleep very well.

"No," I said in answer to Slamet's question. "I don't really like Batavia. It's too . . . organized. Too contained."

He gave me that blank look again, and I tried to make myself more clear.

"The jungle has been beaten back. It's nowhere to be seen." We passed by some of the kampongs—the tiny thatched cottages of the natives—on the outskirts of town. "My favorite parts of the trip were walking Oom Maarten's dog. Torben gets so excited when he goes for a walk, and he barks and barks at anything—people, other dogs, the crocodiles in the canals."

We shuffled along in silence. The sounds of horses clopping through town and barking dogs intermingled with the croaking frogs and buzzing insects of the jungle. I took a deep breath in anticipation of telling Slamet the most interesting part of my trip.

"There's something else, Slamet. The strangest earthquake hit while we were there!"

Slamet was not impressed. "Earthquake is not strange."

He was right. Earthquakes hit Java all the time. "I know, but this one was. It lasted for about an hour."

His head whipped around to face me. "Hour?"

I nodded. "It was terrifying. Tante Greet and I took cover in a doorway, but the ground just kept shaking. Poor Torben sank to his belly and whimpered. Everything went quiet. Even the air seemed to vibrate. I've never experienced anything like it."

We paused while a young native boy ran across our path, followed by a white girl. They hurried to one of the kampongs, reminding me of Slamet and myself when we were that little.

"Strange thing also happens here," Slamet said, his brow creased. "While you are not here."

"What happened?"

"Ash rains down."

"What do you mean?"

"Ash falls from sky." He moved his fingers like falling rain. "Strange."

"When exactly did this happen while I was away?" I pushed my spectacles up.

He thought before saying, "Two weeks."

Chapter 2

Slamet and I hadn't gone much farther when more little children—native and white—ran past us. They were all heading to the same crowded kampong. I shook myself out of my reverie about earthquakes and ash and we followed them. Inside the kampong, a storyteller was beginning to spin a wondrous tale in the same deep, gravelly voice he'd been using since the days when Slamet and I would sneak here to escape our chores. The storyteller didn't speak Dutch, but he was so gifted that I could understand the tales anyway.

As the storyteller spoke, Slamet cocked his head and smiled at me. "It is *Butho Ijo*."

I smiled back. "I know."

Butho Ijo was one of my favorite Javanese stories. It was about a green giant who tells a woman how to have a child, then tricks her into giving up her daughter for him to eat. Fortunately, the daughter manages to destroy him with help from a hermit and a bag of magical objects.

The storyteller warmed to his tale. He made me jump as he raised his arms high above his head and deepened his voice for the giant. He hunched over when he played the hermit and fluttered his eyelashes when he acted out the daughter. I clapped along with the children when he finished the story and bowed.

At that point, Slamet poked my shoulder. "I go. Ibu needs me."

I nodded as he left to help his mother, and slowly I rose to leave, too. I wished I could stay all day and listen to the stories with the other children. I missed being that young, when my mother was still alive and I could run around and play with anyone. But I was thirteen now, and Tante Greet lived with us, trying to turn me into a lady. Girls I used to play with now thought I was odd because of my friendship with Slamet and my insect collection.

My aunt wanted me to be friends with those girls, but I found I had less and less in common with them. They talked about boys and bustles and babies. I wanted to talk about animals and science and natural selection. They giggled a lot, and always seemed to be looking at me when they did. I felt like a zoo animal on display in their presence.

Still, my aunt kept singing their praises. "Brigitta Burkart is a wonderful girl," she often said pointedly. "She's polite and kind and respectful."

But Brigitta Burkart was the worst of them all, and I hated her. Truly hated her. My aunt knew this perfectly well, and it infuriated me that she ignored my feelings and spoke so admiringly of someone I despised.

There was a time, not so very long ago, when I would have agreed with my aunt's opinion. Brigitta and I had been friendly once, thanks in part to our fathers. We were introduced years ago, as small girls, when Vader began working as the controller for Anjer and Brigitta's father assumed the higher-ranking government position of assistant resident. Vader explained all this very carefully to me one day when I asked him about his job. He sat me down at a table and sketched a simple, but accurate, map.

"You see, Katrien, the Dutch East Indies are divided into provinces, like so, then divisions, and then departments," he said, making each section smaller and smaller. "Assistant residents, like Mr. Burkart, are in charge of divisions." He pointed to an area that included Anjer and a few other towns. "Part of the job of an assistant resident is to oversee the regions' controllers. My responsibility as Anjer's controller is to carry out the administration of the department, which includes overseeing the police and collecting taxes."

I understood this to mean that Mr. Burkart was Vader's supervisor, and I was glad of it. Now that our families had begun visiting with each other, I had found Brigitta to be a fun playmate. For several years, the two of us passed those visits playing happily while the adults talked about grown-up things like the fighting in Aceh or other news they read about in the *Java Messenger*. Once we started attending school, Brigitta and I spent even more time together.

But all that changed on the day of Brigitta's tenth birthday party. Every girl in our class had been invited to celebrate at the Burkart family's fine brick mansion on the water. I knew already from my playdates with Brigitta that a small army of native workers was responsible for keeping the home immaculate and the grounds well manicured, but as I stepped onto the Burkart property that day, everything seemed to look even more spectacular than usual. Even the Dutch flag that always flew tall and proud from the pole on the luxurious lawn seemed to be flapping extra hard for Brigitta, and the assistant resident's boat that Mr. Burkart kept tied to his private dock bobbed merrily in the waves. I hoped he would take us all for a ride. What a birthday treat that would make!

I began to feel shy as I approached the house and a housekeeper ushered me inside, but in no time at all, I was on top of the world. Brigitta greeted me with a warm smile and soon made it clear that she was singling me out as special. She insisted I sit beside her at the table. She seemed to prefer the gift I brought her over all the others. And when we went outside to play windmills, Brigitta honored me again. She was the berger, the head of the game, and she picked Rika and me to be team leaders. All went well as we selected teams, but when the time came to begin, I happened to spot a stag beetle climbing on the side of the house. I could not believe my good fortune. In a way, the discovery felt like a present for *me* on Brigitta's special day. I plucked it off the wall and ran to show my friend.

"This is the fourth one for my collection," I said breathlessly, waving my prize under her nose. Brigitta's eyes grew wide in shock. She screamed and rushed into the house. Everyone else came over to see what the commotion was about, and when I held out the insect for them to see, they all backed away in horror. Rika even started to cry, and I started to get angry. I tried to make them understand there was nothing to fear, but their shouting drowned out my words.

Brigitta's father came onto the porch with Brigitta trembling beside him. She pointed at me and cried, "Katrien has ruined my party with that disgusting creature! She's disgusting, too! I never want her here again!" The other girls gathered around her in support.

Moments later Mr. Burkart was escorting me home. I cradled the precious beetle in my hands the entire way, all the while wondering how everything had gone so very wrong.

To this day I didn't know why my beetle collecting disturbed Brigitta so, but one thing was certain: our friendship ended the day she turned ten. And from that moment on, I would have given anything—maybe even my now-sizable beetle collection—to never see Brigitta again.

But of course, I couldn't possibly avoid her. I still had to face her in school every day, and worse, our families continued to see each other socially. Brigitta's and my relationship may have turned frosty, but the adults' was as warm as ever—which is why I was still subjected to monthly Courtlandt-Burkart dinners at the Hotel Anjer. How I dreaded those gatherings! I would rather spend an hour in a pit full of poisonous blue kraits than dine with the Burkarts. But, like so much else in my life, I had no say in the matter.

All these thoughts of Brigitta Burkart were making my head ache. Rubbing my eyes, I forced myself to think about more pleasant things. Today was a lovely day, after all. I had three stag beetles in my net, which increased my collection size to three hundred five, and I needed to prepare them for mounting. With a little hop, I hurried toward home.

But my eagerness vanished when I heard familiar laughter in

the air. Within moments, whom should I see up ahead but Brigitta, Rika and two of their friends, Maud and Inge, sitting on Inge's porch eating ginger buns. Rika was tearing bits of the bread and tossing them to the ground several meters away. A long-tailed macaque sat nearby and scurried over to grab the food.

Inge pointed. "Look how long his tail is."

"It is, however, possible that the long tail of this monkey may be of more service to it as a balancing organ in making its prodigious leaps, than as a prehensile organ," I thought.

"It's a good thing you're tossing those scraps so far," Brigitta said, patting her perfectly styled blond hair. "I wouldn't want him coming any closer to us."

"He wouldn't hurt us, would he?" Rika asked, her eyes wide.

I shook my head. This was ludicrous. Why was she giving her ginger bun to a monkey? "You shouldn't be feeding him at all," I said, walking up to the steps.

Brigitta turned her catlike eyes on me with a scornful glare. "You're one to talk, Katrien. Don't your neighbors feed the monkeys?"

Our neighbors, the De Groots, were an older couple who danced outside under the full moon. They also mashed bananas and smeared the paste onto sticks. Then they placed the sticks in their tamarind tree and encouraged the long-tailed macaques to enjoy a free meal. I loved the De Groots. They were eccentric, but kind and wonderful neighbors. "They feed them what they eat in the wild," I said. "Not ginger buns."

"But he likes the buns," Rika said, pointing to the monkey. He had run under a nearby tree and was clutching the bread tightly in his hand.

I shook my head. Poor thing. Of course he liked the buns. He would probably start raiding people's compost piles and trash now. Vader always said not to feed wild animals. He even tried to get the De Groots to stop, but they refused.

"When he has to be killed after he invades someone's kitchen looking for scraps, you'll only have yourselves to blame," I said.

Brigitta stomped halfway down the front steps and looked down her nose at me. "For goodness' sake, Katrien, he's only had a few bites. Don't take it so seriously."

"It is serious!"

She rolled her eyes. "You're so melodramatic! Not everything is about you."

Flummoxed, I stammered, "M-me? I'm not making this about me."

"If you say so." She crossed her arms and raised her eyebrows.

My arms tingled as if worms were crawling on me, but I couldn't move. All I could do was stare back at Brigitta and wonder how I had ended up in this situation. Tante Greet would not consider accusing people of indirectly killing monkeys a strong foundation to renew a friendship. But I didn't want to be friends with these girls. I only felt sorry for the macaque.

"Why are you even here?" Brigitta asked.

"I'm on my way home." I jiggled my net full of giant stag beetles in her face. "I have work to do."

She let out a little cry and jumped back, tripping over her skirt and landing with a thud on the dirty step. Dusting herself off, she glared and said through clenched teeth, "If you keep playing with bugs, Katrien, you might turn into one."

I responded by dangling the net until it touched her hair. She screamed, and Maud, Rika and Inge tossed their ginger buns aside to drag Brigitta away from me. The macaque dashed over and stole the sweet treats.

Safely back on the porch, Brigitta huffed and shuddered. "Are any of them on me?"

Her friends shook their heads, and I counted the beetles in my net to be sure. Three. *Whew!* "Stupid thing to do. Could have hurt the beetles," I whispered to myself.

"I hear you muttering over there, Katrien," Brigitta spat. "You are so strange. Go home and play with your stupid bugs. Leave those of us who have respectable interests alone."

My hands trembled with anger and tightened around my funnel

net, but I only retorted, "They are insects, Brigitta, not bugs. Try to learn something for once," before I resumed my journey home.

I had comported myself with as much restraint as possible, but inside, my anger shook me with a force that rivaled the tremors in Batavia.

Chapter 3

Plop!

I dropped the last of my newly deceased beetles into a pot of not-quite boiling water and listened as some of the liquid splashed over the sides and sizzled on the hot stove top. In the pot, the water undulated with enough motion to cause the insect—about the size of a deck of cards cut lengthwise—to dance and shimmy across the surface, softening its limbs.

On a piece of wood near the stove sat the stag beetle I had just removed. I carried it from the kitchen into the parlor where I had better natural light. With tissue paper, I carefully dried the specimen's spindly legs, powerful mandibles and other delicate parts, drinking in the details as I worked.

I pushed my spectacles up. This stag beetle had orange eyes. Not so unusual. The darker orange flecks were different, though. I hadn't seen those before.

This beetle also had a solid black body. All my other specimens had brown heads and thoraxes with abdomens that appeared more like polished walnut. Was this a mutation? Or something more important, like an incipient species? I would have to collect hundreds more samples to determine that.

I pinned the unique stag beetle onto the cork and glanced at my watch-pin. Less time had passed than I thought. The insect in the kitchen still needed a few more minutes to soften, so I had time to attack the next step in my stag beetle display, which I happened to dread most: the labeling.

Killing the beetles didn't bother me. That was simply a matter of placing each one in a glass jar with the lid tightly closed, which suffocated them. I explained this process to Oom Maarten once and he was horrified, but then, he didn't even like watching cats chase birds.

Boiling the beetles didn't bother me either, nor did pinning them to the display backing. But writing their names perfectly on those minuscule slips of paper with no drips, splotches, or spills? I shuddered.

It was then that I saw the sunlight was shining onto the varnished teak desk, lighting up my work space as if trying to encourage me. So, with a deep sigh, I set to work. I wrote as neatly as I could, but before long, the wooden pen began to shake in my grip, and black drops of ink splattered across the blotter and onto my fingers. Frustrated, I set the pen down and rubbed my face.

Drat. I forgot the ink on my fingers. I licked my upper lip and sure enough, a bitter taste filled my mouth. I hastily wiped at the ink smears that I knew were decorating my cheeks, and resumed scratching tiny letters onto the tiny paper: *H-e-x-a*...

On my sixth piece of paper, which would yield my second successful label if I managed it, I was startled by a sudden thump at the front door. Seconds later, Mrs. Brinckerhoff whirled through the double doors of our parlor, reminding me of a pink-headed fruit dove with her green skirts and pink hat. Mrs. Brinckerhoff never knocked. If I ever walked into someone's home unexpected, my aunt would have torn into me like an angry Javan tiger.

But Tante Greet considered Mrs. Brinckerhoff a friend, and that made all the difference, apparently. I didn't understand how. Mrs. Brinckerhoff was the type of person Brigitta would grow up to be.

"*Goede dag*, Katrien," she said, patting her brow with a gleaming white handkerchief.

I walked over to greet her, my aunt's reminders about courtesy ringing in my head. She kissed me three times on the cheeks—right, left, right—as was customary.

"Good day to you, too, Mrs. Brinckerhoff." I tried to sound polite, but I think I sounded more irritated. "How do you do?"

She let out a breath of air so massive that even her stiff hat moved atop her head. "The trip across the strait from Ketimbang was quite rough today. May I sit?" Before I could even nod, she eased into the overstuffed chair. "Is Greet home?"

"*Ja*, she is. I'll get her."

Horrid woman. As I left the room I thought of a quote from Mr. Charles Darwin: "*It would, indeed, have been a strange fact, had attention not been paid to breeding, for the inheritance of good and bad qualities is so obvious.*"

When I popped my head into the study, I didn't see my aunt. Instead, our housekeeper, Indah, was there, dusting the bookshelves and humming some Javanese tune.

"Indah, have you seen Tante Greet?" I asked.

"Pantry," she said in her thick accent.

Tante Greet stood inside the small room muttering numbers. She appeared to be counting jars of jam. A pointless exercise. Who cares how much jam is in the pantry? I almost spoke the question aloud, and caught myself just in time. No need to give Tante Greet an excuse to teach me yet another lesson. "You will need to know this when you run your own home, Katrien," she would say.

No, I would not need to know that. I had no intention of running my own home. Especially if it involved counting jam jars.

I cleared my throat. "Mrs. Brinckerhoff is here."

"Johanna?" Tante Greet shifted a bag of flour, rice or sugar—not sure which, they all looked alike to me—on the shelf.

"*Ja*," I said, wondering if she knew another Mrs. Brinckerhoff. I slunk out of the pantry.

"Katrien," my aunt called.

I poked my head back in the doorway.

She handed me a handkerchief. "Clean your face, please. You have ink by your mouth."

My cheeks burned hot enough to melt the ink right off. I rubbed my face. "Is that better?"

She touched my cheek. "I think you're going to need soap and water."

"Mrs. Brinckerhoff saw."

I expected her to be disappointed, but she surprised me and smiled. "She has children of her own. I daresay she's seen ink where it doesn't belong."

Stiffening, I said, "I'm not a child. I'm thirteen."

"Go clean your face, Katrien."

I groaned but did as I was told. When I returned to the parlor, Mrs. Brinckerhoff had not moved a muscle. She sat rigid, like a wooden post being held erect by an invisible string. I longed to poke her. Instead I said, "My aunt will be right with you."

She nodded, staring out the open doors at the Ousterhoudts' across the street. The flowers in their front yard caught everyone's attention. Deep reds, vibrant purples, golden yellows, bright oranges—they grew with wild abandon stretching from the ground up to and above the porch roof as if they were trying to impress God. Tante Greet seethed every time she saw them. Her own flower beds had more weeds than blooms.

I was trying to think of something to say that sounded polite and grown-up when a short screech erupted from the kitchen. I jumped, and Mrs. Brinckerhoff, I was pleased to notice, clutched her chest.

"Katrien!" My aunt's voice carried down the hall.

I rushed out of the room. "What?"

Tante Greet, pale and shocked, stood in the kitchen pointing at the stove. "You forgot something."

"Oh, no." My stag beetle! I peered into the pot of water, now at a full boil. The beetle dipped and dived like a ship in a storm-tossed sea. Pieces of the mandible had broken off, and its legs floated and bobbed beside it. He looked mushy, too. I rubbed my eyes and groaned.

"Get rid of that thing, Katrien. Next time you do this, you do *not* leave the kitchen. And make sure you always use *that* pot!"

"*Ja*, Tante." I grabbed some cloths and hauled the pot of water off the burner.

She shuddered. "I can't abide the idea of a boiled bug."

"Insect," I corrected.

My poor stag beetle. Mutilated beyond repair.

"When you've finished in here, please join Johanna and me in the parlor for some civilized conversation."

Wonderful. Trapped in a room with Tante Greet and Mrs. Brinckerhoff talking about dress patterns. What could be better?

I looked up and saw that Indah had appeared at my aunt's side. Tante Greet shook her head as she left the room and muttered, "Never realized she used our kitchen pots for her bugs." Indah followed her with a tea tray.

Once the water settled, I hauled the pot outside and tossed the water—beetle and all—then joined the ladies in the parlor as I was told. The two women chattered like birds, but I still had labels to complete. I sat at the desk and waited for Tante to object. She merely said, "Sit up straight, Katrien," before returning her attention to her friend. "I have to admit I am surprised to see you, Johanna. I thought you would not be in Anjer until next month."

I adjusted my posture and returned to my labels. Trying to look on the bright side, I reasoned that one less beetle meant one less label, but that still meant I had work to do. Once the new beetles sat under glass, I would place the little identification labels below them and they would officially be part of my collection. I already had twenty-five cases filled with twelve stag beetles in each. I hoped to collect thousands of these insects to see natural selection at work, to see the process Mr. Charles Darwin described in beautiful detail in his book:

> "For during many successive generations each individual beetle which flew least, either from its wings having been ever so little less perfectly developed or from indolent habit, will have had the best chance of surviving from not being blown out to sea; and, on the other hand, those beetles which most readily took to flight would oftenest have been blown to sea, and thus destroyed."

Mrs. Brinckerhoff's haughty voice floated across the room and interrupted Mr. Darwin's words. "I told my husband to go over to the island and see for himself what was happening. I mean, the natives just had to be wrong. A beach does not blow up!" Her hands moved in imitation of an explosion. Then, with a sniff, she pulled herself even straighter. "I imagined it was some simple phenomenon that had merely overwhelmed their smaller brains."

I jerked at the insult and the movement made my pen slide across the paper. Another label was ruined. "Homo sapiens," I muttered.

Tante Greet, who had the ears of a leopard, heard me. "Language, Katrien."

Even though I had said the Latin name for human, I meant it as a curse, and my aunt knew it. "Apologies, Tante."

Mrs. Brinckerhoff ignored me. Or maybe she didn't hear. She blabbered on about commanding her husband to go to the island and investigate, which he did. It was probably a wise decision, or he would have had to listen to her constant nagging.

"And what did he see on Krakatau?" my aunt asked, taking a sip of her tea.

"Why, he said the beach had split open, just as the natives reported!" Mrs. Brinckerhoff gave the side of her cup a firm tap with her spoon.

The beach had *what*? I pushed my spectacles up, suddenly eager to join the conversation. "Was that about two weeks ago?" I asked.

"*Ja*," Mrs. Brinckerhoff said, surprised. "On the twentieth of May."

Tante Greet asked, "Do you remember, Katrien? We felt those tremors that morning?"

I nodded, remembering Slamet's story about ash falling. So the two events were connected.

But Batavia was more than a hundred kilometers from Krakatau. An earthquake on that small island should have barely registered in the capital. And it certainly shouldn't have caused tremors for an hour.

But Mrs. Brinckerhoff hadn't said it was an earthquake. She said the beach exploded.

What could have caused this? An eruption? From an extinct volcano?

"My husband hopes we can all go to Batavia in July," said Mrs. Brinckerhoff, changing the subject. "He said the circus will be there, and the children would love to see the animals."

"If the circus is in town, I can guarantee that Maarten will attend," Tante Greet said. "You've heard me talk about him. He might even have more fun than your children."

The two of them laughed, but I missed what was so funny. I wanted to hear more about Krakatau and growled in frustration.

Tante Greet turned to me. "You may be excused, Katrien."

"*Dank u!*" I fled the room, leaving my labels for later. Right now, I had to tell Slamet what I had learned.

Chapter 4

I thought I would find Slamet in the kitchen, but instead Indah was there now, scrubbing the table with strong, steady movements.

"Indah, do you know where Slamet is?"

She paused her scrubbing and said something in Javanese.

"What?" I understood some of the natives' language, but not much.

Indah sighed. "He is boy."

"I know."

"You are girl."

"*Ja...*" I drew the word out, unsure what Indah meant.

"I want..." She hesitated and stared out the window, muttering under her breath in Javanese.

"Indah, what's the matter?"

"He is"—She struggled with the next words—"at water." She nodded in the direction of the beach.

"Perfect. *Terima kasih*, Indah."

She indicated a plate of sugar-covered doughnuts resting on a table by the oven.

"You made *oliebollen*?" I could sometimes get such treats when we ate at the Hotel Anjer, but they were rare and quite a delicacy.

"First time." Indah held her head high. She excelled at making local dishes like rice and seafood but had trouble with Dutch food.

Tante Greet helped, since she didn't care for spicy Javanese food. My aunt would be thrilled that Indah had made something Dutch without any assistance.

I snatched an *oliebol* off the plate and popped it into my mouth. Still warm. "Mmm. These are delicious," I said around a mouthful of the sugary goodness. *"Dank u!"* Indah grinned, and I grabbed another one before running out the door.

Outside, the humid air slammed into me so hard that I took a step back. Thankfully, though, a gentle breeze sprang up and helped keep me comfortable as I walked. Squinting against the bright afternoon sun, I slowly inhaled the scent of coffee and tea, flowers and fruits, and the sweet smell of my *oliebol*. I took another bite and brushed sugar from my face and skirts.

Anjer songbirds trilled, greeting me with their cheerful chirps. Their chattering reminded me of something. I hadn't heard any birds on May twentieth. During those long tremors in Batavia, there was no birdsong at all.

I always noticed birds and animals, so I knew I wasn't mistaken. I paid strict attention to the sights and sounds of nature. It was how Mr. Charles Darwin made his great discoveries: by observing the lives of those creatures he saw every day.

Since I wanted to be a naturalist, I followed his lead. And I was in the perfect place to do just that, for interesting and unusual and amazing and beautiful creatures covered the entire west coast of Java. *"The Malay Archipelago is one of the richest regions in organic beings."* Mr. Charles Darwin's words spoke to my very soul.

I loved my town of Anjer. I loved the coastline at high tide with its pristine beaches. I loved the coastline at low tide with its exposed corals. I loved the jungle that awaited me less than a kilometer away. It was my temple. My sanctuary.

And the insects there! So many fascinating insects lived in the forest. I don't know what drew me to collect beetles; their appearance really was a bit terrifying. Brigitta wasn't the only person I had seen scream and run away from a stag beetle. Not only girls, but boys, too. Even men.

But somehow I loved them most of all. They were everywhere—clinging to leaves and plants, climbing walls and trees. Easy to catch and collect.

Tante Greet didn't understand my obsession with the beetles, but my father did. He encouraged me. Whenever I had questions concerning my beetles, or any other scientific matter, he would say, "Think, Katrien." Tante Greet may have wanted me to run a home, but Vader wanted me to learn, to use logic, to solve problems.

I strolled past stucco houses and weaved around kampongs while I pondered the silent birds and rumbling tremors of the twentieth of May. They were caused by an eruption, not an earthquake—at least, according to Mrs. Brinckerhoff's husband. I had only met him two or three times, but he seemed like an intelligent man. No reason to doubt his story.

Eating the last of the *oliebol*, I decided my next stop, after I found Slamet, would be to visit Vader. He could answer all the questions rattling around my head. Especially the most urgent one: How was it possible that a beach could explode?

Chapter 5

I was still mulling over the details of Mr. Brinckerhoff's story when I turned the corner by old Mrs. Schoonhoven's tiny cottage and came face-to-face with the open-air market. It was all that stood between me and the beach. The sharp scents of spices, fish, tangy fruits, pepper and tea wafted my way. Vendors yelled. Customers bartered. Babies cried. Underneath all the commotion, the ocean's waves pulsed their steady rhythm, adding a low roar to the market's sounds.

The first booth I passed belonged to our neighbor, Mr. Vandermark, who stood hawking his vegetables. He waved at me. Ever since he painted the doors of his home red, Tante Greet refused to talk to him.

"Brothels have red doors, Katrien," she had said.

"How do you know that?" I had asked.

"I don't, really, but red doors are immoral. Don't ever think of painting something red."

Not only had Tante Greet not spoken to Mr. Vandermark since, she refused to buy any of his vegetables.

Farther inside the market, the crush of people grew stronger. Bodies pressed against me, leaving traces of sweat on my skin. Even though the market had no walls, the sheer volume of people under the pavilion kept any breeze from blowing. I fanned my hand in front of my face, trying to find some sort of relief from the sweltering heat, and shoved my way through the masses.

I should have gone the long way past the Hotel Anjer to get to the beach. But now that I was practically trapped here, it occurred to me that one of the Stuyvesants' oranges would be delicious. Their grove on the edge of town was well known for producing the most delectable citrus fruit on the west coast of Java. Unfortunately, a throng of people swarmed around their stall like winged termites. It would take too much time to wait.

"Katrien," a kind voice behind me said. "How are you this fine afternoon?" I turned to see Sister Hilde, my favorite teacher, beaming at me.

"I'm well, Sister. And you?"

"I am as good as the Lord allows," she said. "Which is always wonderful." Her green eyes twinkled behind her spectacles. She leaned over and whispered, "You have a smudge on your specs."

"*Dank u*, Sister," I said, and moved on past her.

I reached into my pocket for a handkerchief and found nothing but a loose thread. I thought of asking Sister to borrow hers, but when I turned I saw she had been swallowed by the crowd. With a sigh, I wiped my spectacles on my blouse and promptly crashed into a young woman in front of me. I was forced to steady myself against her back, and as I pulled away I left a white mark on her dark blouse. Sugary remnants of my *oliebollen* still covered my hand, and now a stranger's clothes. "Terra firma," I swore, and rubbed my hand on my skirt to wipe off as much of the evidence as possible.

"I should have known it was you," a cutting voice said. I groaned inwardly as the young woman turned to face me. "You're the only person in Anjer who would use the Latin for earth as a curse. How nice of you to share your feelings with the entire marketplace." It was Brigitta Burkart.

A jolt of anger burst through me.

"At least I am honest about the feelings I show," I snapped. "You are all smiles and manners on the outside, but inside you are full of spite!"

She blinked and took a step back.

I pressed my advantage. "Now if you'll step aside—"

But Brigitta cut me off. "You think you're so clever, don't you? Doesn't Katrien think she's so clever?" She turned to Maud, Rika and Inge, her herd of dimwitted friends, who had suddenly appeared out of nowhere.

They nodded automatically. "So clever," Rika said with a blank stare.

I tried to move around them, but the four girls surrounded me and kept me trapped.

"It must be so lonely," Brigitta said, her voice full of false pity.

"What must?" I pushed my spectacles up and again attempted to get by. The beach wasn't much farther away. I could see the sand glistening over Maud's shoulder.

"Being you, of course," Brigitta said.

"What are you talking about?" I finally managed to push through their blockade, but Brigitta grabbed my arm and whirled me around.

"All you do is run around like a wild monkey, collecting those odious bugs. It's no wonder you don't have any friends. Even your aunt is tired of your behavior."

If she had slapped me, I couldn't have been more shocked. Tante Greet thought Brigitta had impeccable manners. If my aunt only knew how hateful and mean Brigitta could be when no one was watching.

I stood gaping at her and she huffed in exasperation. "You know, Katrien, if you weren't so strange, I might feel sorry for you."

Just then, Mrs. Van Tassel approached us. "Brigitta, that hat looks lovely on you," she said, smiling.

Brigitta's hostility vanished. She straightened and beamed. "*Dank u*, Mrs. Van Tassel. I adore it." It was a simple straw hat with one bright yellow silk flower, like those in the Ousterhoudts' garden.

"You must tell your mother to bring your brother by the shop. I normally make only ladies' hats, but I would make an exception for that adorable little brother of yours. He's such a doll."

"I'll tell Mother. We think little Jeroen is special, too."

I fought to keep from retching. The *oliebollen* I ate was less sweet than Brigitta at this moment.

Mrs. Van Tassel glanced at the rest of us. "Ah, to be young and have a bevy of friends again." Maud, Rika and Inge smiled politely, and I stared in disbelief as she walked away. Once again, Brigitta had convinced an adult that she was perfect and wonderful. How did she do that? How could she charm people so easily? Why couldn't I be like that?

Then again, no. I didn't want to be like Brigitta. She was a manipulative phony.

"I pity your brother," I snapped. "Having to grow up with you for an older sister is a fate worse than death."

Brigitta paled and her face fell. Then her gaze hardened. "Katrien, you should consider your words more carefully." She raked me up and down with a condescending glance. "At least more carefully than you consider your clothes. Even the natives look more civilized."

The bottoms of my skirts had mud stains almost up to my knees. And now the sugar from the *oliebollen* clung to the fabric. I didn't normally care about my appearance, but even I knew I must look like a beggar.

My aunt would be furious when she found out. Brigitta would certainly tell her father, who would inform Vader, who would tell Tante Greet, who would punish me.

At this point I knew I should ignore Brigitta's words. But she brought out my worst instincts. "Compared to you," I hissed, "the natives *are* civilized."

She gasped, and her friends recoiled as though they smelled something nasty.

I spun on my heel and stomped off toward the gleaming shoreline.

Chapter 6

I crossed the beach, my heart filled with fury and despair. Every time my heels sank into the sand I pictured them grinding into Brigitta's phony smile.

I would never admit this to anyone, but her words hurt. I didn't want to be an embarrassment to Tante Greet, but I dreaded disappointing Vader even more.

After I read *On the Origin of Species* for the first time, I wrote a letter to the author. Because of my abysmal penmanship, Vader offered to rewrite it for me. "So Mr. Darwin can read it," he had said in all seriousness. "In fact, I think we should translate this into English, since he is an Englishman."

"Can you do that?" I had asked, awestruck by my father's ability to make sure Mr. Charles Darwin could read my letter.

I remembered the excited shiver that passed through me when I signed my name to the letter. For months after that, I pictured Mr. Charles Darwin opening the letter and crying, "I must go to Java. Miss Katrien Courtlandt has offered to be my assistant. There can be no one better."

Only my father would go to such lengths for me. No one else treated me like he did, as a person with thoughts and opinions that mattered. He respected me. Recently, though, he had been frowning more and more at my stained skirts and dirty hands.

I pushed my spectacles up. Perhaps he wanted me to be more ladylike as well. I shouldn't jeopardize the freedom Vader gave me over a fight with his supervisor's daughter, even though it *was* all Brigitta's fault. That girl could make me lash out like a Javan stink badger.

On the horizon, Krakatau rose from the sea. A thin line of gray smoke stretched from its peak and reached into the sky like a strange storm cloud. Closer in, a small pilot boat was heading to the docks where my father had his office, and the Anjer lighthouse, tall and powerful, rested on a rocky spit of land about half a kilometer farther south.

But even closer to me, on the beach itself, stood Slamet, staring across the Sunda Strait. His black hair glowed in the bright light. Seeing him standing there drove thoughts of Brigitta from my mind. She was wrong. I did have friends. I had Slamet, and I hadn't seen him since yesterday afternoon.

"Slamet!" I called over the roar of the waves.

"How is your day?" he asked when I made my way up to him.

"Not well." I groaned and dusted my skirts in a vain attempt to remove any remaining sugar from the *oliebollen*.

"What happens?"

"Well...," I said. I decided to skip over my encounter with Brigitta. "Mrs. Brinckerhoff came to visit Tante Greet."

"Who?"

"Mrs. Brinckerhoff. She lives in Sumatra." I pointed across the Sunda Strait to the landmass directly west of us.

He shook his head and frowned. "I do not know this woman."

"There's no reason you should. She's horrible. You're better not knowing her, believe me."

He didn't say anything.

I groaned again. "I wish my aunt weren't friends with her."

"Maybe your aunt feels same about me. Your aunt does not like me, I do not think."

"No," I said, shaking my head. "No, she doesn't dislike you. But she thinks I should have more friends who are girls my own age and...background." I sighed. I was nothing like those girls, and I didn't want to be. Couldn't she see that?

Slamet and I fell into silence and watched the waves. Tiny bubbles popped along the water's edge as the ocean washed in and out, in and out. The rushing water was clear and bright, like the wings of a Javan kingfisher, and the words of Mr. Charles Darwin came to mind: *"Throughout an enormously large proportion of the ocean, the bright blue tint of the water bespeaks its purity."*

My gaze returned to Krakatau. Looking at the smoking volcano, I was reminded of the interesting part of Mrs. Brinckerhoff's visit. I pushed my spectacles up and proceeded to tell Slamet everything Mrs. Brinckerhoff had related about Krakatau and the exploding beach. "That was on the twentieth, Slamet. Two weeks ago. The same day you said it rained ash, and when we felt those tremors in Batavia. They must be connected."

"*Ya.*" He nodded. "We hear noises here for two days."

"You did?" We hadn't heard any noises in Batavia, but Krakatau was a long way from the capital.

"*Ya*, and ash is soft and warm and sticks to nothing."

"Sticks to nothing?" I thought about this, trying to decipher his meaning. "Oh! You mean *everything.*"

I knelt down to study the beach. All I saw was sand, no ash. "I wonder where it went."

Slamet crouched down beside me. "What do you do?"

"I'm looking for traces of ash." I stood and hurried to a cluster of nearby palm trees. I couldn't see any ash on them either. "Wouldn't it look like ash from the stove?"

"It does, but it rains."

"And it's all washed away," I concluded.

"Not..." He held his fingers a few centimeters apart.

"Not much fell?"

He nodded, relief that I understood him etched on his face. "*Ya.*"

The blue water stretching to Krakatau twinkled like diamonds. Except for the thin plume of smoke, I could see nothing different about the island. From where I stood, it did not look as if its beach had exploded only two weeks ago.

It was high time I spoke to the one person I knew who could make sense of all this. "Let's go find Vader, Slamet. He'll know what's happening."

Chapter 7

Slamet and I scuttled down the beach toward the docks. With the afternoon sun still high in the sky, we were sweating by the time we reached Vader's office. I wiped my forehead with the sleeve of my blouse, moistening the fabric.

As we approached the building, Mr. Burkart walked out the door. His back was ramrod straight, as if he wore a military uniform. I nodded at him, but he only raised an eyebrow in reply. Remembering the stains on my skirts, and my argument with Brigitta, I blushed and scurried inside Vader's tiny office, with Slamet right behind me. The doors and windows stood open, allowing the cooling breeze inside but keeping the hot sun out. Perfect.

Vader sat at his desk with his head in his hands, muttering to himself. "Don't know what I'm going to do...laughingstock... needs discipline."

Was he talking about me? I cleared my throat nervously, and Vader jumped in his chair. "Katrien!" He frowned. "And Slamet." He joined us at the counter. "What can I do for you?"

I repeated Mrs. Brinckerhoff's story in a rush, adding my information about the tremors and Slamet's about the ash. "What do you think is happening, Vader?" I asked him breathlessly.

I trusted my father with my whole being. His intelligence

surpassed that of everyone I knew, including the nuns who ran the girls' school and the priests at church. Vader spoke seven languages and knew geography and advanced mathematics and botany. He was teaching me Latin. If anyone could understand what had happened on Krakatau, it would be Vader.

But for the first time in my life, Vader disappointed me. "I do not know, Katrien. I would have to see the island for myself."

My shoulders drooped, and I felt like I had been dropped in the middle of the ocean, unable to touch the bottom. How could he not know? He had never been unable to answer a question I had.

Vader grinned. "You are in luck, however. I have heard that there are tour boats going to Krakatau from Batavia."

"Tour boats?" I asked at the same time Slamet said, "Why?"

"For just the reasons you explained. So people can see what is happening on the island."

"Can we—" I began.

He held up a hand. "No, we are not going. We will await their reports from here."

I frowned, and Vader smiled fondly at me. But his expression quickly disappeared, replaced by a look I couldn't describe. Not disappointment exactly, but not pleasure either. Realizing he was just now taking in my appearance, I was once more acutely aware of my dirty skirts and sweat-stained blouse. I fidgeted in front of him.

Slamet unwittingly rescued me by asking, "How do they know?"

"What do you mean?" Vader asked.

Slamet gathered his thoughts into Dutch words. "How do they know in Batavia what happens on Krakatau?"

"Tante Greet and I felt the tremors when we were there," I reminded him. "Although I think everyone thought it was an earthquake. I never would have thought it was a volcano."

"Especially one that is supposed to be extinct," Vader added in a worrisome tone. He stepped to the window and frowned at Krakatau.

"But how do they know?" Slamet repeated.

" 'Nor do we know how ignorant we are,' " I quoted.

"Mr. Darwin may have a point." Vader frowned again. "But I believe in this instance we can answer Slamet's question. Think, Katrien. How would people in Batavia be aware of something they had not witnessed? And in such a short period of time?"

My brows furrowed, and I paced. I pushed my spectacles up. Think. How would people know? "They must have gotten word."

Vader gave an overexaggerated nod. "And how would that have happened? Think."

I tapped my lips. "A ship captain could have seen it and told it to the harbormaster in Batavia."

Rubbing his neck, Vader nodded. "That is a good hypothesis, and I do not doubt that happened." Then he smiled. "But in this instance, I also happen to know Mr. Brinckerhoff sent a telegraph to Batavia." He pointed to his own telegraph machine sitting on a table beside him. "As I understand, the tours began yesterday."

I shook my head in amazement. "Technology certainly is wonderful."

Chapter 8

Slamet and I took the longer route past the Hotel Anjer on our way home. The hotel sat nestled in a grove of banyan trees with a porch wrapping around its entire perimeter. As we walked around the building, women in pale-colored dresses and showy hats strolled along the porch. They reminded me of the butterflies darting in and out of the moon orchids lining the porch's edge. I was more like a moth in my stained skirts.

A woman in a yellow dress and a hat covered in red flowers pointed at me and said something in a language I didn't understand. She was one of the many foreign tourists who stayed at the hotel.

"What does she say?" Slamet asked.

"I have no idea." But I could guess. Either she was shocked I was walking with Slamet, or...

The woman gestured to her hat and then to me.

I gasped and slapped my forehead.

"What?" he asked.

"I forgot my hat." I hadn't even thought of it when I left home earlier. It still hung from its hook on my bedroom wall. "Tante Greet won't be pleased."

"Why?"

"She says a lady should never go outside without a hat. She needs to protect herself from the sun, or she'll get spots."

"Spots? Like leopard?" His brow furrowed.

Shrugging, I said, "I guess. I'm not sure what she means. Or what the problem is with spots. Aren't leopards beautiful?"

"*Ya*, but you will look silly with spots." His eyes glimmered, and then he burst out laughing.

I chuckled, picturing myself covered with black spots. "You would probably look better with spots than I would."

"I will." He nodded. "My hair is color of leopard spots."

Slamet had black hair that gleamed, even in the moonlight. My own light brown hair was bland. And it was a mess. No matter how many pins I stuck in it, it always fell down by the middle of the day. Today I had only tied it back with a ribbon. I patted it gingerly. "Oh, no."

"What?"

"My hair is not even done up properly." Tante Greet was going to tear me apart like a crocodile. I was doomed.

Slamet's face puckered in confusion, as if he had bitten sour fruit. "What?"

"You see, I only pulled it back like this." I turned so he could see the ribbon and then blushed, wondering if he thought my hair looked ridiculous.

He shook his head. "I do not understand."

"Tante Greet would not appreciate me going out with my hair like this. It is not arranged correctly. I should have it braided or pinned in a more stylish way." I rubbed my eyes. I thought hair was a stupid thing to worry about. If my aunt were more like Vader, she would be concerned with what was *inside* my head. Or maybe he agreed with her now? The thought made me shudder.

At least Slamet concurred with me. "You will not worry on this."

I sighed. "I wish I didn't have to worry about hair either. Or hats. Or any of the other myriad rules my aunt has. Most of the time, I don't even understand them." What I said was true. Tante Greet had set these ludicrous rules for me, and half the time I didn't even know I had broken one until it was too late. It was like walking through a spider's web I didn't know was there.

"You have small problems," Slamet said.

"Tell that to my aunt," I mumbled.

"Hair. Hats. These are not our problems."

I plodded along beside him. "I wish they weren't my problems either." We were near the shops in the center of town, about halfway home.

"I'm going exploring tomorrow to look for more beetles," I said. "Do you want to join me?"

He furrowed his brow. "I see Raharjo."

"Oh." Raharjo was his older brother. Slamet had talked about him before, but something about Slamet's tone was different now, as if he had spoken out of turn. Was seeing Raharjo a secret?

"Maybe I could meet him," I said hesitantly.

"He lives in jungle."

"I don't mind that." I had been several kilometers into the jungle, sometimes with Slamet and sometimes without.

"Deep in jungle. You cannot go."

"What do you mean?" Slamet wasn't making any sense. He knew I had been farther into the jungle than Vader or Tante Greet allowed. "I wouldn't mind."

"It is time for men." He smiled broadly, and his dimple pinched his right cheek. "No girls."

I tilted my head. "Then why are you going? You're still a boy." I wiggled my eyebrows.

We laughed loudly right in the middle of town. People on the street stared at us with mouths agape. One of them, I noticed with annoyance, was Mrs. Brinckerhoff.

Chapter 9

After supper that night, I curled up on the sofa in the parlor with *On the Origin of Species* in my lap. Rereading Mr. Charles Darwin's words was like coming home.

Vader and Tante Greet stayed behind in the dining room talking. Their murmurs floated through the open doorway, adding to the night noises of buzzing insects and hooting owls. Soon they joined me in the parlor. Tante Greet worked on her needlepoint, and Vader read his newspaper.

The clock ticked in the hallway and chimed its song at nine o'clock. Tante Greet yawned. "I believe it's time for bed. *Goede nacht,* Katrien." She set her things back in their basket.

"Good night, Tante."

As she walked out, she nodded at Vader and something passed between them. "Niels," she said.

He grimaced.

I returned to my reading, but Vader came over and sat beside me. "I need to talk with you, Katrien."

"You do?"

He nodded, and I sat up.

"Did you learn more about Krakatau?" I asked.

"No."

"Homo sapiens."

"Katrien, please do not use Latin in that manner."

"Apologies, Vader. My emotions got the better of me." I placed a ribbon in my book.

"Your emotions seem to be getting the better of you quite a bit lately." He cleared his throat. "I understand you had a confrontation with Brigitta and her friends in the market this afternoon."

Surprised he had already heard about it, I stammered, "H-how did you—"

"So it's true."

"No," I protested, but the disappointment in his eyes made me confess. "*Ja.* But I wouldn't call it a confrontation."

He arched an eyebrow. "What would you call it?"

"A provocation."

"Who provoked whom?"

"She provoked me, of course." That should have been obvious, but Brigitta probably twisted the truth.

He nodded. "I thought you would say that."

"It's true! And how do you know about it?"

Hearing my tone, he gave me a sharp glance. "Mr. Burkart told me when he returned to the office late this afternoon. He was most upset about it."

"I'm sure he was." My legs dangled off the sofa, and I swung them side to side. "I'm sure Brigitta told him how awful I was to her. I'm sure Brigitta never even told him how hateful she was to me."

Vader ran his hands through his hair. "He seemed less interested in what was said between the two of you. He knows that young girls can be, shall we say, less than ladylike. His bigger concern was that this happened in a public place."

"But she started it," I said. "Why am I the only one in trouble?"

"Because of the two of you, you are my responsibility. I am sure Thomas is speaking to Brigitta about this."

"Ha! I doubt it. She's probably never gotten in trouble in her life."

He sighed. "Brigitta's situation right now is not your concern. According to Thomas, she questioned your wardrobe, and you snapped at her."

"That's not—"

"And I have to say," he said, not letting me finish, "that I noticed the state of your dress when you visited me this afternoon."

I felt like I had been pushed underwater. Vader was siding with Brigitta?

His eyes filled with sadness. "Katrien, I realize that your disregard for how others see you is partially my fault."

I shook my head. "I don't—"

He held his hand up. "I accept that responsibility. I wish your mother had not died, and I wish I had sent for Greet sooner. I wish you had siblings. I wish a great many things for you."

"But Vader—"

"The only thing I would not see changed for you is your intelligence and your curiosity. But I'm afraid that will not be enough to see you into adulthood."

"What do you mean?"

He shifted in his seat. "You have to know more than science, more than logic, more than books to get along in this life."

I pushed my spectacles up. Was Vader telling me I should stop reading? Stop wondering about the world? Stop trying to prove natural selection? "Do you mean I need to know needlepoint or something?" I asked, pointing to Tante Greet's basket.

"No." He chuckled. "Although that is not a bad skill. But everyone relies on other people. All my life I've had people helping me along the way—my parents, your mother, Greet and Maarten. Not to mention teachers and neighbors and even strangers."

"I have people, Vader. I have you and Tante and Oom Maarten. Indah and Slamet. Even Sister Hilde."

"For now," he said quietly. "But you are no longer a young child. Your behavior can no longer be justified by saying you don't know better."

"I don't understand. What have I done that's so terrible?"

With a sigh, he said, "It is not a particular thing you have done that is at the root of this problem, Katrien. You haven't committed a crime or created a scandal. But the little things you do—cursing, wearing stained skirts, being impertinent—these things all lead up to people not wanting to be around you, not wanting to help you."

"I don't want help from people who are offended by such simple things." I rubbed my eyes. "For goodness' sake, it's not as if I killed someone." How could I be hurting people if I wasn't causing them pain?

He squeezed my hand. "If Slamet treated you the way you treated Brigitta, how would you respond?"

"I don't know."

"Might you avoid him, so you wouldn't have to be treated that way anymore?"

"I might."

"That's what others will do to you if you keep up this reckless behavior, Katrien. Do you understand?"

I nodded, though I was still unsure what the problem truly was.

He stared at me a moment as if he was debating what to say next. When his words came, though, they were firm. "Tomorrow, you are going to stay home and assist your aunt."

"What?" I sat up straighter. "I'm going to the jungle tomorrow. To collect more beetles."

"No," he said. "Tomorrow you will help your aunt. You will do as she asks, and then we will eat supper at the Hotel Anjer—"

I opened my mouth to speak, but he raised his voice. "—where you will be polite, courteous and respectful. I've talked to Greet about this. If you can't behave tomorrow, we'll be forced to limit your jungle excursions."

"You can't be serious!" I was consumed by rage. He couldn't do this. The jungle was where I felt most alive. The jungle was where I took solace. The jungle was where I found my stag beetles. My work was in the jungle.

"I am serious, Katrien. The one thing you enjoy most is exploring in the jungle. If you can't behave properly, you will only be able to go to the jungle twice a week. Am I making myself clear?"

Still furious, I growled, "*Ja*, Vader."

He smiled. "Now, *goede nacht*."

"Good night," I grumbled.

He left the room, shoulders drooped.

As soon as I heard the click of his bedroom door, I threw myself across the sofa, screaming into a pillow and beating the cushions. I treated those cushions the way I longed to treat Brigitta. Why did I have to be punished for her behavior?

When my arms at last grew tired, I sat up and picked up the pillow, now damp from catching my screams. I stared at it. My aunt had needlepointed a proverb on the front with orange thread. "A good example will gain much following." I flung the pillow across the room. They all wanted me to use Brigitta as an example of proper behavior. But they didn't see the real person she was.

I would not let myself become someone like her. I would not!

And now Vader was threatening to limit my jungle excursions if I didn't behave properly? If I didn't behave like Brigitta? She was a conniving, manipulative phony.

But wait.

Couldn't *I* do that? Couldn't I pretend to be pleasant and polite, just as she did? After all, it wasn't as if I belched or picked food from my teeth. I could be polite at supper. Perhaps I could follow Brigitta's example. I would only really need to be a phony when it came to dealing with her.

And then I wouldn't lose my privileges.

I could do this. I had to.

Chapter 10

It rained the next morning. After breakfast I helped Tante Greet finish organizing the pantry. I took notes while she counted. "We're fairly well stocked, Katrien, but look. We do need to buy some rice and sugar. Perhaps we can get that tomorrow." I dutifully made a note of it. When we were finished in the pantry I had to wind all the clocks and sweep the porches.

After lunch, it was even worse. Tante Greet looked at the clearing sky and took on the appearance of a general. "Come along, Katrien. We still have much to do. Perhaps you'll be glad to know our task will take us outdoors." She pushed her chair under the table. "Don't forget your hat," she said pointedly.

I grabbed my straw hat and took my time tying it on my head before trudging after her to the flower garden.

On my way out I thought of Mr. Charles Darwin. "*It is the damp with the heat of the tropics which is so destructive to perennial plants from a temperate climate.*" I would have laughed if I didn't know how much Tante Greet missed tulips. When she arrived in Java five years ago she had tried to grow some, but they didn't even sprout, so she planted roses instead. They didn't care for the climate either. Vader suggested she try native tropical plants, but she refused. "I will have some culture here, Niels," she had said.

"And culture means roses?" Vader had asked.

When I stepped oustide I found Tante Greet already kneeling in the dirt, yanking weeds.

"Where do you want me to help?" I asked.

She looked at me from under the broad brim of her hat. "Ah, my favorite niece finally joins me."

I pushed my spectacles up. "I'm your only niece."

"Thank the stars. I couldn't handle another one. And please lift your spectacles. Don't push them."

Ignoring her, I said, " '*The more nearly any two forms are related in blood, the nearer they will generally stand to each other in time and space.*'"

Tante Greet paused. "Are you quoting Darwin again?"

I grinned. "If you don't want my help, I can always go work on my beetle collection."

She rubbed her back. "Those filthy bugs. Of course you'll help me. That's what Niels and I agreed to." She pointed to the other flower bed, and I noticed her gloves. Those gloves, caked in years of dirt, kept her hands smooth and soft.

Without some gloves of my own, my hands were unprotected. Not that it mattered. They were already covered in small nicks and scratches from my treks through the jungle.

Tante Greet seemed to know what I was thinking. "There is another pair in the gardening trunk. They should fit you."

Running around the house to the side porch, I dug through the trunk until I found the gloves. They did fit. My aunt and I both had long slender fingers. I hurried back to the flower beds and saw a disapproving gleam in her eyes.

"Katrien, you need to walk, please, and not run."

"But I always run in the yard."

Even though she knelt in the dirt, she straightened her back and seemed to loom over me. "I know, and I am telling you not to do so. Do you understand me?"

I nodded miserably.

A tremendous sigh escaped Tante Greet's lips. "Katrien, what am I going to do with you?"

Even your aunt is tired of your behavior. Brigitta's words buzzed in my brain. I swatted them away like a fly. "Why do you have to do anything with me?" I asked.

"Because you have to grow up. You have to be a productive member of society."

"I will be." I knew my beetle collection would prove valuable one day. It would prove the theory of natural selection. It was my work.

"How?" Tante Greet tilted her head.

I rubbed my eyes and tried to explain myself. "Mr. Charles Darwin says—"

"Darwin," she huffed, "is part of the problem."

"What problem?"

"My dear, you don't even have any friends," she said.

She sounded like Brigitta, and I hated that she was echoing my worst enemy's words. "That is not true!"

She arched her eyebrows.

"Slamet is my friend. And Vader." I bent down and plucked weeds to avoid her eyes. Did she notice I didn't include her?

"I mean you have no girlfriends, Katrien."

"You mean like Mrs. Brinckerhoff? No, thank you."

"Katrien," she warned.

"I do not like that woman."

Tante Greet clucked disapprovingly. "Johanna is a kind woman."

"Kind?" I ripped weeds from the ground with more force, pretending each one was Mrs. Brinckerhoff. "She waltzes into our home like she owns it. Demands I find you. Doesn't say please or thank you. How can you defend her? She's rude."

"I wish you wouldn't be so quick to judge." She wiped her brow. "Put yourself in her place. Have some empathy for her."

"If I put myself in her place, I would realize what a horrible person I was." I yanked at a long bit of greenery and it came loose from the soil. If only I could remove Mrs. Brinckerhoff from my life with such ease. Or better yet, Brigitta.

Tante Greet's lips pressed together. "I find that hard to believe, as you're being a pretty horrible person yourself right now."

I gasped. "What do you mean? I'm helping you weed."

"Katrien"—she crossed her arms—"you arrive at your opinions far too easily. And, I might add, they are usually uninformed. Also, you hardly ever consider changing your mind."

"That is not true," I cried.

"What do you think of Rika Spoor?" she challenged. Her voice had turned sharp, like a knife, and I wasted no time responding.

"She's an empty-headed piece of fluff."

Tante Greet raised an eyebrow. "And when did you form this opinion?"

"Years ago, and she has never done a thing to prove me wrong."

My aunt's expression changed from frustration to disappointment. "Rika may not be as smart as you are, Katrien, but that does not mean you are better than she is. We all have our strengths and weaknesses. You need to learn yours, so you can improve as a person."

"What does this have to do with Mrs. Brinckerhoff?"

"This is not about Johanna. This is about you. I need you to be more empathetic. Can you try?"

"Fine," I grumbled so she would stop talking.

She pulled some more weeds. "And Johanna is my friend, Katrien. You will treat her with all due respect. Believe it or not, she has your best interests at heart, too."

With a loud huff, I said, "She most certainly does not."

"*Ja*, she does." My aunt's voice returned to its usual calm tone, frustrating me further. "She has helped me a great deal with you."

"What?" I choked and pushed my spectacles up. *Helped? How?*

Tante Greet shot me an irritated look. "Lift them, please. Johanna has given me good advice about being a mother—a surrogate mother, in our situation. I'm not sure I would be here right now without her support and friendship."

"If I acted the way she does, you would rip into me like a leopard cat." I jerked at a tenacious weed and fell back on my heels.

"Johanna conducts herself as she does in our home because she knows she is welcome here, Katrien. If you were friendlier with other girls, you would understand that feeling."

"What is that supposed to mean?" Sometimes I thought my aunt spoke in riddles.

Tante Greet turned to me, resting her hands in her lap. "Katrien, all young women need girlfriends. They need someone to chat with, to share their hopes and dreams with, to gossip with, to be silly with."

I grasped another weed and tore it from the earth. "I chat with Slamet, and I'm not interested in those other things."

My aunt raised her eyebrow again. "When you have a girlfriend, no matter how much time goes by between visits, the two of you can begin a conversation as if neither of you has left the room. Do you see what a gift that is?"

I shook my head.

She sighed. "Some things can never be explained. They can only be experienced."

"How does any of this explain Mrs. Brinckerhoff's rudeness?"

My aunt turned back to the weeds. "She is not rude, Katrien. For the hundredth time, she is my friend. She comes a good distance in order to visit, and she is always welcome in our home. We'll leave it at that for now."

I brushed bits of grass away from my aunt's plantings. The poor roses she put in three years ago suffered in the heat and the salty breezes. They were scrawny and full of thorns, but she kept trying to get them to grow. She wouldn't give up on them. Nor would she give up on me.

Still, even with the weeds gone, the rosebushes looked pathetic. *"Eggs or very young animals seem generally to suffer most, but this is not invariably the case,"* I thought.

A strangled noise made me turn, just in time to catch my aunt scrambling away from the spot where she had been weeding. Her face was as white as our stuccoed house, and her breath came in short, sharp bursts.

"What's the matter?" I asked.

She raised a shaky hand and pointed.

I followed her gaze. "Oh!"

"That thing just flew down and landed right beside me!" She clutched her chest. "It flew!"

"It is a flying gecko."

"It flew like a bird."

"No." I patted her shoulder. "They don't fly; they can only glide."

"Please get rid of it." She used her handkerchief to dab her brow.

I scooped the reptile up in my fingers. Holding it gently but securely, I brought it over to Tante Greet. "See?" I showed her the flaps of skin on its side and the webbed feet. "No wings, but these help it glide."

"I do not care, Katrien. That thing is hideous. It looks like a monster. Take it away."

The De Groots had a huge tamarind tree in their yard. The gecko would do well there.

It jumped onto the trunk as soon as I placed my hand against the bark. Its grayish green skin was the perfect camouflage. From just two steps away, I could no longer spot it.

"It's gone," I said, returning to the flower beds.

"Good. *Dank u.*" Tante Greet regained her composure and went back to weeding. I took my cue and rejoined her.

The sun crept across the sky as we worked. Perspiration popped up along my back and tickled as it trickled down my spine. Tiny insects buzzed around my ears. My knees protested. I had aches all over, especially in my arms. I simply had to stretch.

Tante Greet noticed when I stood. "Are you tired?"

"I'm not used to this work," I said, wiping my forehead.

"This should not be that tiring for you. You prowl through the jungle all the time."

"*Ja*, but that's just walking! I don't crawl around in the dirt trying to find insects."

She gave me dubious glance. "Katrien, I've seen your skirts. You would have a difficult time proving to me that you don't go crawling around in the dirt. And now the entire town knows how filthy they are." She shook her head.

Another needling reminder of how unladylike I was. "Do you want some water?" I asked. My question came out a bit harsher than I intended, but I wasn't trying to pick a fight.

She didn't seem to notice my tone. "I do, but I think I'll get it for myself. We both need to freshen up before supper."

I had nearly forgotten we would be dining at the Hotel Anjer that evening. The hotel had the best restaurant in town, and it was the type of place where people dressed for dinner. We didn't normally do that at home, but we certainly did at the Hotel Anjer.

Tante Greet rose and headed for the rain barrels by the kitchen door. "Did you know the *Fiado* has arrived in Batavia, Katrien?" she asked over her shoulder. "The restaurant has beef on the menu tonight."

My stomach lurched in anticipation. So this was the reason for dining out! Whenever Vader or Tante Greet heard the Hotel Anjer had beef, they made certain we ate there. My mouth watered and my stomach growled as I tried to remember the last time I had beef. It must have been many months, maybe even a year.

Rarely did the local farmers have enough meat for all the people who wished to buy it. Fish was far more common. With the appearance of the *Fiado*—a new type of steamship from Australia that could refrigerate perishable cargo—it was everyone's hope that deliveries of beef and other meats would come more often.

I pushed my spectacles up, grateful that Tante was too busy washing up to notice. How would the beef be prepared tonight? Slow-braised? Stewed? Or even Monk's Mince?

I joined my aunt by the barrels, jumping gleefully over the puddles that surrounded them. The rainfall this morning had caused them to overflow. Then, as I dipped water from one barrel into a small bucket, I thought better of my jumping and proceeded more carefully around the mud. I didn't want more stains on my skirts, or Tante Greet's wrath.

Tante Greet stood beside me, rinsing her hands and arms. "One more word about tonight, Katrien," she said. "We'll be dining with the Burkart family."

My fingers froze just under the surface of the cool water and I staggered, nearly stepping into the very mud I'd been trying to avoid. It hadn't occurred to me that this meal would constitute our monthly dinner with the Burkarts. But of course, given Vader's lecture last night, the timing of this month's gathering made perfect sense. Dining with Thomas Burkart and his family meant only one thing: dining with the wily Brigitta.

And I had promised Vader to be polite. "Canis lupus," I whispered—the Latin for wolf.

Chapter 11

A million fig wasps swarmed in my stomach as Vader, Tante Greet and I approached the Hotel Anjer. I tried to concentrate only on the beef I would have for supper and not the company around me.

A strong gust of wind from the ocean lifted my hat and I clamped my hand down on the scratchy straw. The late evening sun tinted the sky a radiant pink as we climbed the steps to the hotel, and the chattering of the people inside grew louder. Their laughter, the tinkling of glasses and the sharp sound of silver scraping against china followed us as we made our way around the porch.

Was Brigitta here already, giggling with her silly friends? Telling even more people stories about how improperly I acted the day before? If so, she was no doubt leaving out the part about how cruel she was to *me*.

A few people stood inside the dim teak-walled lobby when we entered, but none of them were Brigitta or her family. With any luck, they would be late, and I wouldn't have to spend as much time with her.

"Perhaps she won't even come tonight," I murmured aloud.

"Did you say something, Katrien?" Vader asked.

"Nothing, Vader." I removed my hat. The breeze coming in through the open doors blew strands of my hair loose, despite all the pins. Tante Greet made her disgruntled clicking noise at the little wispy bits of hair tickling my neck.

Wilhemina De Graff, a tall blond woman with a kind smile, stood at the reception counter helping a customer. Her dark blue-and-black dress mimicked the feathers of a crested jay.

Wilhemina amazed me. Only a few years older than I, she had traveled here from the Netherlands all on her own. Away from all the awful people she must have known. Such independence! If I could go off on my own, I would go into the jungle and never return. Maybe I would even go to the Amazon.

I waved at Wilhemina and followed my family to the dining room. Mr. Schuyler, the hotel owner, stood at the entrance, looking dapper in his white linen suit. His clothes and the gray hair at his temples made him look like a whiskered tern. He greeted us with his arms spread wide. "Ah, my good friend, Niels Courtlandt." He grabbed Vader's narrow hand in his pudgy one. "And his lovely family." He kissed my aunt on her cheeks. "How are you, Greet?"

"I am very well, Caspar, and you?"

"Oh, I'm quite pleased, quite pleased." He puffed his chest. "Katrien? You look lovely this evening. Are you trying to turn the head of a special young man?"

I choked on my breath and felt my face go up in flames. "N-no, sir," I sputtered. "Tante Greet made me dress for dinner." My aunt did not need to hear about special young men and heads turning. Ugh! Now she would speak of nothing else all night.

Mr. Schuyler smiled, and my father and aunt joined him. I pushed my spectacles up and glared at them. How dare they!

"Will the Burkarts be joining you this evening?" Mr. Schuyler asked.

"Ja," Vader answered, "are they not here yet?"

Mr. Schuyler shook his head and showed us to our table. Of course they weren't here yet. Brigitta probably changed clothes three times before deciding what to wear. She would be the one trying to turn boys' heads.

Why couldn't she do something useful with herself? I truly did not understand her. Even I admitted that she possessed intelligence. In school, she and I were often the only girls who could answer some of the more difficult questions the nuns asked. Why did she waste that talent? How could she stand spending time with Maud, Rika and Inge, who didn't have one brain among them?

As I took my seat I noticed Adriaan Vogel seated at a nearby table with his parents and younger brother. All of the girls in my class talked about Adriaan and how handsome he was, but to me, his mustache looked like a fuzzy caterpillar on his upper lip. Why would anyone find a caterpillar growing on a person's face attractive?

Other familiar faces filled the restaurant. Not surprisingly, we weren't the only ones hungry for beef. I hoped there would be enough for everyone.

Our table stood beside an open window and I was glad of it. A gentle breeze cooled my cheeks and the view of the Sunda Strait stole my breath away. The setting sun sparkled across the water's surface, giving it the glistening quality of topaz and rubies. The sight calmed my nerves and eased my embarrassment. Perhaps the rest of the evening would go smoothly.

Mr. Schuyler interrupted my thoughts. "Niels, while you're waiting for the Burkarts, I'll get you a bottle of wine."

"*Dank u*, Caspar," Vader said.

While we waited for the wine, who should come sashaying up to our table but Mrs. Brinckerhoff. It wasn't enough for her to come into our home unannounced; she had to ruin our meal as well. "Johanna, what a pleasant surprise," Vader said. "Katrien told me you visited the house yesterday. That was quite a story your husband had about Krakatau."

"*Ja*, it was." She appeared distracted. "Greet, may I speak to you for a moment?"

"Of course." She excused herself and joined Mrs. Brinckerhoff in an empty corner.

"I wonder what that's all about," Vader said, shrugging.

My heart sank. Seeing Mrs. Brinckerhoff's gestures and Tante Greet's stricken face, I knew. And I knew it wouldn't be pretty when my aunt returned to the table. It took all my strength not to flee. My fingers squeezed the bottom of my seat as tightly as a reticulated python constricts its prey.

When Tante Greet sat back down, Vader said, "Is everything—"

She interrupted him. "No, Niels, everything is not well." She whipped around to me, her lips white. "Johanna was just telling me she saw Katrien carrying on with some boy in the middle of town yesterday. Some native boy."

"What?" This caught me off guard. I thought Mrs. Brinckerhoff was going to tell Tante Greet about my hair or my not wearing a hat.

Even though he was disappointed in my behavior, Vader defended me. "That doesn't sound like Katrien. Is she certain of what she saw?"

"She is positive." Tante Greet's eyes never left mine.

Vader turned to me, eyebrows drawn together in a solid line. "Katrien, can you explain yourself?"

I opened my mouth, but the wine steward arrived. "Your wine, sir," he said, showing Vader the bottle.

While the steward poured, Vader and Tante Greet kept me locked in their gazes. "Well?" he said.

The steward set the bottle on the table and left. The wine sloshed a bit before settling.

"Katrien, what do you have to say for yourself?" Vader asked. His voice was quiet but forceful, and I heard him loud and clear in spite of the noise in the dining room.

I took a deep breath. "After Slamet and I left your office, we walked home through town. We teased each other and got to laughing. That's all! I was just with Slamet!"

"Ah, well, that explains it," he said, but the little crease between his eyebrows didn't vanish entirely.

Tante Greet's lips pursed. "She should stop being so affectionate with that boy."

"He's my friend," I said.

Tante Greet turned on me so suddenly that I jumped. She reminded me of a mongoose I once saw attacking a cobra in the market in Batavia. Swift and ruthless. "Katrien, you are thirteen years old," she hissed. "You are too old to be friends with a native boy. You are not a child anymore. You need to learn to behave yourself in public. You need to be more ladylike."

Hadn't she spent all afternoon lecturing me on these very things? I pushed up my spectacles and glared at my aunt.

"*Lift* your spectacles, Katrien," she said automatically. "Don't push them."

Vader tapped the table in front of me. "Remember what we discussed."

I balled my skirts in my fists and seethed. Blast Mrs. Brinckerhoff anyhow! I didn't care what Tante Greet said about her. The woman was the devil!

Vader took a small sip of wine and ignored my rage. "This is quite good."

Tante Greet sipped hers and agreed. "What do you think, Katrien?"

Since my thirteenth birthday, Vader had allowed me to have one glass of wine with dinner. I didn't like any of it, but that didn't stop Tante Greet from trying to teach me to savor its nuances. This was part of my education in the social graces, she said.

I resented performing for her tonight, especially when I had just been so thoroughly reprimanded. But I didn't have a choice. If I sulked, it would only lead to them limiting my visits to the jungle. They both sat and watched me like Javan scops owls. I drank a small mouthful and held the liquid on my tongue to taste the flavors before I let it go down my throat. "Ummm...dirt?"

"Your wine tastes like dirt?" asked a familiar, haughty voice.

I did not need to lift my eyes to know that Brigitta and her family had arrived.

Chapter 12

At the sound of Brigitta's voice I closed my eyes and tried to capture the peace I found in the jungle. When I opened them I sipped my wine once more. "*Ja*, dirt." It was always safe to say you could taste the earth in which the grapes grew...wasn't it?

"What a pleasure to see you, Brigitta," my aunt said, standing up and kissing her on the cheeks.

Vader stood as well. "Where are your parents?"

Brigitta waved her hand behind her. "Talking to the Vogels. It seems like all of Anjer is here tonight, doesn't it?"

She sounded like another adult talking to Vader and Tante Greet. I wished I had her ease with people. It would be so much simpler. She socialized so well, and I never could master the art of small talk. Asking people about the weather or other nonsense bored me. I didn't care what people thought of the weather!

My aunt turned her attention back to me. "Katrien, *dirt* is not a flavor you taste in wine. Please use proper terminology."

"Soil, then."

"What else?" she asked.

Brigitta watched me with scornful eyes, and any admiration I felt for her disappeared like sugar in tea. I took another sip. "I think...rosemary?"

Tante Greet smiled. "Very good, Katrien. You are learning. I just wish you would pick up these social graces as quickly as you do your science."

I frowned. I wasn't as bad as she made me sound, and she certainly didn't have to lecture me right in front of Brigitta. It wasn't as if I chewed with my mouth open.

Thankfully, Mr. Burkart and his wife arrived just then and my etiquette lesson ended for the night. Hands were shaken and cheeks were kissed. Even mine.

Then Mrs. Burkart settled little Jeroen into his chair, and the Burkarts took their seats. Brigitta, naturally, took the time to smooth her skirts first. My legs trembled nervously as I sat back down, and I called on God and Mr. Charles Darwin for help to get me safely through this meal.

Brigitta was seated next to me, and as she sank into the upholstered chair she gave her head an arrogant shake. Her blond hair, braided in an elaborate knot, glistened in the evening sun. Tante Greet would love for my hair to be so prettily styled. How did Brigitta do that? Did she rub some ointment on it? I grinned suddenly, recalling a description from *On the Origin of Species* that described her perfectly: "*The insect-species confined to sea-coasts, as every collector knows, are often brassy or lurid.*"

We hadn't even fully settled back into our seats when the waiter appeared. "Good evening," he said. "Let me tell you about tonight's menu."

Mr. Burkart held up his hand with a smile. "We understand you have beef."

"*Ja*, we have veal with red onion dressing."

Mrs. Burkart gave a small clap. "Not just beef but veal! How delightful."

"We also have a pork dish or a fish dish if you prefer," the waiter said.

"The veal," we all said at once.

"Wonderful choice," the waiter said. "I'll bring your soup right away. Would you like something else to drink, or more wine perhaps?"

"Could you bring me some tea?" I asked.

He nodded once and rushed off.

My aunt turned to Mrs. Burkart. "Anneke, I cannot believe what a handsome boy little Jeroen is becoming." Both women were the epitome of ladylike courtesy—erect posture, content expressions, gentle conversation. I could pretend to be civil to Brigitta, but I could never be as graceful as these ladies. I slouched in defeat, and Tante Greet poked me under the table. Yet somehow her concentration on Mrs. Burkart never faltered. "Don't you think little Jeroen is handsome, Katrien?" she asked me.

I had no idea if he was or not. I didn't know what a three-year-old was supposed to look like, but I knew a test when I saw one. My aunt was forcing me to join the conversation and be polite. "*Ja*, Tante, he is."

Mrs. Burkart smiled at her son. "I can scarcely believe he is five years old. So much time passes in the blink of an eye."

"He's five?" I asked. "I thought he was closer to three."

Brigitta let out a soft laugh. "You can certainly tell you're an only child, Katrien, or you would know he's far too big for three."

I clenched my teeth. *Ignore her*, I told myself.

Vader leaned toward Mr. Burkart. "What do you think is happening on Krakatau?"

I shifted my chair to hear the answer, because this was a conversation I wanted to follow. Unfortunately, the men were seated on the other side of my aunt and Mrs. Burkart, and between the women's boring talk and the noisy dining room, I couldn't make out Mr. Burkart's response.

I gave up and instead turned my attention to the waiter, who had returned with the soup and was ladling it into our bowls. As he stretched to fill the last bowl, he overreached and tipped forward, splashing Jeroen's lap with the hot liquid.

The boy cried out and the waiter immediately apologized and jumped to assist him. Mrs. Burkart gasped and fluttered her hands uselessly, but everyone else sprang from their seats to help. Vader ran for water, Mr. Burkart fanned his napkin in the boy's direction, and Tante Greet and I offered our handkerchiefs, which Brigitta grabbed and used to dab at her brother's legs with deft movements.

While she blotted the hot liquid, she sang a soothing lullaby—one I hadn't heard since before my mother died when she sang it to me.

"Do you know the mussels man,
the mussels man, the mussels man?
Do you know the mussels man
who lives in Scheveningen?"

Brigitta's voice wavered like the twitter of a zebra dove. With all the noise in the dining room, I don't believe anyone—except little Jeroen and me—heard the song.

My heart ached with longing. If my mother were still alive, would I feel so out of step with the world? Would she care if I were more like a prickly weed than a beautiful flower? Or would I be entirely different if she were still alive? Would Brigitta and I still be friends? I wiped my eyes before anyone—especially Brigitta—noticed them glistening. I didn't need her to know she could bring me to tears.

Vader returned with a pitcher of water, and Brigitta dipped the cloth and continued her ministrations, her actions sure and precise.

"There now." She wiped her brother's face and gave him a soft tap on the nose. "All better."

He giggled, and we returned to our cooled soup.

While we ate, Brigitta glanced in my direction and frowned. I paid her no mind and instead strained once more to hear Vader's and Mr. Burkart's discussion over the clinking china and Jeroen's babble.

"But the volcano hasn't erupted in centuries." Worry filled Vader's voice. "It's supposed to be extinct."

Mr. Burkart ate a spoonful of soup. "So was Pompeii."

"And we all know how that ended," Vader said.

" 'Many volcanic islands are sufficiently ancient, as shown by the stupendous degradation which they have suffered,' " I quoted.

Every head at the table turned in my direction. I didn't realize I had spoken out loud.

"Thank you for that comment, Katrien," Vader said. Only he didn't look appreciative. This was probably considered rude behavior.

Mr. Burkart wiped his mouth with his napkin. "At any rate, I don't think we have too much to worry about. It is forty kilometers away."

I wanted to tell him Mrs. Brinckerhoff's story, but Tante Greet placed a hand on my knee and whispered, "Please behave," into my ear.

What had I done wrong? I was trying to participate in the conversation, wasn't I? Isn't that what she wanted?

Brigitta kept eyeing me, her head moving side to side like a house gecko. "Is something wrong, Brigitta?" I asked through clenched teeth, trying to maintain my composure.

"You look nice tonight," she said in a too-sweet tone.

"Dank u," I mumbled, keeping myself on guard for a subtle insult.

"It makes a nice change." She returned to her soup.

I glared at her.

"She's correct," Vader said. "You do look nice tonight."

I pushed my spectacles up. Did Brigitta fool my own father? He should be smart enough to see past her false compliment. *"D-dank u,* Vader," I stuttered.

"And it does make a nice change," Tante Greed added.

My jaw dropped. How could my aunt shame me—again—in front of Brigitta?

Vader chuckled.

Even Mr. and Mrs. Burkart smiled. They were all teasing me. They were all insulting me. No one appreciated how hard I was trying to be polite.

Brigitta sipped her soup, oblivious to the hatred I felt toward her. She was the perfect lady on the outside. But I knew her heart was rotten.

Ignore her, ignore her, ignore her.

I couldn't heed my own advice. "Even the most black-hearted

among us can be civilized at times," I said, looking pointedly at Brigitta.

Everyone stared at me again, and a roar filled my head like ocean waves pounding the shore. I knew I would suffer for this. I should have just ignored Brigitta, but she made me want to tear my hair out. Or pour my soup over her head.

Tante Greet said something to my father. I saw her lips move. But the roar was still there, and I couldn't hear a word she uttered. Sliding her gaze in my direction, she raised her eyebrows and indicated the salt cellar in front of me. I grabbed the small glass dish and set it in front of her with a thud.

She opened her mouth—probably to say something about my behavior—but I turned away from her. I felt angry enough for my own eruption.

18 JUNE 1883

My dear Oom Maarten,

Our visit wasn't that long ago, but it seems like months have passed. So much has happened here. I hope your time since we visited has been quieter. I know you must sleep for days after we leave because you're always running like a crazed monkey when we're there, keeping us entertained with parties, dinners, visits, walks in the park. Even Torben must be exhausted.

How have you been? Have you chosen a wallpaper for your parlor yet? I liked the cream one with the vines. It reminded me of the jungle. If you choose that one, I could draw a few beetles climbing in the greenery. I know Torben would love that! He always barks at the geckos that climb the trees in the park.

Tante Greet will probably tell you, too, but I caused quite the stir at dinner last week. Now I am only allowed into the jungle two times a week. This is an effort on Vader and Tante Greet's part to stop my rude behavior.

Vader tried to explain why my behavior was considered so awful, but I'm still not sure I understand. I haven't done anything that terrible. I insulted Brigitta Burkart, but only after she provoked me first.

In case you've forgotten, Brigitta Burkart is the worst person imaginable. She's the girl who thinks I'm disgusting because I collect beetles. I hate her. *She's* the one who's offensive. But she's so good at pretending to be a lady when her parents are around that no one notices how mean she is.

Since I haven't been able to explore the jungle as much lately, I still haven't finished my twenty-sixth case of stag beetles. I only found two beetles on my last walk.

It's dreadfully boring not being able to explore. Tante Greet makes me dust and sweep, and the time passes so slowly. I'm rereading *On the Origin of Species* again.

Tante Greet is calling me. I suppose I had better go. Who knows what she'll have me do if I'm slow to answer.

All my love,
Katrien

Chapter 13

Two weeks after the horrible dinner with the Burkarts, I stood in the front yard of our house, frustrated because I couldn't find Slamet anywhere. It had been far too long since we'd gone collecting in the jungle together, and he was nowhere to be seen.

On the side porch, Tante Greet and Indah cleaned fish for supper. Blood and guts splattered their aprons.

"Is Slamet running an errand?" I called. "I can't find him."

Indah stiffened, and the slender knife in her hands stilled. Tante Greet wiped her hands on her apron and beckoned me to follow her inside.

"Is something wrong?" I asked as she led me to the kitchen.

Tante Greet wiped her hands again. "Slamet will not be spending as much time here as he once did."

"Why not?"

Glancing out the open door, she said, "Indah is concerned about the amount of time the two of you spend together."

"What?"

"And frankly, so are Niels and I."

I rubbed my eyes. "He's my friend. I thought you wanted me to have friends."

"Girlfriends, Katrien. Your friendship with Slamet was fine when you were children, but you're a young woman now. It's unseemly to be so close to him."

"Unseemly? You make it sound like something torrid."

"Katrien, you must understand," she said, now cleaning her fishy hands with a damp cloth. "It is inappropriate for girls your age to be so friendly with boys."

"But I *don't* understand," I said, pushing my spectacles up.

"Lift them, please," Tante Greet said automatically. She walked over to the stove, lit the fire inside and set the kettle on to boil. "Your friendship with Slamet sends the wrong message to other people."

"What kind of message can my being friends with Slamet possibly send? That doesn't make any sense."

"It will make it more difficult for you to find a husband." Her brows furrowed and her voice turned wistful.

"But I don't want to find a husband," I protested. "I just want to go to the jungle with Slamet."

We stood in silence until the kettle boiled, and Tante Greet removed it from the stove. She poured the steaming water into the dish tub and washed dishes while I watched, still confused. "Dry this, please," she said, handing me a cup.

Grabbing a dish towel, I did as she ordered.

"It is time for you both to grow up. Indah has asked her oldest son, Raharjo, to take Slamet under his wing, to teach him things a man should know. Since his father is dead."

"Vader could do that."

She shook her head. "No. Things a Muslim should know. Things a native person should know. Things your father could not teach him."

But Vader knew so much. I refused to believe Raharjo would be a better father figure for Slamet than my own.

"Katrien, there is more than the difference between boys and girls that sets you and Slamet apart."

I growled and threw my hands up in frustration. "I know. He's native, and I'm not."

"And he is Muslim. And other things, too. The point is, the two of you would be quite different even if you were both girls."

"So I won't ever see him again?"

She shook her head. "I didn't say that. But right now he's some-where in the jungle with Raharjo learning who-knows-what."

"I might see him, then. When I go exploring."

"I doubt it. I understand Raharjo lives in a village deep in the jungle. Much farther than you are allowed."

I kept my face blank.

"But I'm sure he will visit Indah when she is here," Tante Greet continued. "So if you do see him, I want you to be as polite and cour-teous to him as you would be to any guest in this home. But you will not converse with him beyond that, and you certainly will not run off with him to play. If he comes here, it will be to see his mother, and nothing else. Do you understand?"

"No," I said honestly.

Tante Greet sighed. "That's fair. Regardless, can I trust you to do as your father and I say?"

I closed my eyes in frustration. Slamet was gone. Who would I talk to? Why did it seem like everyone was conspiring against me? Slamet and I had never done anything wrong. Our friendship had never hurt each other—or anyone else.

I could feel Tante Greet's eyes boring into me, and I knew she was waiting for an answer. There was only one that would satisfy her.

"*Ja*," I said.

Chapter 14

I was so unnerved by my conversation with Tante Greet that I couldn't even think about going exploring in the jungle anymore. Instead I just stood there, feeling as if the kitchen walls were closing in around me. I needed air.

I ran from the kitchen, burst through the door onto the front porch and gulped deep breaths. As I took in the scenery of our front yard, I remembered how once, when we were little, Slamet and I had spent an entire afternoon rolling a ball back and forth between us on the lawn. When that became tiresome, we threw it at each other. He tossed it toward me—not very hard—but I missed the catch and the ball slammed into my stomach and knocked the wind out of me.

That's how I felt now. Blindsided. Hurt.

Bang!

I jumped and turned toward the source of the noise.

Mr. De Groot, our neighbor, was dragging a trunk down his porch steps.

Bang! The trunk hit the next step.

I walked over to his yard. "What are you doing?" I asked over the scraping sound of the trunk.

Mr. De Groot set the trunk on the ground and walked over to greet me. "Little Katrien." The older gentleman clasped my hand.

He had always called me little even though I now stood as tall as he. "Mrs. De Groot and I are leaving."

His news stunned me. "W-why?" I asked. I couldn't handle another upset today and I suddenly felt like I might shatter into a million pieces.

He pointed southwest. "That's why."

I followed his direction. "Krakatau?" In the weeks since I first learned of the eruption, the plume of smoke had become a familiar fixture on the horizon. Sometimes the color was white and hard to spot against the clouds; other days it was gray. Today, it was dark and angry like thunderheads.

He returned to his trunk. I grabbed the other end, and we both shoved the trunk into the wagon that sat waiting by the road. "*Dank u*, Little Katrien."

I pushed up my spectacles. "But why are you leaving? I don't understand."

He ignored my question and walked to the other side of the wagon.

"Hubrecht," his wife called, coming outside, "we have four more trunks, and I want to bring the mirror." Mrs. De Groot was shorter than her husband, but with a long neck. She reminded me of a banded linsang without the spots and tail. "Oh, hello, Little Katrien."

"Hello, Mrs. De Groot. Your husband tells me you're leaving."

"*Ja*, we are."

"Because of Krakatau." Skepticism filled my voice.

She nodded and cast a wary glance in the direction of the volcano. "*Ja*."

"But Krakatau's forty kilometers from here. Maybe passing ships would be damaged by another eruption, but we'll be fine."

Her eyes bored into mine, and I had the distinct impression that I was being judged—as if Mrs. De Groot was deciding exactly if, or how, to respond.

Finally, she spoke. "Come here." She sat on the porch steps and patted the space beside her. I did as I was told. "Hubrecht," she called. "Help me tell Little Katrien."

Mr. De Groot tugged at his cotton-white beard and joined us on the steps. "It's your story, Marijn. You should tell it."

Something important passed between them. The air around me changed the tiniest bit.

Mrs. De Groot took a deep breath. "Did you know, Little Katrien, that my family—and Mr. De Groot's—have been in the East Indies since the 1600s?"

I shook my head. I knew my Dutch history well enough to know the Dutch East India Company had started back then, and that the government took over the colony in 1800 when the company went bankrupt. But I never really thought about the people involved. I suppose that was true for all history. What did we know about average Greek or Roman citizens?

"Over the course of these last two hundred years," Mrs. De Groot went on, "my family eventually settled in Besuki in East Java."

I had never heard of Besuki, but I nodded, not wanting to interrupt her story.

"In 1815, Mount Tambora erupted."

"Mount Tambora?" I asked. "That's on Sumbawa island, isn't it? It's not on Java."

"No," Mrs. De Groot said. "It's not on Java. Lombok and Bali— two different islands—are between Sumbawa and Java. Which is why you should pay close attention to my story."

My eyebrows rose at her imperious tone, but I said nothing.

"Don't scare the girl, Marijn," Mr. De Groot said.

She glared at him. "Sometimes fear is a good lesson to learn, Hubrecht." He grimaced, and she continued. "My mother was twelve years old when Mount Tambora erupted. She used to tell me stories about it. Terrifying stories that would keep me up until dawn."

"What kind of stories?" I whispered, rubbing my arms where gooseflesh had appeared.

"Stories about falling ash and darkened skies. A terrible wave that washed onshore and dragged people from their homes and into the ocean. Her three youngest sisters were swept away and never seen again. She said the noise was so loud she thought a battle was happening somewhere on the sea." Mrs. De Groot's whole body shook.

Her husband placed a hand on her shoulder. "Don't worry, Marijn. We'll be safe."

She regained her composure. "They had warning. Mount Tambora first erupted three years before that. Small eruptions from a volcano everyone thought was dormant. They could have left."

I tilted my head, confused.

She clutched my shoulders and shook me. "We have a chance to leave, too. Before Krakatau erupts again." A chill ran down my spine like a spider scurrying from a lizard.

"Marijn!" Mr. De Groot pried his wife's fingers from me and held her close. "Shhh," he soothed. Tears streamed down her cheeks.

"Where are you going to go?" I asked.

Mr. De Groot answered. "Batavia first. Then we'll see."

"Would you go to the Netherlands?"

"No." He sat up straighter. "We're Javanese. We'll stay on this island until we die."

This I understood. My family had not lived here as long as theirs. Vader had come to Anjer from the Netherlands not long after he married my mother. Oom Maarten requested a transfer to Batavia a few years later, and of course, Tante Greet came after my mother died.

Even after all the years in Java, Vader, Tante Greet and Oom Maarten still considered themselves more Dutch than Javanese. But I was born here. I loved everything about Java. It was my home.

Mr. De Groot stood and escorted his shaken wife inside the house. Then he returned carrying another trunk. Helping him load it into the wagon, I said, "I will miss you when you leave."

"We'll miss you, Little Katrien."

"Who will feed the macaques?" I asked.

Glancing up at the bare sticks in the trees, he smiled. "They can take care of themselves. Of that, I am sure."

"Do you really believe Krakatau will erupt like Mount Tambora?"

He nodded and scratched his beard. "It may be next week or

next year or ten years from now. But it will erupt. I grew up in Yogyakarta, in the shadow of Mount Merapi. It erupts all the time. I know what volcanoes can do." He patted my shoulder, climbed the steps, and with a deep sigh walked inside his home.

I pushed my spectacles up and stared at the smoke from Krakatau. Was it really that dangerous? Did it pose as much of a threat as Mount Tambora? Forty kilometers no longer seemed that far away.

Chapter 15

On the Origin of Species lay open, unread, across my lap. A soft breeze cooled the air pleasantly around me, but the dark plume of smoke from Krakatau kept me from concentrating on Mr. Charles Darwin.

The view from our porch normally delighted me, but not now.

Instead, visions of people being washed away filled me with dread and fear.

Surely Mrs. De Groot had embellished her story a bit? Or if not Mrs. De Groot, then her mother? How could a wave drag people into the ocean from their homes? Perhaps those homes were already on the shore?

I pushed up my spectacles. If only I had seen Krakatau's eruption in May. Then I would have something to reference beyond other people's stories. I would have what I had witnessed with my own eyes. I would have facts.

Tante Greet stepped onto the porch with a basket clutched in her hand. "Indah made a bit too much rice, so I'm taking some of it to Mrs. Schoonhoven. Along with some fruit. And I have Niels's lunch." Another basket hung from her elbow.

I nodded.

"Would you like to join me?" she asked, and I had a feeling I was being tested. This was one of those spiderwebs of a question and I needed to navigate it carefully. But Mrs. De Groot's story had me all jumbled up, and I couldn't see my way around the trap.

"No," I said bluntly.

Tante Greet's disappointment showed in the firm set of her mouth. "It would be polite to visit Mrs. Schoonhoven with me." She held the basket higher. "To help those less fortunate."

"Did you know the De Groots are leaving?" I asked, changing the subject.

She dropped her arm and took a step toward me, the basket hanging by her fingertips. "I did. They told me last week. I...I didn't know how to tell you. I know how much you like them."

"Did they tell you why they're leaving?"

"No, and I didn't ask."

"Krakatau."

She shook her head. "I suppose it is their choice to do as they wish." She patted her hair. "You look presentable, Katrien, since you didn't go to the jungle. Come with me to see Mrs. Schoonhoven, and then we'll bring Niels his lunch."

I sat up. "I'll take Vader's lunch to him. So he won't have to wait, and you can spend more time with Mrs. Schoonhoven."

We watched as the loaded wagon pulled away from the De Groots' house, their silver heads bobbing with each lurch. "Did they tell you where they're going?" Tante Greet asked, waving as they passed us.

I waved, too. "Batavia," I said.

When I turned to reach for Vader's lunch, she jumped. "What are you doing?"

"I said I was going to take Vader his lunch. Do you mind?"

She shook her head, distracted. Her eyes followed the De Groots' wagon. "Fine, fine."

When the De Groots turned the corner, Tante Greet snapped out of her trance. "Please see if we have any mail when you see Niels."

Turning abruptly, she strode down the porch steps and down

the street. I watched until she disappeared around the corner where Mr. Vandermark's home sat. She kept her face turned away from his blazing red doors the entire time.

With Vader's lunch under my arm, I put *On the Origin of Species* inside and set off for the post office, where the postmaster greeted me warmly.

"Ah, Katrien," the postmaster said, smiling. "I have two letters for your family." He handed over two envelopes, both of them from Oom Maarten.

Stepping back outside, I opened the one addressed to me and leaned against the wall to read in the shade.

> *To the lovely Katrien,*
>
> *I believe I have finally narrowed my wallpaper choices to four candidates. First, the green vines that you like, though of course without added drawings of beetles—how could I sit in the parlor with terrifying, enormous bugs staring at me?*

"Insects," I murmured with a grin.

> *Second, the yellow and orange tulips that Greet preferred. Third, a pale blue-and-gold filigree that I don't recall either of you seeing. And finally, a red damask. My inclination is to choose the red—if only because I know Greet would abhor it. And what else can a younger brother do but annoy his older sister? Some things never cease to entertain!*
>
> *I am sorry to hear about your punishment, as I am sure that girl deserves your wrath. It's certain that you have never done anything to bedevil her, have you?*

I swallowed. Oom Maarten's gentle reprimand reminded me that I wasn't entirely innocent in my fights with Brigitta. But that didn't change the unfairness of my punishment. As far as I knew, she hadn't suffered at all.

Perhaps in the future you could try a new approach. The next time you see her, place your hand over your mouth and nose. This will serve two purposes: You will remember not to speak—thereby avoiding any regrettable verbal exchanges— and she will think she stinks. To be fair, she probably does—if not literally then quite certainly in a figurative sense.

Your brilliant uncle—M

I laughed and tucked the note in my pocket. The other letter I placed in the basket with Vader's lunch before skipping off down the road toward his office.

As fate would have it, I soon realized that none other than Brigitta herself was walking ahead of me in the same direction. I hoped she wouldn't notice me, but no such luck. She must have caught me in her peripheral vision because she suddenly wheeled around and sneered at me. "Katrien, where are you off to? Surely not the jungle. I understand you're not allowed to go there anymore."

How did she know that? Did my aunt tell her mother? No wonder I always felt off balance around Brigitta; she knew more about me than I did. And blast my aunt for talking about me behind my back. My punishments should not be made into conversational fodder for the Burkart family!

"That's not true, Brigitta. I can go two times a week. I chose not to go today."

"Two times? My, my, my."

I bit my tongue and walked past her.

Her voice stopped me in my tracks. "Since you're not gallivanting around like a wild animal, are you at least learning some useful skills?"

Useful skills? That was rich coming from her. The only useful skill I knew she possessed was her talent to perpetually insult me and get away with it. I could not stay silent any longer. I turned around and glared. "And what would you consider a useful skill?" I demanded. "Staring in the mirror?"

As soon as the words were out of my mouth, I realized Brigitta had done it again. She was always able to bait me into saying something that she would later claim had hurt her feelings. Not that she truly had any feelings to hurt, but now she had the perfect excuse to run and tattle to her father about how mean I had been, and her father would tell Vader.

This time, though, Brigitta surprised me by responding with a smile. "My goodness, Katrien, there are so many skills you could learn. Needlework, sewing, cooking, gardening..."

I shook my head. She thought those were useful skills? "Nothing you know could ever be considered useful," I said angrily. "It's not as if knowing how to embroider is going to save someone's life."

Brigitta gasped and turned as red as Mr. Vandermark's door. Good.

I whirled off before she could recover.

Chapter 16

When I reached Vader's office, the door was closed, meaning he was out. I waited outside and scanned the horizon. Krakatau's cloud of smoke appeared even darker now. Or was that my imagination?

"Katrien. What a pleasant surprise." Vader's voice startled me from the doorway, and I jumped.

Clutching his lunch to my chest, I said, "You're here."

He opened the door and ushered me inside. "I do apologize. I didn't mean to frighten you."

I shook my head. "I'm fine."

"You must have been deep in serious thought not to notice me." He sat down at his desk, but I remained at the counter. "It's a beautiful afternoon," he said. "I should have had the door open."

I nodded, feeling my worries about the volcano slip away in Vader's company.

He straightened some papers. "Did you go exploring today?"

"No."

"Whyever not? You haven't been to the jungle once this week."

His question reminded me that I had something to discuss with him. I got straight to the point. "Why can't I spend any more time with Slamet?" I demanded.

"Greet spoke to you, then?"

I nodded.

"Did she not explain our reasons?"

"*Ja*, but they're silly. How is being friends with Slamet going to prevent me from finding a husband? I don't even want a husband."

"Not now you don't, no. But, later, you will change your mind."

I arched my eyebrows. "I suppose you want me to be friends with other girls my age, too?" I bumped my foot against the counter. "You know I don't like those girls. They're all empty-headed dodos."

"Perhaps you'd feel differently if you actually tried spending more time with them. As it happens, Thomas mentioned to me this morning that he would like Brigitta to perform more charitable works, and I think that is a fine idea for you, too. The two of you will do so together, volunteering at the convent. Perhaps that will help you overcome your differences."

I grimaced. "That will never work."

"Nevertheless, that is what will happen." He smiled and slapped the desk. "It won't be as bad as you're imagining."

"It will be worse," I muttered. Brigitta and I would likely do more harm together than good.

"Did you come down here merely to ask about Slamet? It could have waited until after supper."

"I brought your lunch." I thrust the basket across the counter, still fuming. How could Vader betray me like this?

"*Dank u*, Katrien," he said, rising to take the food. "That was kind."

I wanted nothing more than to be out of his presence. But through the window, I caught another glimpse of the smoke from Krakatau and my fears about the volcano came flooding back. "The De Groots have left," I said in a leaden voice.

"Have they? I knew they were discussing moving, but I didn't realize it would be so soon." He leaned back in the chair and ate a slice of star fruit. "I shall miss them. They have been wonderful neighbors."

"Don't you want to know why they went?"

"I suppose they have their reasons." He ate another piece of fruit. "It's not for me to pry."

"Because of Krakatau." I could not keep the story inside me any longer and told him everything Mrs. De Groot said.

When I stopped talking, he raised his eyebrows.

"She thinks the eruption in May was a warning," I said. "She thinks we should leave now. While we still have time."

He wiped his mouth with a napkin. "And what do you think?"

I pushed up my spectacles. "I don't know. She was terrified, but parts of her story seemed too incredible to be true. And Krakatau is forty kilometers away."

"Mount Tambora was farther," he reminded me.

"*Ja*, but . . ." I paced. "It's on a larger island. It follows, then, that an eruption from a larger landmass would be bigger. Doesn't it?"

He nodded. "Perhaps. We are still learning about Earth's geology."

I twisted my skirt in my hands and focused on the wrinkles in the fabric.

"You have something you want say?" he asked.

I stayed silent. How could I express myself without sounding ridiculous? Or, worse, unladylike?

"Katrien?" He rapped the desk.

At last I whispered, "I wish I could have seen the eruption."

"Of Mount Tambora?"

"No." I shook my head. "Krakatau. In May."

He grimaced. "Having heard Mr. Brinckerhoff's story—and others, too—I'm glad we were in Batavia with Maarten. Safe from whatever was happening."

"Then maybe we should leave."

He gazed at me for a long moment. "Is that what you want?"

"No," I said with a force that surprised me.

"And why not? Tell me what you're thinking."

I let out a long breath. "I have no reason to doubt Mrs. De Groot's story, but some of it was so incredible. And even if it all happened just as she said, Krakatau is on a smaller island." I gazed directly into Vader's eyes. "I want to be here," I said firmly.

"Then we will stay," he replied, turning back to his lunch. "Especially since I had no plans to leave anyway."

"Then why did you ask me?" The question popped out before I even knew I was thinking it.

He crossed his arms. I didn't say anything, unsure if I was about to be punished or praised. The silence stretched between us, and I focused on the sound of the ocean's waves sweeping onshore.

"Your opinion is important to me, Katrien," he said. "But I am the head of our household."

"But why ask for my opinion if it doesn't matter?" Like Oom Maarten's dog, Torben, cornering a house gecko, I would not let Vader get away from this.

"I never said your opinion did not matter. It matters a great deal. But mine is the one we will be following in this matter. That we agree is important, but not necessary."

"But if yours is the one that matters, why ask for mine?" I asked again. So many decisions were being made for me today that I could not help lashing out.

He ran his hands through his hair. "Katrien, I ask for your thoughts because I want you to be clever and smart and able to function on your own. I do not know what the future holds for you, but there are certain tenets that will, in all likelihood, be true. You will finish your schooling. You will get married, and you will have children. God willing, you and your husband will live a long, happy life together."

I shuddered. Hadn't I just told him I didn't want a husband?

"Don't make that face, Katrien. Marriage is wonderful. Your mother and I were quite happy until she became ill. And she was ill for such a long time, as you know."

I nodded. Rarely did I ever see her outside. She could walk but had to lean on the walls for support.

"And your grandfather—my father—also had a long battle with illness. I became head of that household when I was fourteen years old."

I nodded again, unsure of what to say.

"My mother was unable to do much to assist me, and I do not want you to be in that position. Do you understand?"

"*Ja*, Vader." For once, I thought I actually did. Maybe that was what Tante Greet was really trying to teach me with all the counting of foodstuffs. Independence. In case things took an unexpected turn.

He turned back to his desk. "*Dank u*, again, for bringing my lunch."

With one final glance at the smoky line seeping from Krakatau, I left.

6 JULY 1883

My dear Oom Maarten,

You won't believe what I saw in the jungle today. A silvery gibbon! She was beautiful. I'd never seen one before, and I watched her for as long as I dared.

I spotted her after hearing this terribly loud cry. WOOP! WOOP! WOOOOOP! And then it became a series of barks. Woop. Woop. Woop. Woop. Woop. Quite different from Torben's barks, which are sharper and more piercing.

A puff of bright silver hair surrounded her delicate black face, making her look older than I'm sure she was. She waved one hand at me, and it was so similar to mine. Four long black fingers and a thumb.

When she moved off, farther into the jungle, she had such grace. She was a dancer, a spirit.

Oh, I could almost fly with excitement. She mesmerized me. I don't know if I've ever seen anything so lovely. I wish you could have seen her. I'm going to try to draw her from memory. If you choose the green vine wallpaper, then a silvery gibbon would look wonderful swinging from one vine to another!

Yours in amazement,
Katrien

Chapter 17

Three days after my conversation with Vader, I plodded up to the iron gates of the convent where Brigitta already stood ringing the brass bell on the post. Although the girls' school we attended was connected to the convent, I had never been on the convent's grounds.

An unfamiliar nun opened the gate. "Brigitta Burkart and Katrien Courtlandt?" she asked. Her voice was barely audible over the screeching hinges.

"*Ja*, Sister." We replied together, as if we had rehearsed it.

"Follow me." She led us into a building separate from the church and housing. "Sister Hilde," she called, "the girls are here."

Sister Hilde smiled when she saw us. "Two of my favorite pupils." She had such a forthright manner that I didn't think she was capable of saying anything less than the truth. She took us aside and whispered, "I'm afraid today is not going to be exciting for you. It's laundry day, and unfortunately, it's my turn to assist. However, I can help you out a bit. Washing is such unpleasant work, and we have already begun our labors with it. The two of you can hang the linens, and you'll be out in God's glorious sunshine."

"That will be fine, Sister," I said.

Brigitta sighed and agreed. This surprised me. Why was she being so disrespectful? She could at least feign pleasantness. I had seen her do it hundreds of times. What was different today? I didn't want to hang laundry either, but that wasn't Sister Hilde's fault.

"Wonderful." Sister Hilde handed each of us a basket overflowing with clean white sheets. "The lines are to the back of the building. Oh!" She stopped us with a wave of her hand, and set a cloth sack on each laundry pile. "Clothespins."

I lugged my basket outside with Brigitta beside me. Each of us walked to a separate line to work. The convent had six rope clotheslines set up in a clear area, away from trees and animals.

Setting the basket at my feet, I grabbed two pins and a sheet. The breeze blew in from the ocean as I wrestled the wet material onto the line, careful not to let it hit the dirt. It took three tries before I got enough of the fabric over the rope to keep it from falling. Brigitta, I was pleased to notice, was having as much trouble as I.

The silence between us hung as heavily as the sheets. Chickens clucked near the convent's coop, and the spicy aroma of fish soup drifted from the kitchen. The nuns made soup once a week for poor natives, which seemed more charitable than what Brigitta and I were doing. I felt more like I was being punished. Perhaps that's what Brigitta's problem was today. Perhaps she felt the same as I did, and for once, she couldn't manage to hide it.

Interesting as the idea was, I didn't dwell on it for long. I had Vader and Tante Greet to think about. They insisted I work with Brigitta, insisted I overcome our differences. They would question me about my day at supper, and my life would be much easier if I could tell them I tried. I took a deep breath. "Did you think this is what you would be doing today?"

She grunted in response.

Fine. I tried another tactic. "Why did you choose the convent to work?"

Throwing a sheet over the clothesline, she said, "I was hoping to work in the herb garden."

"The herb garden? Why the herb garden?"

"I like plants."

I froze, dumbfounded. If she had told me that Galileo was wrong and the sun revolved around Earth, I would have been less flummoxed. "You mean botany?"

She picked up her basket. "Certainly not."

"Of course not." I crossed my arms. "Heaven forbid you express an interest in something unseemly like science."

Brigitta stepped toward me until we were almost nose to nose. "If I'm interested in plants in any way, Katrien, it's still more acceptable than your disgusting desire to surround yourself with bugs."

"Insects," I said, shoving her away from me.

Her laundry basket fell out of her arms and bounced away as she stumbled backward. "What is the matter with you?" She pushed me right back.

"I'm sick of getting in trouble because of you." I kicked a mound of dirt toward her.

She gasped and jumped out of the way. Glaring at me with the fury of a rampaging Javan rhinoceros, she marched back over to me. "What is that supposed to mean?" she asked, venom dripping from her voice.

"Every time I defend myself against you, I get punished."

"Defend yourself?" she screeched. "You always insult me! You belittle me! You're rude to my friends!"

"Only because you hurt me first!" I hollered, giving her another shove. As she fell backward, she reached out for something to steady herself. She clutched at a nearby sheet blowing in the breeze, but she was already too off balance and the force of her falling body snapped the clothesline. All the sheets dropped to the ground, along with Brigitta, and the dirt smeared onto the wet fabric like the ink I was forever splattering onto my beetles' identifcation labels.

"What is going on out here?" The anger-filled voice of Mother Superior shot across the yard.

Before I could get a word out, Brigitta blurted, "Katrien pushed me!"

It took Mother Superior only a few strides to reach us. "Come with me. Both of you."

We followed her into the church, behind the altar and into the sacristy. Then Mother Superior turned her cold, snakelike eyes on me and said, "Since the two of you can't do something as simple as hang laundry without fighting, you will work here where you can't do as much damage. Katrien, you will polish the sacred vessels." To Brigitta she spat, "You will remove stains from the vestments."

"*Ja*, Mother Superior," we said.

"You will both work in this room, and you will not act like wild animals. If that means you work in utter silence, so be it. These tasks may take several days to complete, and you will both work together until each task is finished." She gave each of us a pointed look. "Do I make myself clear?"

I nodded.

"*Ja*," Brigitta said.

"I will be back in one hour to check on your progress."

Chapter 18

"What in the world were you thinking, getting into a scuffle with Brigitta?" Vader asked at supper that night, his fingers clenched around his fork.

"I didn't—"

"I don't understand why the two of you can't overcome your differences."

"She's the one who—"

Tante Greet interrupted. "The problem is that Brigitta is a young lady, and she tries to act appropriately. Katrien, meanwhile, is refusing to grow up and acts like a small child."

I banged my fist on the table.

"Katrien!" She glared at me.

Fury coursed through my veins. A small part of me wondered how many times we would have this argument, but I was not about to back down now. I *had* tried to make an effort today, even if it didn't last long.

"If ladies act like Brigitta, then I never want to be a lady. I'd rather stay a child!" I shouted. "At least children can spend time with their friends!"

Vader's voice cut into my tirade like a shark fin slicing through the water. "What do you mean, Katrien?"

I cast a stony gaze in his direction and crossed my arms over my chest. "Slamet," I spat.

Tante Greet protested, "Katrien, I've explained why—"

But before she could launch into whatever lecture she was planning, Vader held up his hand to silence her. Then he put down his fork and stared at it thoughtfully. A moment later, he spoke. "Perhaps we were too quick to prevent you from seeing Slamet, Katrien. I think it came as too much of a shock."

"Niels," Tante Greet began.

Vader shook his head and held up his hand once more. It was so quiet that I could hear the grandfather clock ticking in the hall. "I suggest a compromise," he said at last.

I loosened my arms, relaxing a bit. "I'm listening."

"I will talk with Indah about her concerns. If I can get her to agree, Slamet will be free to visit here as much as he ever did, and you may socialize with one another once more."

A bubble of hope rose within me, and I clutched my hands together in my lap as if in prayer.

He continued. "But in no way should you interpret my generosity as a condonation of your actions today. You will still be punished, and I will address your punishment in a moment. For now, the terms of this compromise are as follows: You may renew your friendship with Slamet, and in return, you must agree to perform one household task a week for Greet, in addition to the assistance you have recently begun providing her. The task will be one of her choosing." He glanced at my aunt. "Does that sound reasonable?"

She pursed her lips. "I would prefer that Katrien agree to acquire a new skill. There are so many she ought to know that she has refused to learn."

New skills? She must be mad. She would have me needlepointing useless sayings on pillow covers in no time. I was certain Vader would take my side, but instead he smiled.

"That will be fine."

"What?" I could not hide the betrayal I felt.

He shot a sharp look across the table at me. "Katrien, you must also face your punishment. From now on, you will only be permitted to go to the jungle once a week."

"You can't be serious!"

"I assure you, I am." He arched his eyebrows. "You may renew your friendship with Slamet and in return you will agree to lessons from your aunt. Unless you would prefer to spend time with Brigitta at the convent. Either way, your punishment stands. Your time in the jungle is now limited to once a week."

"But that isn't fair!" I cried.

"On the contrary," he said, "your behavior toward Brigitta this afternoon was rude, pretentious and boorish. And for that you are being disciplined."

I wanted to run far away. Into the jungle. Perhaps where Slamet was living with his brother.

Oh, Slamet.

If I agreed to this rotten compromise, I could see my friend again. I was certain Vader would be able to convince Indah. After all, she worked for us. But having lessons with Tante Greet? Only being able to explore the jungle once a week?

Furious at Vader for the injustice of his terms, and at Tante Greet for making everything worse, I nodded reluctantly. What else could I do? At least this way, I didn't have to spend any more forced time in Brigitta's presence.

"Good." Vader returned to his meal. "I will speak with Indah tomorrow, and we will start this new phase on Monday."

That gave me three whole days to sulk.

12 JULY 1883

My dear Oom Maarten,

I've been punished again for fighting with Brigitta. She is the bane of my existence.

Beginning Monday, I can only go to the jungle once a week. And I have to start learning new skills from Tante Greet, as well. She's already chosen cooking for the first lesson.

Can I come live with you? You would never force me to do anything I didn't want to do. I could take Torben for walks in the park every day—even twice a day. Though I would miss the jungle.

My last visit was cut short. A Javan rhinoceros rumbled across my path. He was the same height as me, and I know I'm lucky he didn't charge me. Thankfully, he was too busy marking his territory. The smell almost made me retch. It was so strong and vile. The rhino lumbered off into the undergrowth, completely ignoring me. Unfortunately, he took the same path I was following. I had no choice but to turn around and come home.

That was yet another unproductive visit to the forest. My last five explorations have been fruitless. I haven't found any stag beetles!

Desperately yours,
Katrien

Chapter 19

Three weeks later, Tante Greet stood in my room, staring at my collection of beetles while I hurried to get dressed. The cases covered an entire wall and a good part of another.

"How do you sleep at night with these monstrous bugs hanging on the wall?" she asked.

"Insects," I corrected her.

She raised her eyebrows at my impertinence.

I decided to change the subject. "Slamet told me yesterday that he's going to bring food to some friends of his this morning, and I'm going with him."

Tante Greet drew her lips into a tight line, and she made her disapproving click.

"He's bringing food to people! It's charity! Don't you want me to help those less fortunate?"

She closed her eyes for a moment, and I could see a struggle cross her features. "I suppose this is why we relented," she muttered. She retrieved my hat from its hook and handed it to me. "Please don't make a spectacle of yourself, and be polite to these people."

"I will."

"And be back here by midday."

I waved at her and hurried to find Slamet.

He stood in the side yard, hugging a basket close to his chest. He looked tense, but I ignored that.

"Let's go," I said, leading the way around the front of the house.

We hadn't gotten far before I saw Brigitta standing by the Ousterhoudts' porch, talking to Mr. Ousterhoudt. I stopped short, and Slamet bumped into me.

"Apologies, Slamet." I pointed to Brigitta. "I don't want her to see me."

He nodded and we slowly backed away. Remembering Oom Maarten's latest letter—*Obviously, you did not follow my advice!*—I placed my hand over my nose and mouth.

"They are hibiscus flowers," I heard Mr. Ousterhoudt saying to Brigitta.

"Would it be possible to obtain a cutting?" she asked, moving to a bright orange bloom. "Perhaps two?"

Slamet and I made our way over to the Great Post Road, which began in Anjer and ended in Panarukan on the other side of Java. I didn't often travel on the road except for the few times my family went to visit the controller of Merak, the town north of Anjer. Although the road went through Batavia, we traveled by ship to the capital.

"Where are we going?" I asked.

"To mosque."

I stopped. "I thought we were going to visit friends of yours." The mosque was a kilometer north of Anjer along the coast.

"Friends live near mosque."

"Oh." We walked on down the road, and I offered to carry the basket. "Do you know them from the mosque?"

He gave me a quizzical look, and I could tell he didn't understand my question. I tried again. "How do you know them? Your friends?"

"They are from same village as Ibu."

I nodded, and we fell into silence. It had been a long time since I had spent any substantial time with Slamet. Normally, I could be in his company without saying anything and be perfectly content. But an awkwardness descended on me while we walked. My tongue seemed to grow in my mouth, banging into the back of my teeth. The silence between us stretched. If we didn't begin a conversation soon, I wasn't sure we ever would.

"What was it like? Living in the jungle with your brother?"

"Good. I learn much."

"Such as?"

He watched a wagon coming down the road. The driver whipped his horses to make them go even faster. Slamet shook his head.

When he still didn't answer me, I bumped his shoulder. "What are you learning?"

"Arabic. The Qu'ran."

I frowned. If that was all his brother was teaching him, then why did he have to go off into the jungle to learn it? "Vader could have taught you that. He doesn't speak Arabic, but you and he could have learned together."

"Better to learn from teacher."

"That's what I mean. Vader could have found one. You could both learn Arabic."

He didn't say anything.

"How does Raharjo even know Arabic?" I wondered. "He's not in school."

Slamet turned and glared at me, and there was such anger in his expression that I stepped back. "You do not know. You cannot know. You are Dutch. You do what you want. You are not like us."

I felt as if the road had suddenly tilted, and I stumbled, almost dropping the basket. He snatched it from me.

"What? Slamet, what do you mean?" Was he saying I did not understand him? Because I was Dutch?

The air around us had changed. It was prickly and sharp, as if lightning were about to strike.

"You Dutch," Slamet said. "You treat us like dogs." A rough tone had filled his voice, making him sound angrier than I had ever heard him. He had never spoken to me like this. I stared at him in shock.

"Do you truly believe that?" I asked, bewildered. "That I treat you like a dog?"

He slumped. "Not you."

"Then why would you say such a thing to me?"

He shook his head and gazed down the road. His face was set hard like stone. I didn't even see him blink.

"Slamet?" I reached for his hand, but he jumped as if bitten by a Malayan pit viper.

"Raharjo says this."

His brother. Why would Raharjo say these things about the Dutch, about me? He didn't even know me. He sounded as awful as Brigitta.

"What else does your brother say?" I asked.

"He teaches me and tells stories."

"What kind of stories?" I thought of *Butho Ijo*, and the Dutch legends that my mother used to tell me, and the fairy tales I read when I was younger.

Slamet wandered off the side of the road toward the beach. He stared into the distance, his black hair glowing in the bright light. I walked over to him, and he squatted down and drew a pattern of squiggles and dots in the sand. "Bad ones." He stood and erased the pattern with his bare foot, his toes just darker than the wet sand.

His eyes were fixed on the ground. I ducked my head and waved a hand in front of his face. "How bad?"

With a wry smile that showed off the dimple in his cheek, he looked at me and said, "Bad. How much trouble Dutch are."

I waved my hands dismissively. "Not all of us. Only the girls Tante Greet wants me to be like."

He turned back to the road, no longer smiling. More wagons and people moved along the Great Post Road. Slamet stopped and watched them, his whole body tensing with anger. His hand moved toward his side, and I noticed a *kris* sitting at the waist of his sarong. Slamet had never worn the traditional Javanese dagger before. Where had he gotten that? The air turned prickly again, and I pushed up my spectacles.

"Slamet?" I asked. "Is something wrong?"

"Colonial overlords," he muttered.

"I beg your pardon?" The term sounded so strange coming from Slamet's mouth. I myself had not heard it in years, not since the days when the adults would speak of the fighting in Aceh while Brigitta and I played. The natives there had always been fighting the Dutch, but surely Slamet could not feel that way here in Anjer—could he? What had Raharjo told him? What was I missing? I looked around at the people Slamet was watching. Women in colorful dresses and men in pale-colored suits strolled nearby. "They look like birds," I said. "Don't you think so?"

"They are pain."

"Pain?" I let out a laugh. "They're not hurting anyone."

He flushed. "Pain is not word."

I thought for a moment. "Trouble? Annoyance? Problem?"

"Problem. *Ya.*" He nodded. "They are problem."

"But they're not doing anything. They're walking, like us."

"They are problem," he repeated.

With a soft laugh, I asked, "How?"

"They are Dutch."

Taken aback by his response—and the tone in his voice—I stammered, "A-are you serious?"

He kicked at the ground. The silence between us grew once more, and I suddenly felt a barrier forming in our friendship. I had to handle this carefully so no further distance was created. I needed Slamet. He was my friend.

I tried to lighten the mood, saying, "Whatever you have in that basket smells delicious."

His eyes darted from person to person, never resting on anyone for longer than a few seconds.

Poking his shoulder repeatedly until he turned to me, I gave him a sunny smile. "What's in the basket?"

"*Pisang goreng*," he said, handing it back to me.

"They smell wonderful."

"We made them at our home. Not your home."

My jaw dropped. "I never suggested—It wouldn't matter to me if—" I rubbed my eyes in frustration. "What difference does it make where you made the fritters?"

He scratched his arm. "We do not use Dutch food."

"Oh." I didn't know why he was telling me this. "Is that good?"

"We use our food."

What he was trying to say finally made sense. "You mean you only used what you could share. Your own charity."

He smiled and nodded. *"Ya."*

I fell silent, unsure what else to say. We walked farther out of Anjer. Fewer people were on the road, and the jungle crept closer to the sea. Waves washed onshore, and seabirds screeched their harsh cries before diving under the surface for fish.

We reached the mosque, which sat in an open stretch of land facing the beach. Surrounded by palm trees, the wooden structure had a porch around the entire building and two main doors. It looked comfortable and settled, like it had been there for many years.

"What is it like inside?" I asked as we walked past the building.

My question seemed to calm Slamet. "Peaceful."

I never felt that at mass. At mass I felt nervous. Uptight. Uncomfortable. Judged. Peaceful was what I felt in the jungle. "It's lovely."

"It is best place. I learn many things."

"Such as?"

"Stars. We watch them. Follow them."

"You could stargaze at our house," I said. "Vader would teach you."

"Is not same."

"But Vader knows a great deal about astronomy." He knew that.

Vader had pointed out constellations to us when we were younger. Had Slamet forgotten?

"Teacher knows more." He took the basket from me and turned off the road, not even checking to see if I followed. Frowning at his back, I hurried to catch him.

We walked toward the jungle for about ten minutes before we came upon a small village of kampongs partially hidden among the trees. Chickens ran around the houses, and I wondered how anyone knew whose chickens belonged to whom.

Although the village was small, we turned corners so often, I lost my sense of direction.

But Slamet knew where he was going. I stuck close to him, and we stopped in front of a tiny kampong. He stepped up to the door. "Purnama? Wangi? *Ini* Slamet."

A woman came to the door. "Slamet?" I had been expecting these friends to be elderly, like old Mrs. Schoonhoven. But this woman— Wangi—was about the same age as Indah, though she was thinner and looked more tired.

She stared around Slamet at me, and he motioned me forward. "Wangi, *ini adalah* Katrien."

I smiled and gave her a slight bow. Every word of Javanese that I knew fled my mind. "It's nice to meet you," I said in Dutch, hoping she would understand my actions if not my words.

She welcomed us both inside. Slamet handed her the basket of *pisang goreng*. They talked to each other in Javanese, and I stood in the doorway until Wangi motioned for me to sit down.

She offered us the fritters, and I copied Slamet in taking one. Wangi sat next to a man lying on a rush mat. His face was haggard, with lines of pain around his mouth. She raised his shoulders and fed him a fritter.

Slamet introduced him as Purnama. I smiled and nodded at him, but he only grimaced. The three of them talked, and I tried to follow the conversation. But they spoke too quickly for me to make out more than a few words.

We had been there a short time when another voice sounded out-side. "Wangi? *Ini* Raharjo."

Slamet's brother was here? I sat up a little straighter, prepared to be as polite as possible. I would show Raharjo that not all Dutch people were awful. I would make him see what a good friend I was to Slamet.

Chapter 20

Wangi led Raharjo inside. He had a pleasant look about him; not what I expected from someone saying such hurtful things. Like many natives, he was not tall, and he wore a traditional sarong with a *kris* at his waist. The handle of the curvy dagger sat at a cocky angle. He smiled at Slamet and went over to greet Purnama. After a brief chat, Raharjo spotted me.

His friendly expression fell and anger took its place. All my plans for being polite vanished, and I wished I could shrink into the corner to hide. Why was he mad at me? What did I do? I pushed my spectacles up.

Slamet placed a hand on Raharjo's and whispered something in his ear. Raharjo nodded but kept his fierce gaze on me.

I felt like a mouse being stalked by a cat.

Ambulo...ambulare... I tried to conjugate the Latin word for "walk" in my head, but I couldn't. Raharjo scared me. I couldn't even remember Latin verbs. My gaze bounced around the small space before it settled on Purnama.

He had yet to sit upright, despite the visitors. He hadn't spoken much. He wasn't sweating with a fever, and his lips weren't parched with thirst, but something was wrong with him. He looked only a few years older than Vader. When I looked up again, Slamet, Wangi and Raharjo were talking, but I couldn't join them. My Javanese was not as good as Slamet's Dutch. I managed to catch a few words of their conversation—sun, trees, monkeys.

Monkeys. I could say something about that! I had no idea if anyone other than Slamet understood Dutch, but I nonetheless gathered my courage and said, "I saw a silvery gibbon a few weeks ago."

All three of them stared at me. Slamet narrowed his eyes and shook his head the tiniest bit.

"*Ma'af,*" I apologized, my face heating up. The earthen floor under the mat suddenly seemed like the best place to focus my attention, and I traced patterns in the dirt until they began talking again. Raharjo continued to throw ugly looks my way, and Slamet whispered to his brother after every mean glance. I was certain Raharjo said something else about monkeys.

The tension in the house grew the longer we stayed. It swirled around me like humidity on a hot day. When did we plan to leave? I could make my own excuses, but I had gotten utterly lost and wasn't sure I would be able to make it back on my own.

A cool breeze blew in through the door, and I turned my face to catch it. Rain fell outside. Not too hard, but not too gentle either. It was the kind of rain that cooled the air while it fell but made the afternoon steamy when it stopped.

Suddenly Purnama moaned and began shaking his head. "Oh," I cried. In one motion, I stood, snatched my hat off my head and held it over Purnama's face.

Raharjo jumped up and glared, but Slamet laughed and said something to Wangi. She spoke to me directly, but I didn't understand a word.

Slamet translated. "You are good to keep Purnama out of rain, she says."

"The roof needs new thatch," I said, looking up at the leak.

Raharjo walked to the door, speaking the whole time.

Slamet furrowed his brow and said something to his brother, then turned to me. "He will fix."

That wasn't all Raharjo had said, but I didn't want to know the rest.

Wangi and Slamet dragged Purnama on his rush mat away from the leak, and I placed my hat back on my head. My hair would get damp, but I didn't mind.

By that time, the rain had stopped.

Purnama motioned for me to come over to him. I knelt down. "*Terima kasih,*" he said with a painful grimace.

"It was my pleasure." I smiled at him.

At last, Slamet said our good-byes.

"Wait," he said, after we walked outside. He ran over to his brother, who was bundling thatch. They spoke briefly, smiled at each other and parted.

As Slamet rejoined me, Raharjo called after him, "She is dangerous," and pointed to me. My lips parted to reply before I realized he had spoken in Dutch.

How could I be dangerous? I wasn't the one scaring people. I pushed my spectacles up. Raharjo was a hate-filled, nasty person. What had I ever done to him?

Slamet and I followed the circuitous route out of the village. Chickens ran from us, and I remembered the time long ago when we had chased chickens around Slamet's kampong to see how far they would fly. Sometimes the birds ran into the house, and Indah had to chase them out.

Purnama didn't look able to chase chickens. "What's the matter with Purnama?" I asked. "Why was he lying on that rush mat?"

Slamet slapped a mosquito. "He is sick."

"*Ja*, but what's wrong with him?"

He pointed to his back. "He has hurt."

"He's injured?" I remembered the grimaces on Purnama's face. "Is he in pain?"

Slamet nodded. "*Ya*."

"How did he hurt himself?" I asked, stepping around a puddle.

"He falls from coffee tree."

I gasped. "That's terrible."

"He cannot walk. He cannot feel." Slamet pointed to his chest and then swept his arm down his body.

"Oh, no. Poor Purnama. And Wangi takes care of him?"

He nodded again. "*Ya.* She is his wife. She works for coffee owner. She stops when Purnama falls."

"What a dreadful thing to have happen." If something ever happened to Vader, what would Tante Greet and I do? Probably move in with Oom Maarten.

"The coffee owner does not help. Wangi does not work there."

"What do you mean he doesn't help? He didn't send for a doctor to see Purnama? He didn't offer any money?"

Slamet shrugged. "He is Dutch."

"He's a horrible person," I huffed.

"*Ya,* he is Dutch."

"That has nothing to do with it. He's awful and cruel." Slamet's insistence that the coffee plantation owner acted so callously because he was Dutch was unsettling. "And Wangi had to stop working to take care of her husband?"

He nodded.

"They are fortunate to have friends to help them." Vader's words about needing people came back to me. Would anyone help me if I were in that position? Anyone other than my family? The questions made me uncomfortable and I brushed them away.

We walked in silence toward the mosque. When we passed it and were back on the Great Post Road, I asked, "Why did Raharjo say I was dangerous?"

Slamet blushed and turned his face from mine. "He does not say—"

"*Ja,* he did. I heard him. I didn't even know he spoke Dutch."

He shook his head. "He does not mean . . . he says wrong word."

"Then what did he mean?"

"You are Dutch."

"It's hard to confuse *Dutch* and *dangerous.* He sounded like he was warning you about me. Why? What have I ever done?" I pushed my spectacles up.

"You are Dutch."

"I'm not Dutch, I'm Javanese. I was born here. Like you."

"You are Dutch," he insisted.

I growled and threw my hands up in frustration. "You keep saying that. Am I supposed to know why that's a problem?"

"You run our lives."

I stopped walking. "I don't run your life. Didn't we just visit *your* friends?"

"*Ya*, but you come."

"You told me I could," I pointed out.

"You do not ask," he said. "You say, 'I will come.' This is way you run our lives."

Did I do that? I . . . I did. "But you still agreed," I argued. "You didn't say I couldn't come. You could have."

With a disbelieving look, he asked, "Why do you come?"

"I wanted to spend time with you. I missed you."

"You want me around."

"Of course I do. You're my friend."

"What if I do not want to be friends?"

"What?" My heart stopped at his words. "That's not true, is it?"

He sighed. "I do not know."

"Why do you keep saying these awful things?"

"You are Dutch."

Fed up, I rubbed my eyes. "Fine, Slamet. When you decide to treat me like your friend again, when you decide to act like the boy who used to climb trees and swim in the ocean and watch the stars with me, I'll be here. That boy is my friend." I stalked off and left him on the road. He called after me, but I didn't stop and refused to look back.

23 JULY 1883

My dear Oom Maarten,

    Krakatau continues to send smoke up into the sky. But Vader doesn't seem bothered by it anymore. I suppose it's one of those parts of life that we have to learn to live with.

    I've been having problems with Slamet. He said strange things to me about how the Dutch treat native people. I know there are some Dutch people who treat the natives terribly, but I don't think I've ever been mean to Slamet. At least not intentionally. When I asked him to explain why he's angry about it, he said he's heard bad stories about the Dutch from his brother Raharjo.

    What do you think it could mean? Is Raharjo lying to Slamet? Why would he do that?

    When I met Raharjo, he called me dangerous. Slamet said he meant to say Dutch, but I don't believe him. I yelled at him, and I'm not sure we're friends anymore. What will I do without Slamet?

    In other bad news, my punishment has not been lifted. I'm still only allowed to explore the jungle one time a week. But in good news, last week I spotted a wanderer butterfly in a clearing. It had the most beautiful silvery blue-and-black wings, and it dipped and dived around me. I wish you could have seen it. It would make a beautiful wallpaper pattern. Have you decided which one you will choose?

    I haven't found any stag beetles lately. I still have room in my twenty-sixth case for more specimens, but the beetles seem to have vanished from the jungle. It's so strange. I usually find them all around. I wonder where they could be.

It's almost time for dinner, so I'll finish this letter. I miss you and send

Warmest regards,
Katrien

Chapter 21

The next week, butterflies fluttered around me as I made my way toward the jungle. Several Common Clubtails showed off their striking black-and-white markings and yellow spots. Caper Whites and Koh-i-Noors also dipped in and out of my path.

" 'We behold the face of nature bright with gladness,' " I whispered to myself. I could not remember the last time I'd been inspired to quote Mr. Charles Darwin, and I smiled at the familiar words.

A plaintive cuckoo hiding in the tamarind tree let out its distinctive cry: four sharp notes followed by a little laughing chirp.

I walked around a cluster of kampongs. Children scurried from building to building, calling to each other and chattering in Javanese. Their voices mingled with the twittering of the birds.

Ahead of me, Brigitta and one of her servants emerged from a kampong. I froze.

"When we come back tomorrow, we should bring some rice," Brigitta was saying to her servant. "She needs to eat, Kuwat."

"She will not accept," Kuwat said.

"She needs to. I'll make her some *beras kencur*, and you'll have to get her to drink it."

"I will try," he said.

The she saw me.

"Katrien," she gasped, her face white.

Wary of an insult from her, I said, *"Ja?"*

"What are you doing here?"

"I'm on my way to the jungle." I held my funnel net over my head. "What are you doing? What's *beras kencur?*"

Her pale cheeks turned a bright shade of pink. She spun on her heel and walked off, Kuwat trailing behind her.

My jaw dropped. Brigitta had never passed an opportunity to taunt me before. Something was going on with her, but I decided whatever it was, it didn't matter to me. This was my weekly visit to the jungle, and I wanted it to be wonderful—and untainted by thoughts of Brigitta.

I'd already begun to feel the forest's calming effects by the time I reached the path that would take me deep into the interior. As I walked, I wondered for the millionth time how it could be that something I cared so deeply about could cause Vader and Tante Greet such worry. How could I better explain my feelings about the forest to them? They didn't see the tangle of trees as I did. It wasn't only a laboratory for collecting specimens; it was also the place where I felt most at home. In truth, all of Java held wonders for me, from its deep blue sky and puffy white clouds to its glistening shores and the ocean beyond. Even the hideous scar of smoke from Krakatau rising high into the sky had become part of my landscape. But for me, the jungle was the most welcoming part of the island. It was my sanctuary, more sacred than any other place I knew.

As I stepped into its shady solace, I noted as usual that the air—permeated with the sounds of tree frogs croaking and birds singing—was heavy with decay. The jungle, a place so full of life, was also full of death. The very trail I walked was covered in dead leaves and insects, but even that I found comforting.

At my feet, I watched as a dark line of ants paraded on their own path carrying snips of leaves to their nest. I knelt down for a closer look, leaning on the handle of my funnel net for balance. My heels sank in the mud.

" 'It is interesting to contemplate an entangled bank, clothed with many plants of many kinds, with birds singing on the bushes, with

various insects flitting about, and with worms crawling through the damp earth, and to reflect that these elaborately constructed forms, so different from each other and dependent on each other in so complex a manner, have all been produced by laws acting around us,'" I quoted.

I stepped over the busy ants and continued through the maze of trees, following my usual route. Sunlight filtered through the tree-tops and I stopped to observe that here and there, the dappled light would hit a leaf and make it glow like a star. Familiar to me as it was, the jungle still changed every time I set foot in it.

At its outskirts, the town of Anjer encroached on this green wonderland one house at a time. But farther inland, the forest was much darker. The trees grew so thick and their canopy was so dense that little sunlight reached the ground below.

Tante Greet and Vader always insisted I go no more than half a kilometer into the undergrowth. Whenever I complained Tante Greet said, "Any bugs you want to collect will just have to come to you."

But what they didn't know wouldn't hurt them, so I didn't tell them I had been far more than half a kilometer into the forest. Years ago Slamet had shown me a clearing about four kilometers inland. It was one of my favorite places to visit.

In the clearing, banyan trees grew next to a stream. Sampaguita vines climbed some of their roots, and the scent of the Sampaguita flowers filled the air even though they wouldn't bloom until nightfall.

The clearing called to me today, and I headed in that direction with my net ready and my eyes peeled. Since I had left the house, I hadn't seen a single stag beetle. As I made my way deeper into the undergrowth, I could hear the stream gurgling in the distance. I had just crossed the tree line when the pungent odor of wet animal stung my nose. I began to look for the source of the scent when a rapid movement made me freeze.

A pack of dholes, a kind of wild dog, was frolicking with each other in the stream, jumping in and out of the water. Their behavior was a cross between that of a domestic dog and a house cat.

With slender amber bodies and black-tipped tails, the animals—about six or seven of them—nipped at each other. Their white chests sparkled when the sunlight hit the drops of water clinging to their fur. They swatted each other with their paws, and I swore some of them smiled.

One dhole bounced up and down in the water and tried to catch the flying droplets. A bubble of laughter escaped my throat. The dholes acted like children discovering a new toy.

I was just beginning to get comfortable observing them when one of the dholes climbed out of the water and approached me. Crouching low on his haunches, he bared his sharp white teeth. They gleamed in the sunlight, and I took a step back, moving my net in front of me. My heart raced as I imagined the entire pack attacking me at once. I couldn't help thinking right then that this was why Tante Greet and Vader didn't want me wandering so far into the jungle.

But then another dhole, one I hadn't noticed, sat up in the middle of the clearing and let out a series of strange noises, not unlike a hen or a duck. They almost sounded like clucking, where I expected barks.

Whatever the noise, the other dholes understood its meaning. Even the menacing one obeyed. They all followed the lead dhole, who raced out of the clearing and moved inland.

I let out a shaky breath and pushed my spectacles up. "What was that about?" I wondered aloud.

After taking a moment to calm myself, I took my journal out of my bug bag. Oom Maarten had christened my small rucksack with that name when he gave it to me. "For all your tropical traipsings," he had said. I didn't have the heart to tell him he ought to call it an insect bag instead.

Every time I came to the jungle I used my bug bag. I didn't keep a diary, but like any good naturalist, I did keep notes of my explorations, bearing in mind Mr. Charles Darwin's position that *"The opinion of naturalists having sound judgment and wide experience seems the only guide to follow."*

I jotted down a few thoughts about the encounter and dropped the book back in the satchel. Oom Maarten's latest letter rested beside my journal.

As I walked across the clearing, I tried imitating that strange bark the dholes made. "Ah, ah, ah, ah, ah, ah." I licked my lips and tried again with a higher pitch. "Ah, ah, ah, ah, ah, ah." When I reached the banyan tree, I stopped.

Banyan trees do not grow like most trees. They do not start life as a tiny seed and grow up, reaching for the sunlight. Banyan seeds take root in crevices on other trees. Once they sprout, they feed off the host tree. As a banyan grows, roots shoot off from its branches and stretch down to the ground.

This banyan was old. It had thick branches with four trunks intertwined in an elaborate root system. They fanned out like the toes of a water monitor lizard. When I stepped up to the trunk, the tallest roots came almost to my knees. I needed to be careful.

After leaning my funnel net against the tree, I placed my foot on a root and grabbed another growing to the ground. Its circumference was about the size around of a man's fist, and I knew it would be strong enough to hold me. A branch about four meters above reached its sturdy arms over the stream. Using notches in the wood as footholds, I pulled myself hand over hand up to the extending branch, finally swinging my leg over it and resting my back against the trunk.

This was the perfect place to read Oom Maarten's latest letter. Settling more comfortably on my perch, I pulled it out of my bug bag.

To my adored niece,

I am sorry to hear you're having difficulties with your friend. And I admit Slamet's brother does sound rather harsh. However, as you grow older you will discover it becomes more and more difficult to maintain childhood friendships. I myself am no longer friends with any of the boys and girls who were our neighbors and friends as children. And that has nothing to do with my moving to Java. We grew up. We found new interests. We grew apart. It is, unfortunately, the way of the world.

I sighed. This wasn't the kind of support I wanted. I wanted him to tell me how to stay friends with Slamet, not to let him go.

You will make other friends. Perhaps even friends Greet would prefer, but don't fret too much if she doesn't. She always needs something to worry about. If it's not your friendships, then it's my bachelorhood. And you can see how much I let that affect me!

Oom Maarten's tiny house could never accomodate a wife. Tante Greet asked him every time she saw him when he was going to get married and buy a larger home. He always chuckled and said, "After you, Greet," and Vader would just laugh at them both.

As to your bugs,

"Insects," I whispered.

I can't say I'm saddened to hear that you haven't found any in a while.
But I know that upsets you, so I'm upset on your behalf. But not really.
You know I find those things terrifying. I have nightmares about your collection coming to life and eating you whole.

"That's a gruesome image, Oom Maarten."

But I wish you good luck with your bugs all the same.

Happy hunting—M

His letter didn't offer the advice I wanted, but at least it made me smile. That was something.

"Ah, ah, ah, ah, ah, ah." I tried making the dhole's noise again. It was such an odd sound for an animal to make. "Ah, ah, a—"

A rustling noise made me stop and look down from my perch. I could scarcely believe my eyes.

At the opposite end of the clearing stood a Javan rhinoceros, the second one I had seen in less than a month. Since I was up in the tree, I didn't think he would be a threat, but my heart still beat like a sparrow's wings. If he decided to stay here overnight, I would be trapped, and Vader and Tante Greet would be furious.

He moved across the clearing, leaving a trail of crushed grass in his path. Stopping at the stream, he scratched his enormous feet against the ground. The deep folds of thick hide reminded me of leather saddles. I wondered how anything could injure such a tough skin. Gray hairs, slightly darker than his flesh, grew thicker on the folded parts of his hide.

When he finished drinking, he followed the stream farther inland.

I pushed my spectacles up. Why had I seen two Javan rhinos so recently, when I'd never seen one before in my life?

" 'Rarity is the attribute of a vast number of species of all classes, in all countries,' " I murmured.

That silvery gibbon, too. I had never seen one of those before either. To see two creatures for the first time in such a short period? It was odd.

And these animals seemed to be on the move, all heading inland. Deeper into the undergrowth. What had Mr. De Groot said? *The animals could take care of themselves.* Were they doing that? If so, why now?

The jungle closed in around me. The cool damp no longer felt welcoming. A gloom filled the air and my spine tingled as if someone were blowing on my neck.

I was suddenly consumed with the need to talk through what I had seen, and I scrambled down the banyan tree. Vader would still be at work, and I hated to disturb him. But he would listen, even if he didn't have any answers. Leaving the wilds of the bush, I returned to the cultivated landscape of Anjer.

Part Two

AUGUST 1883

Anjer, Java, Dutch East Indies

Chapter 22

By the end of August the heat had grown oppressive. Even the ocean breezes did little to help circulate the air. The sun shone all around Anjer. People avoided the open roads and strolled along under the trees. Some ladies carried parasols; others found relief with lacy fans. Everyone wore white and looked like clouds come down to visit Earth.

In the distance, the sunlight danced on the waters of the Sunda Strait, making the surface twinkle. The pale cloud of smoke hanging over Krakatau created the sole ugly spot, and even that line of gray had a kind of majesty in its ability to remind us all of the power of nature to impress mankind. Every time I saw it, I couldn't help thinking of Mr. Darwin's words: *"There is grandeur in this view of life, with its several powers, having been originally breathed into a few forms or into one."*

I kept those words to myself, though, on the afternoon that Tante Greet said, "That smoke. All it does is hang over the island. Like a guest who refuses to leave."

"Let us not be bothered by the ugliness over Krakatau," Vader responded. "The sun is shining and all is well."

It was true. Despite the heat, the afternoon was so glorious that I couldn't even worry about the sewing lesson awaiting me later in the day.

We stood on the beach. The tide was out and the sharp dark coral poked up out of the shore. "It's marvelous, isn't it?" he asked.

I grinned. "I love it. There isn't a more beautiful place."

"It is even more lovely and tranquil than the North Sea," Tante Greet agreed.

"How different can the North Sea be? It's all ocean."

She brushed some stray hairs behind my ear. "Oh, Katrien, it's one of the reasons we should visit the Netherlands. You have—"

But I never learned what Tante Greet was about to tell me.

For it was then that a blast, a tremendous blast, far louder than any cannon fire I had ever heard, reverberated around the strait with a thundering boom.

Every head on the beach turned toward the fearsome noise in astonishment and surprise.

"Katrien," she said, her voice urgent, "we need to go home."

"*Ja.*" But I didn't budge until she jerked my hand. Once I was moving, I felt an urge to run and hide, but I couldn't see anything.

My ears heard every little noise, though—the hitch in my aunt's breath as she struggled to walk, the frightened whinnies of horses, the howling of dogs.

Tante Greet dragged me down the beach. The darkness pressed around us.

"I can't see, Katrien," Tante Greet squeaked.

"I can't either." I felt my aunt whip her head in my direction. "But I know the way. I'll lead."

We inched along the beach, stopping when the air choked us. It had not been that long since the eruption, but my throat grew raw from coughing up the filth. The smell made everything worse. Not even ruined fish or boiled cabbage had this odor—like thousands of eggs left to rot in the sun.

A single spot of light wavered ahead of us. "I think it's the hotel," I panted. The sense of relief that washed over me must have been what sailors felt when they saw a lighthouse beacon during a terrible storm. The Anjer lighthouse was farther down the beach from the hotel, but I couldn't see its light in this pitch dark. Another shudder of fear ran down my spine.

"I need to rest, Katrien. I can't breathe." Tante Greet's words came in short, sharp bursts.

We made our way—step by slow step—to the hotel porch, and I waved my hand in front of me to help guide me to the stairs. Tante Greet clung to my waist as I climbed them and headed for the doors.

The glow from the windows was faint but seeing it helped. I had never been more happy to set foot inside the Hotel Anjer. We pushed the door open and collapsed inside.

Prettily dressed men and women crowded the lobby and stared at us with fearful eyes. On any other day they would have been enjoying the sunshine—outside. But here they all were, coated with a light dusting of ash and stepping away from us as if we had brought the volcano in with us.

Tante Greet drew her handkerchief from her sleeve and coughed into it with a force that shook her shoulders.

Wilhemina De Graff raced over and grabbed my hands. "Katrien, what is going on?"

"Krakatau has erupted."

"How long will it last?"

"I don't know." I pushed my spectacles up.

Her eyes, round and rimmed with tears, shone in the light of the lamps. "This is far worse than it was in May."

I had suspected so, but I couldn't say anything. I had been in Batavia then. Safe. The De Groots had been right to leave.

Tante Greet continued to cough beside me, her hacking finally easing into delicate, ladylike sounds.

"When I came here from Rotterdam, I only wanted to find a rich man to marry. I never thought I would have to deal with this." Wilhemina's face crumpled, and she pressed her fingers against her eyes. I reached over to comfort her but stopped. I was covered in ash. She wouldn't want to be dirty as well as terrified.

I wanted to go home. To get out of this filthy, hot air. I could feel the grit everywhere. My eyes burned behind my spectacles, and my clothes weighed at least an additional kilogram.

Worst of all, my throat was coated. I knew it was unladylike, but I couldn't think of another solution. I stepped away from Wilhemina and my aunt and spat mouthfuls of ash into my hand, again and again.

"Katrien!" Tante Greet cried.

"Apologies, Tante," I said, wiping my hand on my skirt. Grit remained in my mouth, but I didn't spit anymore.

Instead I coughed and almost retched from the effort. When I finally caught my breath, I turned to my aunt. "We should go," I managed.

She nodded. "Do you have a handkerchief with you? After that display, I certainly hope you don't."

I shook my head. "No, why?" Leave it to my aunt to be caught in a volcanic eruption and still be concerned about my manners.

"We could hold them over our noses and mouths. They may help us breathe."

"Oh, that's a wonderful suggestion." Surprise at her good idea filled my voice. "Let me see if Wilhemina has one she'll lend me."

Wilhemina stood back at the reception counter. She gave me a handkerchief with a generous smile. "You know you can stay here. You don't have to go home."

"*Dank u*, but we'll get in your way here."

I returned to my aunt. We took one last breath of relatively clean air and left the hotel.

Chapter 24

By the time Tante Greet and I reached home, we were completely covered in ash. Our hat brims were bent from the extra weight, and our shuffling steps had kicked up the powder on the ground the entire way, which in turn had thoroughly coated our legs and undergarments.

Tante Greet and I fell into the hall and slammed the door behind us. The clock chimed three times. The walk home typically took about twenty minutes, but it had just taken us two hours.

"You are home!" Slamet cried from the parlor. He had been sitting on the floor and he popped up as we stumbled through the doorway.

"What are you doing here?" I croaked through a throat full of dust. Since our fight, I had seen him exactly twice. We hadn't spoken, and he darted away from me both times.

"I come here after noise. I help Ibu close doors, windows."

"*Dank u. Terima kasih.*" It was such a thoughtful act that I hoped the old Slamet was back. I moved toward him, but he ducked away, fidgeting, with his head bent.

"Slamet, what is the matter?" I pushed my spectacles up.

He took a deep breath and glanced away. "*Ma'af.* I think here is safer."

"There's no need to apologize, Slamet," Tante Greet said in that forceful way of hers, although I didn't think he was talking to us. "You did the right thing coming here. It is safer." Her voice gentled. "And *dank u* for closing the doors and windows. The furniture in this house would be buried in ash if you hadn't. If you don't mind, we're going to try to wash some of this off."

He nodded. "I am with Ibu."

In my bedroom, a pyramid of powder sat under the large window. I ignored it and instead pulled off everything I wore and threw the clothes in a corner. They collapsed like saggy elephant skin, all gray and wrinkled. My nicest outfit. It would never be clean again.

I took off my spectacles and grabbed a handkerchief. But no matter how hard I rubbed, I could not wipe the ash off the lenses. It just moved from one side to the other. Homo sapiens. Thank goodness I had another pair in a drawer. They were tarnished and scratched, and I didn't see as well with them, but at least I wouldn't be looking through a smoky haze when I wore them.

After removing the pins from my hair, I shook my head like a dog. Ash flew everywhere, but I didn't care. *"For each has to live by a struggle; but it is not necessarily the best possible under all possible conditions."* I grimaced. Conditions were certainly not the best possible now.

As I brushed my hair, more ash floated to the floor.

Next, I tackled the grit stuck to my skin. Fortunately, I had water in my pitcher and basin on the vanity. After moistening a small cloth, I rubbed my face and managed to get it clean, for the most part, but the ash didn't dissolve in the water. It turned to mud.

I couldn't use the basin again.

Grabbing another cloth, I scrubbed my whole body without water. The grit still clung all over, but there was nothing else I could do. I would have to wait until Krakatau stopped rumbling before I could have a proper bath.

I stared at the mud in the basin and thought of our water barrels standing outside, no doubt covered in residue. Or mud, since that's what happened when the ash and water collided.

I dressed in clean clothes and allowed myself one last glance in the mirror. I saw pink cheeks and red-rimmed eyes. Dirty hair. Bits of gray still clung to my arms and neck. Never mind a bath. When this was all over, I would go for a swim in the ocean to clean myself off. I grabbed my old spectacles and left the room.

Down the hall I found Indah and Slamet standing in a corner of the kitchen with their heads bent together. Rapid whispers in Javanese floated across the room. I cleared my throat.

Slamet kept whispering to his mother. His face was a mixture of anger and disappointment. She brushed him away, straightened and walked toward me. "I have favor."

"Ibu, do not—"

Indah cut off Slamet's protest with a hard look. "I have favor," she repeated.

"Of course," I said, surprised.

Slamet fingered the *kris* at his side, and I gulped. His furious expression made me wonder if he might use the dagger. Why was he so angry?

Just then Tante Greet breezed into the room. She had changed clothes, but ash still clung to her arms and hair, too. She had also pinned her hair back into a bun, while mine hung loose around my shoulders. "Is it possible to make some tea?" she asked.

"I don't think we have any water," I said.

With a sigh, she said, "Oh, well." Then she noticed Slamet and his angry look. "Is something wrong?"

"I have favor," Indah said once more.

"What favor?" Tante Greet asked.

"We go to mosque."

"But that's over a kilometer away!" I looked at my aunt. She couldn't allow this. It had taken us two hours to walk half that distance!

Tante Greet, always a bit aloof with Indah, softened. With the barest nod, she consented. "Of course. I understand."

"It will take them forever in this ash and dark," I protested. "They should stay here."

"I am strong. I help Ibu," Slamet said. He seemed to grow taller as he spoke. "We want to pray."

"You can pray here." I waved my arm toward the kitchen corner where I had seen them kneeling many times. "We won't interrupt you."

Utter astonishment filled his face before his expression hardened. "Allah hears prayers better from mosque."

"Is that what Raharjo says?" I could not believe I asked the question, but their desire to leave the safety of our home made no sense. It had to be something to do with Raharjo's influence. Slamet—and more importantly, Indah—could not be this illogical!

"It is truth," he said.

"It is ridiculous!" I rubbed my eyes and stormed out of the room.

"Take a lantern with you," I heard my aunt saying behind me.

I yelled back to them, "And tie something around your mouth!"

I was going to go back to my bedroom, but something made me reconsider. I stomped to the front door and waited for them, instead. A quotation from Mr. Charles Darwin floated through my mind: *In some cases, however, the extermination of whole groups of beings, as of ammonites towards the close of the secondary period, has been wonderfully sudden.* Why would I think about ammonites at a time like this? I pushed my scratched spectacles up.

When Indah and Slamet reached the door, she touched my arm. *"Selamat tinggal,"* she said.

"Good-bye. Be careful," I told her.

She hugged me. *"Terima kasih."*

I turned to Slamet. The angry set of his mouth. His haunted eyes. This was not the face of my friend. Some other boy had replaced my friend with an impostor.

I wanted my friend back.

But I knew—just as I knew that Earth revolved around the sun—that with my unfeeling words in the kitchen, our relationship had shattered.

I remembered Oom Maarten's words about friendships ending. I remembered Slamet saying there were things about him I would not, could not, understand. Maybe they were both right. But I did not want us to part in anger.

Slamet and Indah moved to leave. I knew I had one final chance to see my friend—my old friend, my only friend—before they left.

"Slamet." My voice cracked on his name. "I apologize for my outburst."

He looked at me, and for one brief moment, the Slamet I knew shone through his eyes. Some strange impulse compelled me to fling my arms around him. To hold onto him forever. He stiffened, but I squeezed him tight.

He took a step back, but I only rocked forward, clinging to him. I would not let my friend go. But he finally managed to escape my grasp, his face as red as the Ousterhoudts' flowers.

"*Selamat jalan*," I said.

"*Sampai jumpa lagi*," he said.

"*Ja*. Until we meet again." I didn't know if that would be true. And if only his angry impostor returned, I wasn't sure I wanted to meet again. But I would not think of that now.

Indah opened the door, and she and Slamet stepped into the black afternoon.

Chapter 25

As evening fell, Tante Greet and I kept busy. By the time the clock chimed seven, we had dusted the ash off all the furniture and swept it into piles in the corners of every room. The rumbling from Krakatau continued like constant, rolling thunder. I traced patterns in the thin layer of powder that had somehow managed to coat the inside of the windows. Outside, the view was now pitch black.

Please keep Indah and Slamet safe. Please keep Indah and Slamet safe. I prayed this silent plea over and over. I was sorry for what I had said to Slamet earlier, but I still didn't understand what Tante Greet had been thinking, letting them leave the house. "Why did she do that?"

"Did you say something, Katrien?" Tante Greet asked.

Did I? I pushed my spectacles up. "Why did you let them leave?" I asked.

"Lift them, please." She sat on the sofa and patted the cushion next to her, but I crossed my arms and refused to budge.

"I let them leave for the very same reasons we left the hotel," she said.

"What do you mean? It made sense for us to leave the hotel. We were taking up space there. We didn't live there. It wasn't our home."

"Katrien, the same thing could be said for Indah and Slamet here."

"They weren't taking up space!" If she said they were, I would shove her back outside.

"No, they weren't," she agreed. "But did you want to stay at the hotel?"

"Of course not."

"Why not?" She stayed calm, despite the maelstrom outside and the edge that was creeping into my voice.

"It wasn't home," I repeated. I looked around. Every lamp in our parlor was lit. The furniture had some of the awful powder coating it, but everything was still familiar and comforting in the scary turmoil of the eruption.

"Precisely," said Tante Greet. "This is not their home."

"But they didn't go home." I pointed in the direction of their kampong. "They went to the mosque." I flung my arm behind me and accidentally pushed the window open. A whirl of ash blew inside before I could hook it closed again. "Terra firma," I muttered at the new layer of filth on my blouse.

"Language," said Tante Greet. "Katrien, the mosque is where they feel comforted," she explained. Again, she patted the seat next to her, and this time I joined her. "I think we both need some comforting ourselves right now."

"What do you suggest?" I asked in a tiny voice. The thunder from Krakatau echoed in my head.

"When I was a little girl, I always liked hearing about the Netherlands. I loved the history, the stories. Would you like to hear something like that?"

I nodded.

"I'll be right back." She went into the study with a lamp and returned a few moments later carrying a leather-bound book. When she settled back on the sofa, she pulled me toward her. I rested my head on her shoulder. The book was dusty, but I didn't know how much of that was ash and how much was from sitting unread for years. She opened the cover and began, *"The History of the Netherlands* by Thomas Colley Grattan. Chapter one. B.C. 50 to A.D. 250."

"So long ago," I said. "It's a solace. To know the world has been around so long."

Tante Greet nodded and began to read. " 'The Netherlands form a kingdom of moderate extent, situated on the borders of the ocean, opposite to the south-east coast of England, and stretching from the frontiers of France to those of Hanover. The country is principally composed of low and humid grounds, presenting a vast plain, irrigated by the waters from all those neighbouring states which are traversed by the Rhine, the Meuse, and the Scheldt.' "

She read with a low, reassuring tone, and her voice drifted over me. *I should be furious with her*, I thought, *for letting Indah and Slamet leave. For keeping me from the jungle. For so many things.* But her arm around my shoulders was so warm. The soft murmur of her voice so soothing. I tried to block out the rumbling, the worry, the fear. I clung to the comfort my aunt provided like a drowning man clings to driftwood.

" 'The history of the Netherlands is, then, essentially that of a patient and industrious population struggling against every obstacle which nature could oppose to its well-being; and, in this contest, man triumphed most completely over the elements in those places where they offered the greatest resistance.' "

Another blast outside caused both of us to jump like startled cats.

"That—that wasn't Krakatau, was it?" Tante Greet asked, panic in her voice.

"I don't know."

It hadn't been as loud as the blast from this afternoon. I walked to the door and opened it to try to identify the source of the noise.

"You can't see anything," Tante Greet reminded me.

"Yes, but..." I trailed off as I took in the blackness. She was correct. But just as I swung the door back to close it, she stopped me.

"What is that?" She pointed toward the docks.

An orange glow shimmered in the darkness. It appeared to be near Vader's office.

"Is it a fire?" I asked. Someone must have set an oil lamp too close to a curtain.

Tante Greet's hands were on my shoulders, squeezing them like a boa constrictor. I grimaced and shifted, but she didn't stop. "Tante, you're hurt—" I began.

But then another blast sounded, and the orange glow grew larger. It was certainly a fire.

"Oh, my God," Tante Greet whispered. "Niels."

I turned cold with fear. So cold I wondered how my aunt could keep touching me. Vader's office *was* near that fire. Vader was near that fire. I shoved Tante Greet away and ran down the steps, slipping in the ash piled on them. I couldn't see anything ahead of me.

"Katrien! Come back!"

"No," I screamed. "I have to get to Vader."

"Katrien!"

A streak of bright orange lit the sky. It arced overhead and fell with a thud in the center of town. Flames leaped into the sky and sparks flew into the air, fizzling out in the darkness. I cried out in fear, skidding to a halt. What was happening? My stomach clenched. I couldn't breathe; the ash was too thick.

"Katrien!" Tante Greet grabbed me and dashed back under the porch.

More balls of fire rained down, some extinguishing before hitting the ground and others setting more buildings alight.

Mrs. De Groot had not mentioned anything like this. This was more like stories I had heard of Pompeii. All those people who died there. Was that going to happen to us? Were these my last few moments on Earth? Standing under our porch with Tante Greet's fingers grasping mine? Vader in his office, so close and so far at the same time?

No!

I ran back inside. Tante Greet followed me and shut the door. She took a sharp breath and coughed. When she looked at me, she had tears in her eyes. I had never seen my aunt cry, and the sight unnerved me. Suddenly I felt like tiny insects were crawling all over me. I scratched my arms and my neck and my fingers and my head. My hands would not stop moving.

Tante Greet shook me, and I stilled. "Calm down, Katrien." Her voice was firm. "Stay here, and do not move."

I did as she said, watching as she stepped back outside and stood on the porch.

"Are they still falling?" I called.

She didn't answer. The clock chimed eight times. I did math in my head to distract myself. It had been seven hours since the eruption, five hours since we made it home, and four hours since Indah and Slamet left.

I gasped. Indah and Slamet! They were walking to the mosque. They might be out there in this rain of fire. "Oh, God," I moaned. "Tante Greet?"

She came back inside and shut the door again. "I think it's over."

I collapsed, shivering, against her. "What about Indah and Slamet? Did you see anything falling toward the mosque?"

She shook her head. "We'll pray that they are safe."

Chapter 26

The night dragged on. Tante Greet and I stayed in the parlor where the glow from the fires was now visible through our front windows. Eventually they died down. The only good thing about the heaviness in the air tonight was that wind couldn't blow, and flames couldn't revive and spread.

This knowledge eased my fears about our house catching fire, but it did little to calm my nerves about Vader. His office was so near the first fire. I hoped with all my might that he had been able to get to safety in the hotel. He could still send telegraph messages from the hotel's machine. He could still do his job from there.

My stomach rumbled like Krakatau, and I realized I hadn't eaten since before the eruption.

"Are you hungry?" Tante Greet asked from her seat on the sofa.

I rubbed my arms. I was hungry but didn't know if I could bring myself to eat anything.

"We may as well eat," she said. "Perhaps then we can try to get some sleep." She trotted to the kitchen.

She expected me to sleep in this? Krakatau grumbled in reply. I couldn't sleep now. Too many fears and worries rushed through me anew. My mind wouldn't quit churning up images from Mrs. De Groot's story and my own imagination.

"Katrien," Tante Greet called, "come help me, please."

I dragged myself down the hall, wondering if food would help ease my fear.

My aunt rummaged through the shelves in the pantry before popping out with a wax-covered wheel of Edam in her hand. "Cheese!" She set it on the table and returned to the pantry. "Is there any *volkorenbrood* left?"

"*Ja*, I can tear the loaf in half."

"Do that, please."

After breaking the bread into chunks, I stared at the cheese.

"We've also got *belimbing*," Tante Greet said, coming back into the kitchen carrying two star fruits. "That will work." She plucked the cheese from my hands. The knife went through the waxy surface with only slight force. Then she sliced the star fruit while I grabbed a wooden tray.

"I think we still have tea in the pot," I said.

Her face wrinkled in disgust. "It will be cold."

"It's better than nothing."

She shrugged and poured the tea into two cups. Each of us had bread, cheese and star fruit—the only stars visible on Java, I imagined. The thunder from Krakatau rumbled in the distance, drowning out the sounds of our chewing.

"Do you think Oom Maarten is safe?" I asked.

She took a deep breath and nodded. "I'm sure he is." She didn't sound sure.

"We should have left." Even to my own ears, I sounded shrill, and my hands shook. "Like the De Groots. We should have listened to them. We're not going to make it." Then my voice broke like a shattered cup.

"Shhh, Katrien." Tante Greet patted my hand. "Shhh. Don't think like that."

The tea did nothing to wash the grit from my mouth, and the food tasted like it had been sprinkled with dirt.

It made me think of the earth and worms, of rotting flesh and death. "*Nevertheless so profound is our ignorance, and so high our presumption, that we marvel when we hear of the extinction of an organic being; and as we do not see the cause, we involve cataclysms to desolate the world, or invest laws on the duration of the forms of life."* Cataclysms. I was in a cataclysm now. Had Mr. Charles Darwin ever been in such a cataclysm? Would I escape this one? Was the world headed toward extinction? Or just me?

"The ash was piling up when we were outside," Tante Greet said, worry filling her voice. "It's probably higher now."

I shrugged, unsure why the ash was worrying her. It was messy and choked the breath out of you, but inside the house, breathing was much easier. As long as we didn't disturb the piles of powder.

"If it keeps up, the roof could collapse."

"What?" I cried. "It's ash! It weighs no more than a feather!"

"*Ja*, but think of how the ash bent your hat earlier." She glanced at the window. "Now it's piling up like snow."

"I don't understand." I pushed my spectacles up. "What does it matter if it's like snow?"

Tante Greet reached across the table and squeezed my hand. "Snow can collapse roofs when it gets too heavy. It happens, and it can be deadly for anyone inside the building."

I stared at her. Could this be true? I had never seen snow. I had read about it, of course, but it never snowed in Java. "Should we leave the house?" I asked.

"No. We'll take our chances. Better to be inside and able to breathe than outside and struggling."

I was now consumed by this new worry. I thought I heard the roof groan with the weight of the ash, but I knew it was only my imagination. I hoped it was only my imagination.

We finished our meal. Tante Greet dusted again, and I stood by the parlor window. My reflection in the glass didn't look like me. My hair was even more of a mane than before, and fear filled my red-rimmed eyes. The rumbles from Krakatau reminded me of a rampaging rhinoceros. What if it never stopped? What would happen to us? Would it be dark forever? Was it dark in Batavia? Was Oom Maarten safe? Had Indah and Slamet reached the mosque? Was this the end of the world?

"I don't know, Katrien."

I didn't realize I had spoken aloud. Tante Greet and I stared at each other. Her lips trembled, but she didn't cry. She enveloped me in her arms. My face squashed against her shoulder, and my spectacles floated up to my forehead.

We stood there a long time. Clutching each other. She had never held me like this before. I wanted to cry, but the tears wouldn't fall. "I'm scared," I whispered.

Her arms tightened around me. "I am, too, Katrien. I am, too."

The clock in the hall ticked louder and louder, but the two of us stayed together, wrapped in each other's warm embrace.

Chapter 27

Despite the incessant rumblings from Krakatau, Tante Greet said we should try to get some rest. "Who knows what tomorrow will bring?" she said.

After pulling on some nightclothes, I crawled into bed and stared at the stars Vader had painted on my ceiling years ago. *On the Origin of Species* lay on my bedside table, but I couldn't read it. Not tonight. I had too many thoughts and worries dancing through my mind.

Was Vader safe?

What about Indah and Slamet?

Did Oom Maarten know what was happening?

I blew out my candle and tried to calm myself by naming animals I had seen in the jungle. "Silvery gibbon. Javan rhinoceros. Javan lutung." It was difficult to remember them all. "Dholes. Oriental whipsnake...wanderer butterfly...long-tailed macaque." I yawned. "Flower pot toad...black giant squirrel." I yawned again. "*Hexarthrius rhinoceros rhinoceros...*"

I must have fallen asleep because I was groggy and disoriented when a loud explosion shot me right out of bed.

"I think that one was louder than yesterday's." Tante Greet stood in my bedroom doorway holding a candle.

"It sounded like it was." She was blurry, and I reached for my spectacles. "Is it morning?"

"Almost. It's early. You ought to get dressed."

"*Ja*, Tante." The cold, scary darkness still cloaked Anjer and I lit the candle on the bedside table.

Ash, seeping in through the windows and the cracks around the doors, coated the furniture again. The pyramid under my bedroom window had grown.

Tante Greet met me in the hall and handed me a banana. "It's still falling," she said with a glance to the ceiling.

Monsoons were never this terrible. Even those rains came in ebbs and flows. This ceaseless torrent would bury us. "Like Pompeii," I whispered.

"We shouldn't talk about that," my aunt said. "Come here." Leading me into my room, she brushed my hair off my shoulders, pulling it into a tight braid. "Much better. It won't fall in your eyes."

"*Dank u*, Tante Greet," I whispered. The arrival of a new day did little to quash my fears.

She smiled. "Come along, Katrien. Eat your banana. We need to keep busy. Let's sweep this new dust into piles. It will be that much easier to straighten when this is all over."

"But what—"

She whipped her head around and gave me a glare that would have stopped a Javan tiger in its tracks. My mouth snapped shut.

"I left the broom in the pantry," she said. "I'll brush off furniture and you can sweep the floors. We'll start in the parlor."

Gulping down the banana, I tossed the peel onto the kitchen table, along with the remains of last night's pathetic meal. The clock chimed six. So early. Yawning, I went to get the broom.

As I swept, the powdery ash swirled around the floor with my thoughts. Tante Greet had been worried about the ash last night. I rubbed some between my fingers and decided it was like beach sand mixed with flour. It still seemed strange to think that something so fine could damage a roof, but if Tante Greet was worried, then the possibility must exist.

Tante Greet stared out the window. The sun must have risen somewhere on the other side of all that filth because the sky had lightened a bit. Now the dark was gloomy but no longer oppressive. Not that it mattered. We still needed candles and lamps to light the room.

Half of the parlor had been dusted and swept when another eruption shook the house, rattling the windows. One pane cracked but did not shatter. "Why won't it stop?" I cried.

Tante shook her head.

More rumbling from Krakatau. But under the thunder, another noise started. The dark haze of smoke kept me from seeing anything. Racking my brain to figure out what it sounded like, I dropped the broom and pushed my spectacles up.

"Katrien, please get back to work. We have oth—"

"Shhh!" I thrust my finger in front of my mouth to hush her.

"Is that rain?" she wondered.

In that moment I knew. Mrs. De Groot's story echoed in my memory. My mouth went dry. My stomach clenched. "Oh, God. It's the ocean." Grabbing Tante Greet's hand, I yelled, "RUN!"

Chapter 28

We tore out of the parlor doors and whipped around the house. My aunt, whom I half dragged behind me, cried, "Careful, Katrien! The rosebushes!"

I swerved to avoid crashing into the spindly things, but my skirt snagged on some of the thorns. I did not stop moving and heard the fabric rip.

The thick blanket of powder slowed us down. It was worse than trying to run on the beach. We pushed our way through the drifts and the falling ash.

"Keep running, Katrien," Tante Greet panted behind me, her hand slipping in mine. I tightened my grip.

Our slog through the ash was taking too long. I could hear the ocean roiling behind me, and I pictured a wall of clear blue water coming to sweep us away.

Tante Greet stopped in the cemetery by the Dutch Reformed Church. She leaned against the side of the little wooden building. "I'm not going to make it, Katrien."

"*Ja*, you will," I insisted, reaching for her hand. "I'll carry you into the jungle if I have to."

She brushed me away. "No, Katrien, you keep going. I'll wait here."

"I'm not going to leave you." The rushing sound got louder, more distinct, over the rumblings of Krakatau.

"Your father will have to come this way. I'll rest, and he and I will join you."

"Vader—" I stopped. Vader would never leave his post. She was making excuses.

The thunderous roar of the ocean grew even louder. I couldn't hear my own breathing.

We couldn't hide behind the tombstones. They weren't tall enough.

But the trees could work. They were tamarinds with solid trunks and thick branches. Perfect for climbing. "We have to get up there." I pointed to a low-hanging branch.

"Have you lost your mind?"

"It's our only hope."

"I can't climb a tree."

"Your life may depend on it."

"You climb. I will cling to the trunk."

"No—"

"Do it, Katrien!" She shoved me toward the tree.

The ash still fell like rain. I shimmied up the trunk, my feet slipping numerous times on the powder-coated tree. But my experienced fingers clung like a house gecko crawling up a window. They sifted through the grit and gripped the rough bark. I had just gotten my legs and arms over the lowest branch when the giant wave attacked Anjer.

Crack!

As the water smashed through town, the sound of splintering wood was the first noise I could identify above the roar. Then a sharp crash followed as glass shattered, and a grinding screech as metal buckled, and heavy thudding as large objects shifted from their foundations.

The wave itself was worse than I imagined. Much worse. It was not a clear blue, but a roiling gray-green mass, as tall as the tree I clutched. It washed over buildings, casting them aside like houses of cards.

"I love you, Katrien!" Tante Greet cried from below.

She flung her arms around the base of the tamarind as the water washed over us. My body lifted off the branch, and I held my breath. I squeezed my arms and clung with my fingertips.

The water pummeled the tree, whipping me around and around as objects banged against my legs and side. My hands stayed glued to the branch. My chest ached.

Keep holding your breath. Keep holding your breath. Oh, God, please let me keep holding my breath! I had never prayed so hard.

My fingers began to ache as the bark bit into them and the water continued to gush. But I vowed not to let go, even when the salty, dirty sea seeped between my clamped lips and my legs caught the current, making my body shift. I was pinned to that tamarind tree like my stag beetles were pinned to the cork in their cases.

Just when I thought I could stand it no more, when I was sure I would have to open my mouth out of desperation to breathe, the water receded. My legs dropped against the tree, and I wrapped them around the branch.

I gasped and began gulping long, deep breaths. Air never felt so good.

Then I started coughing, for the air was still thick with grit.

The water had shoved me farther out on the branch, and I crawled toward the trunk. My arms felt like stone. My legs were raw. The bark poked and scratched me all over. Half of my skirt was missing, torn straight from my body by the force of the water.

A long, thin gash in my leg oozed a small trickle of blood. Not too deep, but I would have to try to wrap it back at the house.

"Tante Greet!" I called. "The water took some of my skirt!"

But Krakatau's rumblings were the only reply I heard.

Chapter 29

The little wooden church? Gone. Only a pile of broken boards against the base of the tamarind tree remained.

The tombstones in the cemetery? Ripped from the churchyard. They lay in a trail, leading to the ocean as if a giant Hansel and Gretel had dropped them for guidance.

Tante Greet? Vanished.

No.

No, that couldn't be right. She had to be there—the saltwater must have affected my eyes. I reached to push my spectacles up, but my finger didn't hit the familiar metal band that bridged my nose.

The wave had stolen my spectacles. "Tante Greet!" I cried.

No answer.

I shimmied down the tree. The bark scratched my calves and thighs all over again and tore more of my skirt.

Where was my aunt? She had been right here, clinging to the trunk. She couldn't have disappeared. I had clung to the same tree. I was still here.

Then I noticed that somehow, the top third of the tree was gone, and even the large statues in the cemetery had been moved by the powerful wave. Big, imposing stone monuments weighing many tons had shifted as if they were made of nothing more substantial than paper. The Rutgers Monument—a marble, life-sized angel standing on a meter-high base—rested next to the Groesbeck statue.

Wait.

The Groesbeck statue?

That was from the Catholic cemetery at least half a kilometer away. It shouldn't even be here.

Yet here it was, a two-meter-tall statue of the Holy Mother leaning against the Rutgers angel with a broken wing.

I wanted to tell Tante Greet about the power of the water. To point out how it had moved rocks buried in the ground. But she was gone.

A terrible dread enveloped me. What if...

Tante Greet wasn't a stone. She was a living being. She could cling to the tree like I did. It was a living thing, too. It was still standing. I willed her to show up. Why wasn't she here?

I was on the verge of panic when a clamoring noise filled the air, joining the rumbles from Krakatau. It came from all around me. It was the sound of children wailing, women moaning, men screaming.

It was agony.

Despair.

Devastation.

"I want to go home," I said aloud.

Home. *Ja.* That must be where Tante Greet was. I didn't know why she hadn't waited for me, but I would go home and find her. And change my clothes.

I reached to push my spectacles up, forgetting they were gone. My vision was poor without them, but I could still tell that tree branches, leaves and debris littered the ground. My spectacles were probably down there somewhere, but I would never spot them.

I could remedy that at home, too. I would simply grab my dust-covered spectacles again. After I found Tante Greet.

I set off, crashing into bizarre obstacles along the way: broken bits of furniture, mangled trees, hunks of coral. Strange structures loomed in the gloom before me. Without my spectacles, much of the world blurred into one giant indistinct mass, and the smoky air did not help. My legs grew more bruised with each step. *Don't think about the pain, Katrien, you'll recover. Get home. Get Tante Greet.*

The ash continued to fall, and in my wet clothes, the grit couldn't be brushed off. The ash turned to mud wherever it landed, whether it fell on the ground or on me. I wiped my face but only smeared the awful stuff. Layers of filth covered me now. Even my eyelashes were heavy.

The muck squelched beneath my feet. Wherever the wall of water hit piles of ash, a massive gray quagmire had formed. The mud weighed down my feet like bricks and oozed over the tops of my shoes, squishing between my toes.

I passed a house. At least, I thought it was a house. It had most of its roof but only one wall, like a child's unfinished drawing. Nothing remained inside.

Would our home be standing? What if I couldn't find our house? What if I couldn't get my other spectacles? What if Tante—

Oof!

I crashed into a dining room table. The teapot and cups still resting on it rattled. Leaning on the table to catch my breath, I coughed in the filthy air.

Almost everything around me showed signs of devastation. I had no idea where I was. All my points of reference—Mr. Vandermark's red door, the De Groots' tamarind tree, the Ousterhoudts' beautiful flowers—were gone.

Where was my home? All my life I had lived in Anjer. I knew every street and corner. I moved to push my spectacles up before remembering, yet again, that they were lost.

Mud, trees, more piles of debris. I skittered over everything in my path.

Closer to town, the cries of Anjer's citizens grew louder, more distinct over the rumbles of Krakatau. My legs sagged beneath me, and I collapsed into the mire.

"Mother!" cried the voice of what sounded like a little child. "Father!"

His wails melded into howls from other people calling for their loved ones.

"Annalien!"

"Nicolet!"

"Stefanus!"

"Ernst!"

"Luuk!"

"Drika!"

The wave didn't spare the natives either.

"Harta!"

"Buana!"

"Nirmala!"

"Lestari!"

What about Indah and Slamet? Were they safe? Had they even made it? The mosque was a kilometer from Anjer. They had gone there to pray. Surely God wouldn't let His followers die in a house of worship. Then again, the Dutch Reformed Church had been smashed to bits. I hoped desperately that no one had been inside.

The thought forced me to stand once more. Fumbling my way ahead, I walked under a roof being held aloft by posts and beams. There were no walls. It was like a pavilion.

Glancing up to keep tears from leaking out, I gasped. Painted constellations decorated the ceiling. Scorpius was above my head— just as it was every night.

It was my room.

I was standing inside my room.

But nothing was left.

My bed. The dusty pile of clothes. The vanity. All of it had vanished. I swallowed.

I would not be getting my other pair of spectacles. Without them I had the eyesight of shrew, at least for seeing distances.

And where was Tante Greet? Why wasn't she here?

She had been clinging to the tree when the wave hit. I had, too. But she was gone.

In my head, Vader said, "Think, Katrien."

"A grain in the balance will determine which individual shall live and which shall die."

I tamped the thought down to keep it from taking root in my mind. I would not let Mr. Charles Darwin's words turn against me.

But they kept gnawing on me like a Brahminy kite feeding on a dead fish.

I whispered, "If the wave destroyed our house...then it could have..." *Destroyed Tante Greet.*

I couldn't finish the sentence out loud.

And Vader?

He was in his office at the docks, closest to the giant wave.

Giving no thought to the violent ocean before me, I walked toward the beach.

Chapter 30

I hadn't gotten far when another explosion from Krakatau ripped across the Sunda Strait.

People on the beach screamed and clambered for the jungle, away from danger.

One man ran by and used me like a log, pushing off my head with his hand. Grime from his palm trickled down like worms wriggling in my hair.

"Vader!" I cried. Even on a good day I was standing too far away from him to hear me, only about halfway to his office.

The air around me moved as people continued to rush past. *Should I continue to look for Vader? Or should I run?*

Again, I heard my father's voice. "Think, Katrien."

The answer came from Mr. Charles Darwin: *"The slightest advantage will lead to victory."*

I sprinted toward the forest.

About three-quarters of the way there, I tripped over a downed tree and crashed face-first into the muck. I stood right up but the tree shifted, and I fell again. Bracing myself, I managed to stay upright on my second attempt, and I rubbed my eyes.

When I opened them again, I stared at the tree, and realized it wasn't a tree at all.

It was a man.

I scrambled away from him and ran once more, wiping my hands down the front of my dress. A cold, tingling feeling ran through my fingers as my imagination turned all the strange shapes around me into dead bodies. Those inert shapes couldn't be humans... could they?

When I reached the jungle's edge, people crowded near the trees. Was my aunt here? My father? Several thousand people lived in Anjer.

But several thousand were not sitting here now. It was more like several hundred. At most. Where was everyone?

"Katrien!"

"Tante?" I cried.

"Katrien! Over here!" Someone grabbed my hand and jerked me around. I couldn't believe my eyes.

It was Brigitta who stood before me. Her hair was a mess, as if six different types of birds had tried to build a nest in it. My own braid was a series of tangles and knots.

She clutched my hand. "I've been calling for you."

"*You* called *me*?" I stared in disbelief. Half the town had been washed away, and she still wanted to antagonize me?

"*Ja.*" Her grip on my hand tightened. It hurt, but I refused to wince in front of her. She would pounce like a leopard.

But she was scared. Her face twisted with anxiety. I softened. "Are you all right, Brigitta?"

She ignored my question. "Do you know what's happening?"

Had she gone simple? "Krakatau erupted."

"But why is the sky black? Why did a giant wave attack us?" She clung to my arm like a terrified child desperate for answers.

Placing a hand on her shoulder, I tried to comfort her. "The air is black from the ash. From the volcano. The wave... well..."

A memory from years ago leaped to the front of my mind, of Slamet throwing pebbles into a large puddle. I had watched the circles form where the rock hit the water. They had moved from the point of impact in precise, concentric rings to the edge. I had talked him into throwing larger, heavier rocks in the water "to make a giant splash." We had succeeded, but the experiment drenched our clothing. Tante Greet and Indah had not been pleased.

I was certain something similar was happening with Krakatau and the ocean in the Sunda Strait. Krakatau's eruption was impacting the water in a massively powerful way. That's why the wave had been so large. I was about to explain this to Brigitta when a man standing nearby cried out.

"Listen!" he yelled.

Every head turned toward the beach. There was that sound again, like a thousand pots of water boiling all at once. I couldn't see anything, but I recognized that awful roar.

"Not again," Brigitta whispered, and even under all the ash and mud, I could tell her face was ghost white.

"Climb the trees," I shouted to the people gathered near us.

"I can't," Brigitta said.

"What? Why not?"

"It wouldn't be proper. Mother would not like it."

"Hang being proper, Brigitta! Your life is at stake!"

I climbed up a nearby cempedak tree. She followed reluctantly, like a snake being forced to slither after a big meal.

Steadying myself on a sturdy branch, I reached down. "Brigitta, give me your hand."

She stretched her arm out to me.

"Climb a little higher." She wasn't even half a meter off the ground.

"I can't, Katrien."

"*Ja*, you can. Come on!"

Other people around me moved into the trees, but some, like Tante, refused to climb. *They will probably die like her, too.*

No.

I couldn't think like that.

Tante was fine. I just had to find her. And Vader. Everything would be fine.

With bark biting into my legs and arms once more, I stretched as far as I could for Brigitta without tumbling down. I couldn't reach her.

The second wave moved toward Anjer with the sickening rushing sound of a million whirring bees. I gave up trying to save Brigitta and concentrated on saving myself. Wrapping my arms around the branch, I shut my eyes and waited for the wall of water.

More splintering sounds. People screamed. Others prayed. I waited and waited with eyes scrunched shut tight.

But the wall of water did not reach us this time.

After what seemed like hours, I opened my eyes again. The awful boiling sound had vanished.

Cheers erupted from everyone around me. "Thank God," someone cried. *"Allahu akbar,"* praised another.

Brigitta still clung to the tree below me. With a thud, she plopped to the ground, and I scrambled down after her.

Even though the ocean had quieted, Krakatau continued its incessant rumble. Would it ever stop?

"Think, Katrien," said Vader's voice in my head.

"We should go farther into the jungle," I said, more to myself than to anyone in particular.

Brigitta whipped around to face me. "What? Why? The water didn't reach us here."

"Because that volcano is still making noise." I pointed to Krakatau. "It hasn't stopped since yesterday afternoon. It may never stop. Who knows? But I don't think it's finished erupting, and I would like to be as far away as possible when the next bout comes."

She crossed her arms. "What about your father and your aunt?"

"Tante Greet and I were running for the jungle when the first wave hit." Even in those last desperate minutes, my aunt wanted me to reach safety. She insisted I go on without her.

"Where is she?"

Hesitant to tell Brigitta the truth and not wanting to voice my own worst fears, I finally said, "We got separated."

"And your father?" Each question was an accusation. She thought I didn't care about my family.

"He's at the docks. He's sending telegraph messages to Batavia. He's doing his job." Pride rang through my voice.

"Then he is dead," Brigitta spat. "Your aunt is dead, too."

I jumped back from her words, as if they were living things floating in the air. If I avoided their touch, then they couldn't be true.

"How can you say that?" I demanded.

"Because my father is dead." Her voice cracked. "My whole family is dead. The water took them all."

Chapter 31

Brigitta's words hit me like another wave. Aghast, I asked, "What do you mean, your whole family is dead?"

"The water came and swirled me around my room like I was a spinning top. When it receded, mine was the only room still standing. The rest of the house was destroyed." She choked back tears. "Mother was under a collapsed wall with my brother in her arms. Father was not far away."

I reached for her. "Brigitta, I'm so sorry." It was a terrible thing to lose a parent. My experience with my own mother taught me that.

"We were right on the water," she shrieked. "Your father works at the docks. In that little shack! He's dead!"

I stopped reaching for her and my arms snapped back to my sides. How could she be so spiteful? Why was I bothering trying to comfort her? Why had she even made the effort to get my attention?

"Why did you call to me today?" Rage filled my voice.

"I thought you might know what was happening. You consider yourself so smart." She poked my shoulder. "Even now, you act like you're so superior," she sneered with another poke. "But you don't know any more than the rest of us." One last shove.

I stumbled. My fists clenched, and I fought to keep from pushing her back. She and I were nothing alike. "*They may metaphorically be called cousins to the same millionth degree.*" Mr. Charles Darwin was correct. She and I were both humans, and that was the only common ground we shared.

Forget Brigitta. She would never be anything but a mean, hateful shrew.

But Tante Greet's voice rang in my head. "Don't be so quick to judge, Katrien."

Brigitta was behaving like an injured animal, lashing out at anyone and everyone.

This was my chance to do something ladylike. To rise above petty bickering. To help someone I despised. To make my family proud.

But it was hard.

Her eyes flashed fury. Her teeth bared. I half expected her to bark and bite me. "Don't judge, Katrien." Tante Greet's voice again.

I swallowed my pride. "Brigitta, I am sorry for your loss. And I don't want to sound cruel when I say this, but we have to go into the jungle. We have to try to save ourselves."

"I don't want to go anywhere with you." She shot me a mutinous glare.

I forced myself not to walk away. "It just so happens that I don't particularly want to go with you either. But we should try to help each other. Right now, we're all each other has."

"We're safe here," she protested. "The water didn't even reach us last time."

As if in response, Krakatau rumbled once more. "We got lucky," I said. "I doubt we'll get so lucky a second time."

"I don't want to go in the jungle."

"It will be fine." The mud on my face was starting to dry, and I brushed it off.

"No!" She stamped her filthy boot.

"Why not?" I cried. She was wasting time. We needed to get to the clearing. It was four kilometers inland. We would surely be safe there. But we needed to leave. Soon.

"Brigitta?" I turned to see Adriaan Vogel approaching us. His trousers were shredded, and mud covered his shirt. Even his mustache was stained with filth. "What is going on?"

She pointed at me. "She wants to take me into the jungle."

His jaw dropped. "What? Why?"

I rubbed my eyes. It wasn't enough that Brigitta was dragging her heels; now I had to deal with Adriaan. "It will be safer," I yelled at him. Grabbing Brigitta's hands, I pulled. "Come on, Brigitta. You should come, too, Adriaan."

She resisted.

"Let's go," I said.

"No."

"Why won't you come with me?"

She took a watery breath, and her shoulders drooped. "My father always told me there were creatures in there that would eat me. He said I should stay away."

"What?" Her father had done Brigitta a disservice telling her that. There were animals that were dangerous, to be sure, but only when threatened or desperate. "That's not true. Besides, Mr. Charles Darwin says, *'The present condition of the Malay Archipelago, with its numerous large islands separated by wide and shallow seas, probably represents the former state of Europe.'* So you see? We're practically in Europe! What would your father say to that?"

"What about the bugs?"

Bewildered, I asked, "The insects? What about them?"

"They'll crawl all over me and bite me and—" Her voice rose in panic.

I grabbed her shoulders. "It will be fine, Brigitta. I know the forest. I know what's in there. I'll keep you safe."

"No," Adriaan said, yanking her toward him. *"I'll* keep you safe. Won't I?"

He was only a year older than us. I didn't know how he thought he could protect Brigitta in the jungle, but she apparently trusted him. The tendons in her neck stood out sharply as she gave a short, stiff nod.

I addressed the crowd. "We should all go in the jungle for safety."

Some people ignored me entirely, keeping their eyes pinned toward the ocean. The water remained hidden with all the smoke and ash in the air, but that was the direction of danger.

The others waved their hands as if to be rid of me.

"Come on," I implored. "We should move farther inland. Away from the ocean!"

Someone asked, "Why should we listen to you?"

Another person said, "You have no interest in us."

My face grew hot enough to make steam. This was what Vader meant about needing people. Only he didn't mention how that could work two ways. It wasn't that I needed these people right now. They needed me. But they wouldn't listen. And it was all my fault. Because I had been so judgmental. "Please," I begged, "you have to listen to me. Go to the jungle!"

Grumblings and dismissals. "We were fine last time." "There won't be another wave." "The jungle is more dangerous than the sea."

Were they all mad? Were they so scared of the forest they would rather face another lethal wave?

I didn't have time to convince anyone else. Grabbing Brigitta's and Adriaan's hands, I dragged them with me. With one last look over my shoulder, I cried, "Please come into the jungle!"

No one moved.

Chapter 32

I led Brigitta and Adriaan into the familiar emerald landscape. My oasis. My sanctuary. Even though I hadn't been here in a month, even though Brigitta and Adriaan stood unwillingly by my side, even though the world seemed to be ending, the jungle welcomed me.

Brigitta was about two seconds from running away like a rabbit, so I babbled. "One time, I came through here and saw a Javan lutung. He was a splendid monkey! He watched me for a while, and then he ran down the tree, turned to look me directly in the eye, bowed and ran off. I swear if he had been wearing a hat, he would have doffed it. It was one of the most amazing things I've ever seen!"

Anxiety rolled off Brigitta and Adriaan placed her arm on his. I continued, "There's no need to worry about any of the animals here. They're just as frightened as we are right now. They don't know what's happening either."

"Would you please be quiet?" she said in a snotty voice.

My mouth snapped shut, and I moved faster.

"Slow down," she called.

I rubbed my eyes. Be quiet. Slow down. Couldn't she do anything without ordering me around? I wasn't her maid! "Don't judge, Katrien." My aunt's voice again.

"Where are we going?" Adriaan asked.

"I know a place we can stop." I pointed with a vague motion. "It's a sort of clearing, and there's a little stream there. It should be far enough inland."

"How far?" Brigitta asked.

"About two hours if we hurry."

They stopped. "What?" she said.

"We have to keep going."

She turned in a complete circle. "I can't see anything but trees, Katrien. Surely we're safe right here!"

"Certainly we're safe." Adriaan patted her arm.

I glared at him. "We've only been walking for a few minutes. We're hardly away from Anjer."

He crossed his arms. "We should be far enough inland."

"Let's keep going," I urged.

Brigitta stamped her foot. "Katrien Courtlandt! I am not moving one more step from this spot!"

"We need to keep walking."

"Why?" Adriaan said. "What exactly do you think is going to happen? Why don't you think we're far enough away from the ocean?"

"I don't know. But I do know I would feel safer deeper in the jungle."

He threw up his hands. "This is ridiculous. I'm going back."

"You can't!" I cried, reaching out to him.

"Why not?"

"I just told you, I don't think you'll be safe."

"Then neither will my brother. I have to go get him."

Brigitta placed a hand on his shoulder. "Why did you leave him?"

Adriaan turned bright red under the mud coating his face. "I . . . I don't know." He spun on his heel and ran like a startled rusa deer.

"Adriaan," I called. "Come back!"

But his blurry outline disappeared.

I faced Brigitta. "We need to keep moving."

"No," she said, her mouth drawing into a straight line. "Why should we?"

"For the last time, Brigitta, I just know we'll be safer the farther away from the ocean we are. *'Success will often depend on having special weapons or means of defence.'* "

She blinked, bewildered, before she gave her head a quick shake. "I'm not going anywhere. I think we're fine." She plopped down and gave me a look that dared me to go on without her.

I was tempted. I longed to leave her to her own devices. Let her get washed away by a mountain of water like—

No.

Don't even think it, Katrien.

What did I owe Brigitta? Nothing. But Tante Greet had not raised me that way. She tried to instill a sense of empathy in me. I rarely listened to her in the past, but now that she wasn't here her daily reminders buzzed in my brain.

She had come all the way to Anjer from the Netherlands when my mother died. Vader asked, and Tante came. It was simple for her. Even though, as she said, she missed "weather and seasons and snow and tulips."

"Piles of snow, Katrien," she would say. "Sometimes a meter high."

With the ash, I was beginning to understand more about snow.

I looked around and noticed there was less ash on the ground here than there was out of the forest. "It must be caught on the leaves," I murmured.

"What?" Brigitta gave me a withering look.

"Nothing." I studied the trees as best as I could without my spectacles. Normally they teemed with life—ants, beetles, butterflies, maybe even a python or monkey. But they were empty today.

How could that be? There must be some sort of creature hiding in their branches. I had never once been in the jungle and *not* seen an insect or an animal of some kind. "Brigitta, could you come here a moment?"

She sat rooted to her little patch of dirt. "I told you, Katrien, I'm not moving."

I sighed and rubbed my eyes. "I'm not asking you to walk. I just need to borrow your eyes."

"Why?"

"I lost my spectacles in the wave. I can hardly see."

"And you've had me following you?" she screeched.

"I know precisely where we are."

"How can you know that? You can't see anything!" She crossed her arms and muttered loud enough for me to hear. "I knew you looked more ridiculous than usual. I should have stayed with the others."

"Listen, Brigitta, I have explored this forest almost every day since I was seven years old. I know where we are. Trust me."

"Why should I trust you?" Her voice turned suspicious. "Can you see me?"

Although she was blurry, I could make out her movements. "You're mostly a blur."

"Then you can't see this?" She stuck out her tongue and made a rude gesture with her hands.

My first instinct was to slap her, but I fought the urge. "I don't know what you're do—"

Suddenly I hit the ground as the loudest noise I had ever heard came from Krakatau's direction. It sounded like every cannon on Earth had been fired directly at me.

Brigitta giggled. "What are you doing?"

Something terrible had happened. Another wave would surely come. I was right, we weren't far enough into the undergrowth. We weren't safe. "We need to climb the trees," I said, standing up, urgency filling my voice.

"Oh, please! Not that again."

Why was she laughing? Didn't she hear that explosion? Didn't she know how dangerous things were? Didn't she want to live?

She chuckled and grinned that silly grin. Enough was enough. I stomped over to her, yanked her to her feet and slapped her with a satisfying thwack.

"Ow!" She cradled her cheek. "What did you do that for?"

Brigitta always brought out the worst in me. I put all my contempt for her in the tone of my words and spat, "Just climb the blasted tree."

"Why do I have to climb a tree all of a sudden? Just moments ago you were telling me we needed to move farther into the jungle!" Her arms flailed about like a macaque's tail.

"Did you not hear that blast? There's no time to move!"

"What blast? Are you making fun of me?" Her voice grew suspicious again.

"No. The blast! From Krakatau! The loudest one yet!" She might have been a tree for all the reaction she gave. How could she not have heard that noise?

She leaned in, her face centimeters from mine. Her fury was visible despite the mud and ash coating her. "Listen to me, Katrien. I do not like you telling me what to do. I don't even know why I followed you, but that ends now."

She turned, and as she did I caught sight of her jawline and suddenly understood. I grabbed her shoulder and whipped her around. "Brigitta. I know why you didn't hear the blast." I wiped a finger by her left ear and ran it a few centimeters toward her neck. When I pulled my hand back, I showed her the blood trickling down my finger.

When she rubbed her own hand against her face, she saw more blood. She then clawed at her right ear, but it wasn't bleeding. "What is this?" she screamed, shaking like a scared dog.

With both my hands on her shoulders, I steadied her. "It's going to be fine. It's probably from the blast. Your right ear is fine. We can look at it more closely later. But right now we have to get to safety. I need you to go up that tree. I'll be right behind you."

She still trembled. "I can't do that."

"*Ja*, you can." I copied the low, measured tones Tante Greet used on me when I grew flustered trying to cook.

She shook her head, trying to back away.

I squeezed her shoulders. "Come on, Brigitta. You can do this. You have to do this. You don't have a choice."

Chapter 33

Brigitta seemed to take hours going up the cempedak tree, but at least she climbed it. I crawled behind her the entire time, reassuring her along the way. "You're doing great. Keep going. Just a little bit more."

Finally she reached a long, thick, sturdy branch.

"Brigitta," I called to her, "I need you to climb onto that branch."

"What?"

"Climb onto the branch," I said a little louder.

She moved over and clung to it like a sick monkey.

"Keep going, Brigitta."

"What?"

Was her hearing getting worse, or was she just being obstinate?

"Keep going," I repeated. "I need space, too."

Inch by inch, she crawled farther out on the branch until I had just enough room. We wouldn't have long until the water found us. I recited my favorite quote from Mr. Charles Darwin. " 'We should not forget that only a small portion of the world is known with accuracy. We should not forget that only a small portion of the world is known with accuracy. We should not forget that only a small portion of the world is known with accuracy.' "

"What are you saying?" Brigitta cried.

"Nothing. It's not important."

"What?"

"Nothing!"

Then the thundering, rushing noise of water suddenly echoed through the jungle. "Here we go," I muttered, before I yelled, "Hold on, Brigitta!"

"I don't think I'll be able to, Katrien!"

"*Ja*, you will!"

"No!"

"I won't let you fall!" I wrapped my arms around her ankles and the branch.

"Oh, my God!" Her piercing cry came over the crashing of the wave. "It's enormous!"

Even without my spectacles, I could see the wall of water. It roared into the forest, taller—much taller—than the wave that took Tante Greet away. This one was taller than the trees.

We weren't going to make it. This wave was Death.

The water slammed into us with the speed of a steamship, shifting me on the branch. I clung as tight as I could, holding my breath as the water washed over my head. *Dear God, please let my breath hold.*

As the wave crashed around us it churned over and under. What was left of my skirt swirled around me. The water pried my legs off the tree. I clamped my arms tighter against the branch and Brigitta's ankles.

Debris smacked into me. Something heavy hit my arm, and my eyes popped open with the pain. I squeezed them shut again. The saltwater burned the cut in my leg. I longed to cry out, to moan, but I kept my lips clamped tight like a locked trunk.

Then the water disappeared, just as suddenly as it had arrived.

Brigitta and I gasped for air.

"Are you well?" I called, struggling to right myself on the branch. She coughed and croaked, "*Ja.*"

We lay heaving against the cempedak branch, taking in great gulps of air. And then, to my horror, the boiling noise came again, drowning out the sound of our heavy breathing.

"Hang on!" I screamed.

"Oh, no," she moaned.

I fixed my arms around the tree and Brigitta's ankles once more. The water slammed into us. Did I have the strength to hold on this time? My grip loosened, and I waited for the wave to yank me off the tree, out of the jungle, and into the ocean.

No!

I wouldn't let that happen! I couldn't. I couldn't do that to Vader and Tante Greet. I forced myself to squeeze the branch as the water churned.

When at last it receded, we panted for air again.

Brigitta pushed herself into a sitting position. "That one wasn't as bad."

I nodded, too tired to speak and only half listening to her. I strained to hear the sounds of rushing water, hoping they wouldn't come again.

Then Brigitta screamed.

"What?" I cried, popping up off my stomach.

She whimpered and pointed above us.

A shape hung in the top of the tree. "What is it?" I squinted.

"It's—it's a p-person." She shuddered.

"Oh." Now I could see it was clearly a person. Arms, legs, head, torso all wrapped around branches giving the body the look of some ancient beast.

Brigitta scrambled to turn around.

"What are you doing?" I asked.

"I want to get down," she said, pointing to the ground about three meters below.

"What? Why?"

"I can't be in the same tree with a dead person."

"Brigitta, we don't know if another wave is coming."

"I don't care. I'll take my chances." She brushed at my legs, trying to get me to move.

"You'll die," I said forcefully. "You'll end up just like that person up there."

As if on cue, the boiling sounds returned, and Brigitta whimpered like a scared dog before wrapping herself on the branch. I grabbed her ankles and clutched the tree yet again.

But this time, the water didn't find us.

We waited and waited and waited.

My arm ached where it had been hit. Brigitta rubbed her ankles. Tree bark had cut into one of her legs, and blood oozed down and inside her shoe. I grimaced. I hadn't meant to hurt her.

We stayed in the tree for hours. She spoke of climbing down several more times, but I would not budge.

I couldn't tell if the body above us was a man or a woman. "Who do you think that is?" I asked.

"My father. Your father. Who knows?"

I shook my head. Even at her most vulnerable, she still lashed out.

"What?" she demanded.

Why did I insist on keeping her alive? If our roles were switched, she would never have rescued me. "Nothing," I said, and I went back to listening for the ocean.

Chapter 34

I startled awake and clutched the branch to keep from falling. When I looked up I found Brigitta staring at me. "Are you well?" she asked.

"I'm fine." Sitting up, I rubbed my eyes. Bark bit into my legs. Everything hurt, and I could feel a bruise on my arm. My stomach rumbled in the silence.

Silence...

"Do you hear that?" I asked.

"Hear what?" She scrunched up her face and pointed to her left ear. "I can't hear from this ear, remember?"

I ignored her. "No rumblings from Krakatau, no roaring ocean."

"It's over?" she wondered.

"Perhaps."

"We can go back home?" She clasped her hands, pleading.

"Neither one of us has a home to go back to." Even here, farther inland, the jungle had been ripped apart like a paper diorama.

She clenched her teeth. "I didn't mean that literally. I just meant Anjer."

"I think we should still head for the clearing."

"Why?"

"Just in case."

"But I want to go home," she whined.

I placated her. "I know. I do, too." Vader and Tante Greet would be waiting for me. But they might also be looking for me, and they knew I would be in the jungle.

"Then we should go!" She slapped her knees.

Even though I longed to find my family, they would want me to be safe. Tante Greet had insisted I climb that tree in the churchyard. "Brigitta, I think it would be best to walk to the clearing."

"What if I don't follow you? What if I just go back to town?"

I rubbed my eyes. Pain and exhaustion coursed through me. Hadn't I done what I set out to do? Hadn't I helped Brigitta? Hadn't I kept her safe? Krakatau was silent now. If she wanted to go back to Anjer, who was I to stop her? "Do you know the way?" I asked.

She drooped. "No." Her voice a miserable sob.

Would it be too much to insist she go with me? Perhaps she would be better off in Anjer. I had no idea whether the clearing was any safer. It was just a gut feeling I had. But what if the wave had reached there, too? Maybe we should go our separate ways.

"That way." I pointed toward home. "Go that way, and you'll reach Anjer."

Her eyes brightened.

"It shouldn't take that long," I said. "We didn't walk very far before the wave hit. You'll be on your own, though. I'm going to the clearing."

She nodded.

My hands and arms hurt so much it made gripping the tree difficult as I climbed down. It felt like a hammer had been bashing my fingers. I had never been in such pain.

When I reached the ground, I guided Brigitta, telling her where to put her hands and feet. She leaned her head against the tree and took a deep breath. "I never want to climb another tree as long as I live."

I flexed my fingers and stared at the ground. "Well... I suppose..."

"*Ja,*" she said, brushing off the front of her blouse.

"Be careful."

"And you." She offered me her hand. Surprised, I took it. "*Dank u,*" she said.

With an awkward shake, we split apart. She followed my directions toward Anjer, and I headed for the clearing.

I hoped I did the right thing letting her go off on her own. "Keep her safe," I whispered aloud. Then I added, "Keep me safe, too."

Downed trees crisscrossed the ground. My strength was gone. I couldn't climb over the ones in my path, so I walked around them. It made my route longer, but it didn't matter. The sky was still gray. Ash still fell.

By myself it was much harder to keep going. I needed a reason. Vader and Tante Greet were behind me, back in Anjer, and now Brigitta was heading that way. I knew I needed to reach the clearing, that I needed to move, but I could not take one more step. Even Mr. Charles Darwin couldn't help.

So I sat on the ground, leaned against a fallen tree, held my head in my hands and thought, just as Vader taught me. Maybe I *didn't* need to go to the clearing. After all, Krakatau was silent. Then again, if it started rumbling again, the clearing was farther inland. It was certainly safer.

I simply could not make a decision. I stood up again, looked around, and found my distance vision was even worse than before. My eyes were tired, too. I rubbed them yet again, hoping an answer would present itself by the time I opened them.

Instead, a scream ripped through the ravaged jungle.

I knew that voice. I ran toward the sound and found Brigitta hanging from a low tamarind branch. She'd managed to hoist her chest over the branch, but her legs dangled, and she was scrambling to pull them up.

At the base of the tree stood a lone, growling dhole. The hair on its back was raised. Whenever Brigitta's legs fell from the tree, it jumped.

"Help!" Brigitta called.

I wanted to tell her to be quiet, but I couldn't let the angry dhole know I was there. Where was the rest of the pack? I scanned the area but didn't see anything.

Picking up a stick from the ground, an idea formed. Those dholes I had seen weeks ago hadn't barked, so my imitating a large dog wouldn't be much of a threat. But that strange cluck? I could copy that.

"Ah, ah, ah, ah, ah, ah," I whispered until I was confident it sounded like the noise I remembered. With a deep breath, I did it louder. "Ah, ah, ah, ah, ah, ah, ah, ah, ah, ah, ah, ah."

The dhole looked in my direction, and I launched the stick. It flew in a high arc and bounced off a downed tree before landing. The dhole took off after it.

"Help!" Brigitta cried.

"I'm coming!" I hurried to the tree.

Brigitta was dangling a little over a meter off the ground when her grip slipped and she dropped back over the branch. I leaped to stop her slide, but when she stood before me, safely on the ground, I could see the front of her dress had shredded like cabbage.

Brigitta didn't seem to notice. Clutching me in a tight hug, she sobbed. *"Dank u, dank u, dank u."*

Stunned, I gave her an awkward pat on the back. "He's gone. The dhole's gone."

Pulling herself away from me, she wiped her eyes. "Which way is the clearing?"

Chapter 35

I was taken aback by Brigitta's change of heart, but I pointed wordlessly toward the clearing.

"Lead the way," she said, squaring her shoulders.

"Are you certain?" I asked.

She nodded and brushed absently at the mud on her blouse. As she did, she finally saw the ripped linen under her collarbone. "Well, I always wanted some décolletage," she giggled.

I gaped at her in wonder.

"Don't look like a fish, Katrien. You can be such a prude."

My jaw snapped shut, and I blinked.

"Are we going to the clearing or aren't we?" she asked.

I set off deeper into the jungle and she followed me. There was something I needed to say.

"I wasn't being a prude," I said.

"What?"

Her ear. I forgot. Louder, I repeated, "I wasn't being a prude."

"Oh, no?"

"No." I faced her. "I was just amazed you made a joke about your blouse. I expected you to cry even more."

"You really don't know me, Katrien." She limped closer. "You only think you do."

"Really?" I arched my eyebrows. "You think I don't know you?"

"I know you don't."

"Tell me one thing about yourself that I don't know. One thing."
I folded my arms across my chest and waited.

She sniffed. "Last year I read that book you're always reading.
That Darwin book."

I gasped. "You aren't telling me you read *On the Origin of
Species.*"

She nodded.

"By Mr. Charles Darwin?"

"Is there another book by him?" She placed her hands on her
hips.

Vader only had that one. "You read a book about science?"

"*Ja,*" she growled. "Try to wrap your mind around the idea that
I am not stupid."

"What did you—" I stopped. Did I want her opinion? Would it
matter? It wouldn't change how I felt...would it?

But she knew what I was going to ask. "What did I think?" She
tapped her lips. "I thought it was an interesting idea, but in the end,
I didn't believe him."

"How can you not believe him? He lays out his evidence so
clearly."

She shrugged. "I just didn't. Why haven't we seen evidence of
natural selection at work?"

"Because it's a subtle process that takes years!" I exclaimed.
"He explains that. *As natural selection acts solely by accumulating
slight, successive, favourable variations, it can produce no great or sudden modification; it can act only by very short and slow steps.* Don't
you see?"

She stared at me with her mouth hanging open. "You have it
memorized?"

I blushed. "Not the whole thing. Only sentences I particularly
enjoy."

"Is that what those weird things you're always saying are from?
Darwin's book? Good grief, Katrien. You need to get a hobby."

"I have—"

She held up a finger to stop me. "I mean a hobby that does not involve Darwin."

I glared at her before stomping off, infuriated.

"Wait," she called, and hobbled after me. My fury ebbed slightly when I saw her limping. I must have pinned her ankles tighter to the tree than I realized.

Our progress was also hampered by the changed landscape. The waves had uprooted trees and tossed them about like matchsticks. Giant fig trees that had been growing for centuries and that I once used as landmarks were gone. I hoped we were headed in the right direction.

"Waaaah!"

Brigitta and I stopped when a strange cry burst forth from somewhere nearby.

"Is that—is that a baby?" she asked.

"Waaaah!"

"It sounds like it," I said.

"Hello!" she called. "Where are you?"

"Waaaah!"

I pointed to the right. "I think it's over there."

We followed the crying until we reached an uprooted tamarind tree that leaned at a strange angle, supported by its branches. Trapped under those branches was a young boy, crying and struggling to break free.

"We have to help him," Brigitta said.

"Of course we do," I responded.

"We're going to help you," she told the boy, who looked native and probably couldn't understand a word she said.

I positioned myself near a branch. "I'm going to try to lift it. You pull him out."

She nodded and squatted on the ground, ready to grab the boy.

Taking a deep breath, I whispered, "One, two, three," and pulled with every ounce of strength I had left. "Uuunnh." The branch was heavier than I imagined. "Hurry, Brigitta."

"I need a bit more room."

I heaved it higher, standing on my toes. "That's it. Quick!" I cried.

Her hand snaked under the branch, grasped the boy by his arm and yanked him out. She had just gotten him clear when my strength left me. The branch crashed back down and impaled the ground where the boy had been.

His cries grew louder, and he hiccuped.

"Shhh." Brigitta rubbed his back and held him close. "Shhh. You're fine. Everything is fine." She rocked back and forth.

I had no idea what to do. Thank goodness for Brigitta.

"Is he hurt?" I asked.

She shook her head. "I don't think so. Just scared." She soothed him until he settled. "We have to take him with us."

I nodded. "Let's go, then."

"How far is it?"

"About a kilometer from here." I spoke with more confidence than I felt. I had no points of reference anymore. It was worse than Anjer. "Maybe two," I conceded.

We walked. My eyes grew ever more weary from the strain of trying to see without my spectacles.

We walked. After a time, Brigitta asked me to carry the boy.

We walked. Our surroundings blurred into one giant ashen mass.

We walked. Brigitta pointed out odd sights. "There's a small boat over there." "I think we just passed someone's roof." "This is half a grandfather clock."

After what felt like a lifetime, the jungle returned. It looked like my beloved tangle of trees again.

"Thank God," I muttered.

The boy wriggled in my arms, and I set him down. He scrambled ahead of us. "Don't go far," I called.

"Frits, come back," Brigitta called.

"Frits?"

"It's what I'm calling him."

He turned around and toddled back to us.

I scrunched my nose. "How old is he?"

"Probably two or three." She bent down and opened her arms. He walked right to her. "Hello, Frits."

He giggled and babbled something in Javanese. Or maybe it was his own made-up language.

"I'm thirsty," Brigitta said, kissing Frits's hands.

"We're almost there, and we can get some water from the stream. It's very cool and tasty."

"Maybe we could wash a bit, too."

I nodded. "That's a wonderful idea."

Sweat and grime, tiny bits of tree bark, saltwater residue, and blood covered us both. I not only felt sticky but also prickly, filthy, weak and sore.

She picked Frits up. "I'm just glad we haven't seen any snakes or anything."

"You're right," I agreed, though the thought troubled me.

Krakatau was silent now. I hadn't heard a single rumble since that last devastating boom.

So now, I reasoned, buzzing insects and calling monkeys and a thousand other sounds should be echoing around the forest. But the only sound was our footsteps and Frits's babble. Earlier, my eyes were telling me that the trees were devoid of animals. My ears seemed to be doing the same for the entire forest now.

"It's so odd," I whispered. "So much silence." Had the ash muffled the noises? It still fell, but not as heavily.

"Pardon?"

"Oh." I spoke up for Brigitta. "It's just unusual not to hear anything here. Or see anything."

"I'm grateful we haven't."

"Where do you think they are?"

"Where do I think what are?" she asked, setting Frits back down and holding his hand.

"The animals. The insects. Where do you think they are?" My voice rang out in the quiet, making me flinch as if I had spoken aloud in church.

She shrugged. "Dead. Why wouldn't they be? Snakes couldn't out-slither that wave."

"Perhaps. But..." I trailed off.

"But what?"

"But we haven't seen any bodies. We should have seen some evidence by now. Even if it was just insects."

"What do you mean? Because we haven't seen a dead snake, there can't be any dead snakes?" Her nonsensical leap of logic made my head hurt.

"Not entirely, no. I've walked through the jungle many times," I explained. "Sometimes I see a python or a constrictor or some other snake and other times I don't. So the fact that we haven't seen a dead snake is irrelevant."

She rolled her eyes and let Frits drag her. "I think you're talking in circles."

"Here's my point. I always see insects. Hundreds of insects. They're everywhere—on trees, flying through the air, scurrying along on the ground. They're all around."

Brigitta pulled Frits toward her, eyes darting back and forth.

I finished my argument. "With so many insects, some of them should be dead. We should see their bodies. The wave could have easily washed away those insects closer to the beach." I swallowed suddenly and blinked to keep the sharp tears that sprung up at bay. My *Hexarthrius rhinoceros rhinoceros* collection! Three hundred four specimens. Years of hard work. Gone in minutes. Rubbing my eyes, I continued, "Here, where the waves never came, we should be seeing evidence of life."

"Maybe this is like natural selection. No evidence exists."

I growled. "Evidence does exist, just not the evidence you want."

"Then maybe the ash killed them," she speculated.

"Maybe," I conceded, "but it couldn't have killed *everything*. And if it did, we should still see some evidence. Bodies. Exoskeletons. Something. We haven't seen any. Where is the life?"

Frits fussed and whimpered, and Brigitta picked him up again. "He's probably hungry."

I didn't answer, because up ahead, I saw a familiar sight. At long last we had reached the clearing. The banyan trees still circled the small space, and the grass was a verdant green. The Sampaguita vines climbed up the banyan trees.

Everything around the stream remained unchanged.

Only the stream itself was different.

Chapter 36

The stream was drained. Its muddy bed was completely exposed.

I hoped my weak eyes were playing tricks on me.

"Lovely, Katrien. Just lovely." Brigitta's sarcasm told me they weren't.

Frits's crying grew louder.

"I wasn't expecting this," I said.

"That's good. I'm glad you weren't expecting this. I would hate to know you marched me all the way up here. In the dark. With the bugs—"

"We haven't seen any—"

"—and with the snakes. And the wild animals, all the while *expecting* to find a stream drained of all its water. But you weren't expecting this, were you? That's a relief. I feel so much better. And now I'm stuck up here in the middle of the jungle. With you," she added, as if that was the worst part of all. "And there's no water! I haven't eaten since this morning. I haven't had anything to drink either. Who knows when Frits last ate. I'm hungry. I'm wet. I'm thirsty. My ankle hurts—that's your fault, too, for gripping it like a vise. My feet feel like they want to fall off my legs. My arms hurt."

Frits wailed, and I interrupted her tirade. "And you're scared. I know, Brigitta. I am, too. But we should stay here. We should try to get some sleep tonight and decide what to do in the morning."

She bent down and picked up Frits, patting his back. "We're going back to Anjer tomorrow."

Rubbing my eyes, I said, "Do you want to sleep on the ground or in the tree?"

She glared at me. "On the ground, of course. We can't get Frits into the tree. He might fall and hurt himself."

I hadn't thought about Frits's safety. "Why don't we pick a spot close to the tree?"

Her willingness to sleep on the forest floor surprised me, but it probably had more to do with her concern for Frits. She stretched out under a banyan tree and got the little boy to lie down. While he tossed and turned, she sang.

"Under trees so big and giant
in the forest of the gnomes
is a nice and little cottage
between tree roots on the moss."

It was just like the evening in the Hotel Anjer when she sang to Jeroen at the dinner table. "I haven't heard that since my mother died," I said aloud. I realized then that there had not been much singing in my life since my mother passed away. Hymns at mass weren't the same thing.

"Shhh," Brigitta soothed. She hummed some more, keeping a gentle rhythm until Frits was asleep. Then she eased her shoes off and winced as she rubbed her feet.

"I am sorry about your ankle," I whispered. "Is it still bleeding?"

She shook her head and brushed dried mud off her legs and arms.

"I didn't mean to hurt you. I only wanted to keep you on the branch." I removed my own shoes. Oh, that felt good!

My feet breathed their thanks as I wriggled my toes and made circles with my ankles, letting the air—warm and stuffy as it was—soothe my skin.

Brigitta didn't say anything for several long moments, but then responded gently, "I know." She let out a watery breath and sniffed.

I scooted closer to her. "It's going to be fine. We're going to be fine. We're alive."

"I know," she said again with a whimper. "But my mother and father aren't. Little Jeroen, too. Even Utari. And Ratu and Kuwat."

"Who are they?"

"Ratu is—was—our cook and housekeeper. Utari, the nanny. Kuwat was the gardener." Her voice broke on Kuwat's name.

What would Tante Greet do in this situation? "Empathy, Katrien," I heard in my head. I did have some empathy. I reminded myself again that I knew what it was like to lose a parent. "Would it help if you talked about them?" I asked.

"I don't know." Tears filled her voice. "It hurts so much. Why does it hurt so much? How long does it take to get used to them being gone?" Her question was drowned out in a sob.

Frits shifted beside her, and she rubbed his back.

"Vader likes your father," I said. "He thinks he's a wonderful supervisor. He never says one cross thing about Mr. Burkart."

"You do know your father is dead, don't you?"

Why did she do that? Why did she lash out? I was trying to comfort her, to ease her hurt. I moved away, not wanting to be any closer than necessary to her vile words. "No. I don't know that. You should get some sleep."

She wept a bit longer, her soft sniffles the only sound in the darkness. I couldn't sleep. My mind would not stop whirring. What happened to the animals? Where were they? We had tromped through the jungle for hours, and except for that lone dhole, the only life we saw was each other. And Frits.

"A group, when it has once disappeared, never reappears."

Brigitta's sniffles turned to snores as she fell asleep.

As I sat awake, the scent of the Sampaguita flowers filled the dark air and reminded me of other smells that always seemed to permeate the air around Anjer. Tea and coffee, spices and raw fish, the salty ocean and sweet fruits. But Krakatau had taken all that loveliness away.

Anjer would never be the same.

My life would never be the same.

A wave of sorrow washed over me, and I could feel tears leaking from my eyes. I didn't know what to do. I had dragged Brigitta and Frits up here, and I wasn't sure if it was the right thing or not. What if this had been a mistake?

What if another wave attacked us? I didn't think I had the strength to hang onto a tree another time.

What if a wild animal cornered us, instead? Even though we had only seen a dhole, that didn't mean other animals weren't lurking in the recesses of the jungle. We were near a stream that was normally filled with water. Animals would need to drink, too, and they wouldn't know it was drained.

Why was it drained?

I focused on that. State the problem. "It is drained of water," I whispered to myself.

Hypothesize answers. "Drought." That was the simplest answer. It was also unlikely. Although we were in the dry season, it had still been raining off and on.

However . . . it hadn't rained in over a week.

But a week or so without rain wouldn't cause the stream to completely dry out. Besides, the bed was muddy.

No. It couldn't be drought.

Another answer. "All the water was drunk." Ridiculous! Every animal in the jungle would have to drink from this one stream at the same time. Impossible!

A different answer. "The wave?" That didn't make much sense to me. There ought to be more water. It should be flooded, shouldn't it? The stream should be brackish with saltwater. Or at least I thought it should.

But none of those things happened.

"Maybe we should go farther into the jungle?" I whispered aloud. "Follow the stream. We might be able to find some water farther inland."

That was it. That was the plan.

Chapter 37

I swung from tree to tree. The wind whipped through my hair and made my skirts ripple. Vader swung along behind me, and Tante Greet followed him.

"Woooo!" my aunt cried, joy coursing through her voice.

Silvery gibbons brachiated beside us.

"Katrien, keep up with them," Vader called.

"I will." My legs swung harder, and I picked up a little speed. The gibbons didn't pass me, but Vader and Tante Greet fell behind.

The gibbons stopped, and I teetered on the branch when I landed near them. "Vader! Tante Greet! I'm here!"

They were gone.

Where could they be?

I burst into tears, a little girl lost in the jungle. Loud cries ripped from my soul, causing the gibbons to scatter.

"Wake up, Katrien," Brigitta said, shaking me.

I yawned and wiped my eyes. Frits bawled beside us.

"You need to get up," she said.

"I'm awake," I said groggily. "Why is he crying?"

She pulled the boy into her lap. "He's hungry, and I want to go home."

"We need water."

"*Ja*, we do." She reached for her shoes and pulled them on.

"I think we should follow the stream farther inland."

The glare on her face could have sunk a fleet of ships. "What?" she asked hostilely.

"We might find water."

"What makes you think that? The stream is empty. There *is* no water."

"It's a stream," I said. "I can't explain why it doesn't have water here, but there may be some farther inland."

"I thought you fancied yourself a scientist," she said with an accusatory sneer.

"I do."

Frits's wails increased in volume, and Brigitta bounced him on her knees. "Then why don't you know what happened to the water? Why? Give me a reason."

"Believe me." I ran my hands through my knotted hair. "I wish I could. But one of the first things scientists learn is how little they know."

Brigitta growled in frustration. "Why am I even listening to you?" She stood, picked up Frits and paced. "You made me come with you into the jungle. You made me climb a tree."

"I saved your life," I protested.

"Perhaps." She gave me a dubious look and continued ranting. "You made me march all the way up here. You said there would be water. There is no water. And now you want me to march farther inland? Because you think there *might* be water? When my father hears about this, he'll—" She stopped short, realizing her mistake, and glowered at me.

"I also rescued you from a dhole, but I notice you've already forgotten that."

"I wouldn't have needed rescuing from that thing if you hadn't dragged me into the jungle in the first place."

Frits screamed.

"Can't you get him to be quiet?" I asked. His wails bored into my brain and made me want to smash something.

"He's a baby, Katrien. And he's hungry." She kissed his cheek and whispered in his ear, but his cries continued.

I stood up and rubbed my eyes. "Then our best option is to follow the stream inland. The wave didn't hit here. We could find something to eat. It's our best plan. Don't you see that?"

Brigitta's entire being sank like a wilting flower. Frits almost tumbled from her arms. She mumbled something, but I couldn't make out the words.

"What was that?"

"Ja," she said tiredly. "I'll come with you."

"Good." I nodded. "Let's go."

We followed a path along the bank, created by years and years of animals treading to and fro. Frits continued to cry and moan.

We hadn't walked more than twenty minutes when a rustling noise came from the forest. I threw out my arm and forced Brigitta to stop. "Shhh!"

She placed a hand over Frits's mouth, but his whimpers still echoed.

The rustling grew louder.

"What is that?" Brigitta whispered.

I shook my head. "I don't know." I half expected a Javan rhinoceros to burst through the undergrowth.

But it was Raharjo and four other men who emerged from the foliage.

I couldn't believe it. What was he doing there? Shouldn't he have gone to the mosque like Slamet and Indah? Maybe they had come to him instead. I tried to see past the men, to see if Slamet was farther back in the trees.

Raharjo stared at me and pointed a finger. "You!" He narrowed his eyes and leaned toward me. "You are reason Slamet is not here with me where he belongs. You are reason Ibu is"—He paused before sneering—"not in her home. Not with her family."

I felt as if I had been slapped. Was he saying that Indah was dead? That she had not made it to safety with her people? Or was he just berating me because she worked for my family?

I didn't understand Raharjo at all. I had never met a native person as confrontational as he was. Normally, they just smiled and backed away from conflicts. What was wrong with him?

But as soon as that question crossed my mind, I heard Slamet's words in my head. "You do not know. You cannot know. You are Dutch." I remembered his story about the coffee plantation owner's callous indifference toward Purnama. I remembered how Wangi had to care for her husband, day and night. Purnama and Wangi were not about to get into an argument with the owner. Who knows what would have happened to them if they did? But just because they chose not to fight didn't mean they weren't in the right.

Now, standing in the middle of the jungle, filthy, thirsty, hungry and exhausted, I found myself growing angrier by the second. No matter what Raharjo meant about Indah, his malice toward me was unjust, and what he said about Slamet was not true. I did not keep Slamet from him! Slamet chose to be with his mother when the volcano erupted, not with his vile brother. And I did everything I could to protect them. After everything that had happened, I found I did not have the strength to walk away from this fight, regardless of the consequences.

"I tried to keep them safe!" I shouted. "When they wanted to go to the mosque I tried to keep them at home. Where it was safe!" I wished I had done more to protect them. For a brief instant, I even wished they had gone to Raharjo, deep in the jungle, instead of the mosque.

"Safe?" He turned to the other men and spoke in Javanese.

One of them responded and Raharjo turned back to me. Even in the dim light with all the ash in the air, his eyes gleamed with hatred. I took a step back.

"You tried to keep them from mosque?" Raharjo's voice dripped with contempt. "To keep them at your home? To do as you say? Like prisoners or slaves?"

"That is not—"

"What has happened to your home?" he interrupted.

I pressed my lips together and felt myself grow hot. I would not give Raharjo the satisfaction of an answer.

Brigitta stepped out from behind me, still holding Frits. "I'm sure it fared better than the mosque. Our homes are not made of wood." Her eyes met mine, and I could tell she was frightened. But she wasn't going to be bullied either. Good for her.

The men all talked at once, now gesturing toward Frits.

Then, graceful as a leopard, Raharjo moved and in one swift motion took the boy from Brigitta's arms. Brigitta stumbled backward and fell, landing with a sharp cry on the damp mud.

"Raharjo!" My voice cracked like a whip. "We have been caring for that boy!"

"You are Wewe Gombel." This was unfair. Wewe Gombel was a supernatural woman who kidnapped children.

"I did not steal him! We found him, and we've been caring for him. He's frightened!"

"You are dangerous," he spat.

Brigitta reached out. "Frits."

Raharjo sneered at her. "You give him Dutch name? He is not Dutch! We will take him. We are his family now."

"No!" I grabbed his arm. "You can't!"

As soon as I touched him, one of the other men pulled his *kris* from his waist and pressed it to my throat.

I froze, and Brigitta gasped.

"The boy is Javanese," the man said. "He is ours."

Terrifed though I was, I cried out, "Raharjo! I'll tell Slamet about this."

He gazed at me, and in his eyes I now saw grief mixed with hatred. I forced myself not to move. Even the slightest shiver would cause the *kris* to puncture my skin. "The Dutch are not welcome here," Rahajaro hissed in my ear. "The Dutch never were. Slamet learned this, but he made a mistake. He trusted you. And you have killed him."

Tears pricked my eyes, but I refused to let them fall. Slamet had listened to his brother's stories about the Dutch. I knew the stories were probably terrible, and I knew some of them might be true. And I knew Slamet had believed them. But I also knew that in spite of all this, Slamet had been my friend. He *had*. Even Raharjo said Slamet had trusted me.

"I didn't kill him," I said, putting as much rage in my voice as I could. "I don't even know if he's dead, but I certainly don't plan to give up on him so easily!" The tears that had been threatening finally spilled over.

Raharjo stared at me for a long moment. Then, without another word, he walked away with Frits wriggling and twisting in his arms. My captor removed his *kris* from my neck and drifted off with the other men, his eyes never leaving mine until he faded into the forest.

I gasped in relief and held my head in my hands.

I stood there a long time, thinking about what had happened. I might have stayed in that spot forever if it weren't for Brigitta, who began whimpering from where she still sat on the ground. I squatted beside her. "Are you hurt?"

She shook her head, and tears streamed from her eyes. "I want him back, Katrien."

"I know." I rubbed her back as she had done with Frits. "I know."

Wrapping her arms around my neck, she sobbed. "I miss him so much."

She had grown quite fond of the boy for knowing him less than a day. And not really knowing him, even then.

"I m-miss him s-so m-much," she repeated, hiccuping.

I continued patting her back. Trying to find the right words, I said, "Frits is a sweet boy." *When he isn't screaming*, I thought. "Maybe they can find his family." Even as I said the words, I doubted them. His family was probably dead.

"Not Frits," Brigitta said, clutching my blouse. "Little Jeroen. I miss him so much."

It must be awful to lose a sibling. I couldn't imagine what that would be like. Would it hurt more, less, or the same as losing a parent? I rubbed her back again until her sobs died down and eventually stopped.

She pulled herself away from me and wiped her eyes. "Shall we keep going?"

"Inland?"

Nodding, she said, "By the stream. You said—"

"I know. But do you want to? I mean, with Raharjo and those other men in the forest . . ."

"No." Her voice was soft, but resolved.

"Nor I."

She stood up. "So what are we going to do?"

We. I liked the sound of that. We were a team now. We had faced Raharjo together.

"Go back to Anjer," I said. "By way of the streambed." I just hoped that if the water rose again, we would have a standing tree to climb.

Brigitta's shoulders drooped with relief. "Thank goodness. I was terrified to follow those men."

Chapter 38

When we passed the clearing again, Brigitta's sarcasm returned. "I see our rooms from last night."

"We were safe, though."

"Only because those men didn't find us." She ducked under a branch. "How do you know them?"

"I don't."

She put her hands on her hips. "I heard you call one of them by name."

"Raharjo." I sighed. "I don't really know him. He's Slamet's brother."

"Isn't Slamet that native boy you're always running around with?"

I nodded. "Raharjo hates me."

"I can't imagine why," she said archly.

"The only other time I saw him he called me dangerous. I had never even met him before."

"You may be many things, Katrien," she said, walking a bit ahead of me, "but dangerous isn't one of them."

"Slamet said he meant to say Dutch."

"But you aren't Dutch," she stated, "you're Javanese."

"I know," I said, amazement filling my voice. Brigitta understood.

Of course she did. She was Javanese, too. Born and bred in Anjer, just like me.

"How far is it to home?" she asked.

"Several hours."

She groaned.

I encouraged her. "We'll get there. Don't worry. Keep your eyes open for any puddles we can drink from."

"I am not drinking from a puddle, Katrien."

"Are you expecting to find a glass and a clean rain barrel?"

She puffed up like a proud bird. "I'm not stupid, you know. It's dangerous to drink from puddles."

"You're correct."

She gave me a smug smile.

"But in this case," I said, "it might be more dangerous not to."

Snapping her mouth shut, she shot me a defiant glare.

I smiled prettily, enjoying having an edge over her. "Come on, Brigitta."

We had covered about fifteen minutes' worth of ground from the clearing when we saw the first downed tree. Not far beyond, bodies lay scattered.

There was a woman in her underthings. Brigitta and I both turned our heads.

There was a native man with his hands clasped in prayer.

Neither of us said anything about the bodies we passed. We made the sign of the cross each time we encountered a corpse, but we kept our thoughts to ourselves.

After a while, a pink fluffy pile of cloth caught my eye.

"What is that?" Brigitta asked.

"Fabric," I said, looking down at my torn skirt. "I could wrap it around me like a sarong!" I picked up the bundle and was immediately surprised by its weight. I turned it over to examine it closer and suddenly a tiny face emerged from the folds.

"Oh!" I gasped in surprise.

"What?"

"It's a doll." I laughed and brushed the face with my fingers. It was cold. Waxy. Not porcelain. I froze. "Oh, God."

Brigitta stared at the bundle in my hands, yet I got the impression she wasn't seeing it. She seemed lost in some somber world of her own. But then she took a watery breath and came out of her reverie. Her voice cracked as she said, "It's a baby, isn't it?"

I nodded.

She stepped over to me. "We should bury her."

Grateful for a task to get the cold feeling of death off my hands, I thrust the baby into Brigitta's arms. "I'll dig." I scrambled in the mud, the dirt caking my fingers as I dug, until I had a hole large enough for the baby. Brigitta placed her gently in the grave, and we both covered her. I moved to leave, but Brigitta stayed. She stood as still as the dead baby.

"Brigitta? We need to keep going." I touched her shoulder.

She startled like a mouse and wiped her eyes. "Amen," she whispered and crossed herself.

"I'm sorry. I didn't know you were praying. We can stay a bit longer."

She shook her head. "It's fine."

We walked on. I couldn't absorb all the loss. The fallen trees became thicker and more numerous. Like the bodies, they lay scattered everywhere. We climbed over the ones that crossed our path.

"Oh, my," Brigitta said.

Ahead, a monstrous tamarind tree blocked our way. It stretched across the streambed and buried itself in the ground on the other side.

I scrambled over it first, my feet slipping and one heel catching in the bark. I had to yank it free. Once I reached the top, I stretched down for Brigitta's hand. She grabbed it, and I hauled her up. We caught our breath before sliding down the other side.

She landed with a thud and tumbled into me. "Ooof. Sorry," she said, righting herself.

"That's fi—"

Brigitta screamed.

I grabbed her. "What? What is it?"

"It's a—it's a man!" She shuddered.

"Good heavens, Brigitta. You just helped me bury a dead baby."

"*Ja*, but I've done that before."

I stopped. What was she talking about? I wanted to ask aloud, but now wasn't the time. When I got a good look at the corpse, I understood why she screamed. He didn't look peaceful like the others.

The upper half of the man's body lay across the path. His legs were wedged beneath the tree at a strange angle. His face was bloated— one eye shut, but the other wide open. Bright blue and staring.

But then I noticed his clothes. One sleeve of his shirt was ripped off, but otherwise it appeared to be in good condition. And Brigitta needed a shirt since the tamarind tree shredded hers yesterday.

Bending down and closing my eyes, I yanked the shirt off the body and held it out to Brigitta.

She took a step back. "What do you expect me to do with that?" she asked in disgust.

"I expect you to wear it. Your shirt is ripped. You need something to cover yourself."

She shook her head in short, quick movements like a vibrating string. "No. No. I cannot wear that shirt."

"Why not? There's nothing wrong with it. It's just missing a sleeve. You don't need the sleeves. But you do need something to cover your—" I made a vague gesture in the direction of her chest.

"You can't see anything! Can you?" She looked down at her torn blouse.

"No, but you can't go home and change clothes, Brigitta! You told me your house is gone!"

"My room was still standing," she said, her voice growing more shrill.

"Brigitta, be sensible. I doubt your wardrobe full of blouses and dresses is still there."

"I cannot wear a dead person's clothes, Katrien! I can't!"

Taking a calming breath, I tried to copy Tante Greet's soothing voice for what felt like the millionth time. "Brigitta, it is very important that you put this on. You don't want to shame your father by showing up in town in a state of undress."

She relaxed a little.

I continued. "And what would your mother say? She would be appalled."

"But that is a dead man's shirt," she whimpered, reminding me of a frightened animal.

"I know, Brigitta. But we don't know what we'll find when we get to Anjer. And right now, this"—I held the shirt out again—"is all we've got. Please put it on."

She took the shirt from me and shook the fabric with several violent flaps as if she were trying to force the stench of death out of it. Or maybe it was just to get the dirt off.

She retched before she slid it over her shoulders, but she did manage to get it on and button it.

As we left the man's body behind us, I said a silent thanks to him.

Chapter 39

We slogged on. My thirst grew. The mud grew, too, and the deeper it was the more it tried to suck the shoes off my feet.

"I don't see any water, Katrien," Brigitta panted. She sounded exhausted.

"Neither do I."

"My mouth is too dry to even swallow."

I did not respond, because just then, my shoe stuck decisively in the muck. The lace on my boot broke, and my foot popped out. "Terra firma!"

Brigitta gasped. "What's the matter?"

"My shoe's stuck."

She yanked it out of the mud. "That's no reason for such language, Katrien."

"I wasn't even cursing. You sound like my aunt." I took the boot from her. The heel had broken off, and the lace was frayed in two places. I couldn't wear it. Sitting down, I removed my other shoe and tossed them both aside.

"What are you doing?"

"I can't wear just one shoe," I said, standing up. "I'll have to go without."

"But—" She stopped.

I spread my hands out. "I'm open to suggestions."

She fingered the hem of her new shirt. "Perhaps we can find another pair. Like..." She pointed to the dark fabric. "Like this." Her voice trailed off. I had expected more of an argument from her, but the fact was, she hadn't argued with me since I'd given her the shirt.

"Are you well?" I asked. It was a ridiculous question. Of course she wasn't. Neither of us was. And if we didn't find water soon...I refused to dwell on the thought.

She turned to me. Her eyes were unfocused, and her face as blank as an unpapered wall. Then she collapsed.

"Homo sapiens." I knelt over her and patted her hand. "Brigitta? Brigitta?" I raised my voice, remembering her damaged ear. "Brigitta?!"

If only there were some water I could splash on her face. Where was the water?

But no, I needed to focus on one problem at a time.

Still patting her hand, I called again. "Brigitta? Brigitta?"

No reaction.

Her skin was as white as the feathers on a Brahminy kite's head. "Brigitta? Brigitta?"

She hadn't died, had she? Not now. Not after we had survived volcanic eruptions, a monsoon of ash, enormous walls of water, and even a confrontation with Raharjo. "Please don't let her be dead," I prayed. I listened for a heartbeat or the sound of her breathing.

I heard nothing, but then I felt the faint rise of her chest.

"Oh, thank God." I didn't know I had been holding my breath until I spoke.

"Brigitta?" I gave her a gentle slap. "Brigitta?"

Still no reaction.

I tried again.

"Brigitta?" I swung my arm and this time gave her cheek a hard thwack. "Brigitta!"

She stirred, and I clutched her shoulders, giving her tiny shakes to revive her.

"Come on, Brigitta, wake up. Wake up. Wake up!"

Her eyes stayed shut, but she spoke. "Mother?" She mumbled a bit after that.

I shook her harder. "Brigitta. Brigitta. Wake up. You need to wake up now!"

"*Ja*, Mother, I'm awake." Her lids fluttered open, and her expression went from pleasant to puzzled to panicked. "What happened?"

"You fainted." I sat on the ground.

"I did?" Her eyebrows rose in shock.

Nodding, I said, "You just fell to the ground."

She struggled to sit up.

"Don't rush," I warned her. "I don't want to have to revive you again."

"Why did I faint? I don't, normally."

"You don't?" She was so feminine that I pictured her keeling over any time a ship passed through the strait.

"Why do you sound so shocked?" she asked. She was definitely alert now.

"I—I—"

"I'm not half as delicate as you think I am, Katrien."

"I never said you were delicate!"

"No, you didn't," she said. "But I can see it in your eyes. Admit it. You think I'm some weakling who needs nothing but help."

"Fine," I said. "I think you're feminine and frilly and far too concerned with appearances. You should be concentrating on improving your mind rather than your looks."

She glared at me. "Do you know something, Katrien?"

"What?" I snapped.

"You can be quite detestable when you want to be." Then, she offered me a slight smile. "To be honest, I didn't think you had it in you to say what you really felt about me. Although I don't know why I didn't. You've always been catty to me."

Wait. What?

I must have misheard. Brigitta sounded . . . proud. Proud of me? I rubbed my forehead in confusion. Maybe it was the lack of food and water that was slowing my brain. "I don't understand. Are you mad or not?"

"I should be furious." She sighed. "But I'm too tired."

So was I, and I didn't want to argue. "I have an idea. Why don't we stay here for the rest of the day? We're probably halfway home. We can go the rest of the way tomorrow."

She dragged herself over to a downed tree and leaned against it. "That would be wonderful."

"You stay here." I stood, steadying myself on the same tree. "I'm going to try to find food. Or at least some water."

She nodded, yawned in a most unladylike manner, and closed her eyes.

I took in our surroundings. A gray blur was all I could see. Mud covered everything. Very few trees—perhaps one in fifty—still stood. The gloom from the ash that still hung in the air made everything more bleak and dreary.

Not wanting to get lost, I headed south in a straight line, walking with great care so I wouldn't injure my bare feet, and counted my steps. "One. Two. Three…"

After eleven steps, I stumbled upon more bodies. Some were in the few trees that were still upright. Most were scattered throughout the forest as if some giant had tossed them in the air and let them fall, twisted and mangled like neglected dolls.

At thirty-seven paces, I tripped and landed on my hands and knees. "Ow," I muttered. I kneaded my wrists to make sure they weren't hurt. "Whoever said mud is soft was lying."

I turned to see what caused my fall, and the familiar face of Sister Hilde greeted me. Still in her long habit, she lay half buried in the ground. I stared in disbelief and wiped my eyes even though no tears formed. A tingling sensation skittered under my skin. I knew Sister Hilde. I *knew* her. This was the first dead body of someone I knew that I had ever seen. Even at my mother's funeral, Vader hadn't allowed me to look at her in her coffin.

Sister Hilde looked like she was sleeping. I had heard people say that of my mother, and I wondered how it could be true. My mother hadn't been sleeping. She had no life left to need to sleep. But now, seeing Sister Hilde, I understood what they meant. The barest trace of a smile still graced my teacher's face, and I was reminded, then, of her many kindnesses to me. Like the time at mass one Sunday when she had lent me a handkerchief to wipe my spectacles. When I tried to return it, she placed her hands over mine and said, "I believe you will have more need for this than I ever will. Keep it."

Even in school she never raised her voice to scold. She encouraged my interest in science and had told me, "Look to the Heavens, Katrien. You can see the face of God in the stars."

Why had she died? Why had someone kind and generous been taken in such a manner?

Now, even in death, she wore a peaceful expression, as if she had accepted her fate.

But I couldn't.

I screamed. I beat my fists against my legs. I kicked at the dirt.

"Ow!" Some tree bark jammed into my big toe. Grimacing, I pulled the bark out in one swift motion. "Holy God, that hurt!" Clamping my hand over my bleeding foot, I rocked back and forth trying to stop the throbbing.

I needed something to stanch the blood, but I didn't have a handkerchief.

"Sister, do you—"

What was I doing, talking to a corpse? Except this wan't any corpse. This was Sister Hilde. My favorite teacher. She always had a handkerchief.

I dug around until I found her pocket. There! The thin piece of linen was just what I needed.

I tied it around my toe and stared at Sister.

She was still gone. Nothing was going to change that. With a wavering breath, I reached under her spectacles and closed her eyes.

I needed to press on. What number of steps had I been on? I couldn't remember. Maybe I should just turn around and head back to Brigitta. North would probably be a better direction anyway. *Ja.* That's what I would do.

Suddenly I froze.

Spectacles!

Sister Hilde was wearing her spectacles!

How did they stay on her face during the wave? Perhaps her wimple held them in place?

I stared back down at her. Should I take them? I took that man's shirt for Brigitta. That hadn't been difficult. I didn't think of it as stealing since it was filling a need. Even taking Sister Hilde's handkerchief didn't seem odd since she lent one to me before.

But taking spectacles from a nun? That seemed like stealing, even when the nun was dead.

But...she *was* dead. She wouldn't need them anymore. And I did. I was tired of straining to see through a hazy blur.

Fine. I would try them.

They might not work.

If they didn't, I would return them.

"Forgive me," I muttered, plucking the spectacles off Sister Hilde's nose and sliding them onto mine. In an instant, my surroundings were clear and sharp.

Trees, stripped bare of leaves and branches, pointed toward the sky like angry claws.

Mud, drenching the ground, turned where I stood into an ocean of gray.

Bodies, twisted and mangled, lay everywhere with their clothing ripped and even missing.

Still I whimpered with relief, having forgotten how wonderful it was to see a clear world. Even if that world had become Hell.

Glancing back down at my teacher, I hoped once more that she wouldn't mind. "*Dank u*, Sister Hilde. I'll never forget your last generosity." I kissed my fingers and pressed them to her forehead.

Limping back to Brigitta, I counted, "One. Two..."

Chapter 40

My heart pounded, and my breath came in short bursts. My thirst had nearly overwhelmed me by the time I reached Brigitta.

She didn't move when I plopped down beside her. Holding a hand under her nose, I was reassured by the cool breaths I felt on my fingers.

I rested my head on my knees and waited for some of my strength to return. Walking exhausted me, but we still needed water and food.

Staggering upright, I headed north. "One. Two. Three..." So tired. So hungry. So thirsty.

Twigs and branches and debris cut further into my feet as I shuffled. I had no energy to lift them. I should have taken Sister Hilde's shoes, too. Except they were buried in the muck.

Crawling over another huge tree—this one a strangler fig—I stopped. In front of me was a small area that must have been a clearing at some point. Now, what was once a grassy field was covered in bodies. Men, women, children. They lay battered and broken, facing every direction.

I collapsed against the fig. I had never seen such loss of life, like the end of a battle.

Only these people had not been fighting. They had been living their lives. They didn't deserve this!

"Come on, Katrien," I told myself. "You can't help them. You need to find water."

But I also needed shoes.

From the pile of bodies, a woman's boot stuck up at an odd angle, about six or seven meters from me. It looked to be about my size. Three corpses lay between me and the shoe.

I grimaced and shuddered as I made my way forward. My feet brushed the bodies and I felt their cold, waxy skin. Then a frisson passed over me, as if Death himself had run a finger down my spine.

I reached for the boot. I was only close enough to grab the heel, but I clutched it anyway, intending to use it for balance as I pulled myself closer.

Unfortunately, my weight was too much. The boot couldn't hold me, and bodies tumbled as I tried to get nearer. I fell face-first onto the stomach of a dead man lying below me. When I landed, his stomach made a belching noise. I yelped and jumped backward, smashing into the face of a child. His teeth grazed my toes.

Horrified, I fled back to the fig tree, and only when I got there did I realize I now had the entire boot in my hand.

A leg, from the knee down, filled the shoe. It didn't belong to any of the bodies I'd just seen. Somehow it had become separated from its owner. The jagged bits of flesh and bone reminded me of the guts Tante Greet and Indah ripped out of fish.

The image made me retch. "Oh, my God!" I cast the boot aside.

Heaving great gasping breaths, I firmly turned my back on the field of bodies.

Again I sensed Death crawling all over me. My feet. My hands. My legs. My face. This feeling would never leave. Never. I shivered.

My toes tingled. I rubbed them, and my hand came away bloody.

I pushed Sister Hilde's spectacles up. A thin red line stretched along three toes. "That can't be good."

When had this happened? Now both my feet had injuries.

When my breathing returned to normal, I left. I would find shoes elsewhere. I needed to let these poor people rest in peace.

I walked on, cursing the lack of water, when I noticed a pile of strange green spheres wedged under a tree trunk. Reaching down, I pulled and yanked one out. The welcome scent of citrus greeted me as the sphere came free. I couldn't believe it. It was five unripe oranges that sat resting there, nestled like a clutch of eggs.

"They must have come from Mr. Stuyvesant's trees!" His grove of orange and lemon trees grew at the northern edge of Anjer. Had I walked that far?

I pushed Sister Hilde's spectacles up and scoured the area for more oranges but didn't see any.

I dumped the fruit into what was left of my skirt and returned as quickly as I could to Brigitta.

When I reached her, she hadn't moved. I dropped down beside her and shook her shoulders. "Brigitta, wake up. I found something to eat."

Her eyes snapped open, and she inhaled deeply. Rubbing her face, she said, "Oh, Katrien." The disappointment was thick in her voice. "I must have fallen asleep."

"*Ja.*" I thrust the fruit in her face, like a hunter returning with food for his family. "I found oranges."

"But it's green."

I frowned. "It's just not ripe yet."

"Is it safe to eat?"

"Of course," I answered with as much certainty as I could. I didn't truly know if the fruit was safe or not, but it was food. And I thought any food—especially food we didn't have to cook—was worth eating.

Brigitta gave me a skeptical look, but she took the orange and began to peel it.

I did the same. The inside was a pale, translucent color. I tilted my head back, tore off a segment, and bit into it.

My lips puckered around the fruit, sealing shut like the lid on a pickle jar. It took all my effort not to spit it back out. I had never eaten anything so sour.

Fighting back a gag, I managed to swallow the bite.

"Katrien," Brigitta said. Her lips pursed, her eyes narrowed and her nostrils flared as she choked down her own segment.

"*Ja?*" I struggled against the laughter that threatened to bubble up and took another bite.

"This is the worst orange I have ever eaten in my life."

My laugh escaped, and the sound surprised me. I thought I would never laugh again. "I know, it's terrible. But it's food. Doesn't it taste wonderful for that reason alone?"

"Well." She dragged the word out before shrugging and eating another segment.

"I have another one."

"I can't eat another one, Katrien."

"*Ja*, you can. We need to eat. Mr. Charles Darwin says, '*Though food may be now superabundant, it is not so at all seasons of each recurring year.*'" *Or when a volcano and giant waves obliterate the landscape*, I thought. I handed Brigitta a second orange.

She gave the green fruit a dubious look. "Superabundant?"

I waved my hand and chuckled. "He was using it in a different context. But we'll stay here, eat our abundant oranges and regain our strength."

We both gave in to the absurdity and roared with laughter.

Chapter 41

Sunlight warmed my face. My aunt would knock on the door soon, telling me I had slept too long. Spent too much time staring at the stars on my ceiling or reading. Or both.

I cracked my eyes open. The stars weren't over my head. The sky—a beautiful blue sky—was.

The sky!

I shot up, ignoring the aches and pains in my body.

The sun!

I could see.

Some ash remained, floating to the earth, but the sunlight glowed on our surroundings.

"Brigitta, wake up!" I shoved her. "Wake up! There's sunlight!" I grabbed Sister Hilde's spectacles and put them on.

"Oh, my goodness." She rubbed her eyes. "I forgot how bright it was."

"Me, too." I squinted.

Brigitta stared at me. "Where did you get those spectacles?"

She must not have noticed them the day before. "I ... found ... them." My throat closed around the words.

"What, just lying on the ground?"

"No." I traced my fingers in the dirt and avoided her gaze. "They're Sister Hilde's. I found her."

Her lips parted in surprise. "Where?" Her question was a solemn whisper.

"Back there." I pointed south, behind us. "She was lying on the ground. Half buried in mud."

Brigitta's lip quivered. "She was my favorite teacher."

"Mine, too."

"She let me help her in the herb garden. Those were my favorite days." Her voice turned wistful.

We sat in the bright silence. No birds chirping. No frogs croaking. No insects buzzing. The remaining leaves didn't even rustle.

Brigitta took in my swollen, crusted feet and the handkerchief tied around my big toe. "Perhaps you should wear my shoes today," she suggested.

I shook my head. "No. I can't take your shoes. I'll find some somewhere. Besides"—I scratched my arm—"I think they're too swollen for your shoes." My normally long toes resembled rookworst sausages. The skin stretched tight and shiny as if it were too small. My toes only moved the tiniest bit when I wiggled them.

"Can you even walk?" Her expression was filled with concern and worry.

Taking a deep breath, I said, "I...don't know."

"Should you even try?" she wondered.

"We can't stay here," I said, wishing I could hide my feet under a blanket. "We have to get to Anjer. Why don't we split the last orange, and we'll see if I can walk then."

We finished our meager breakfast, and Brigitta helped me stand.

"Oooh." My feet screamed, like a thousand pins were plunged into the soles at one time.

"Do you want to sit back down? Do you want to rest some more?"

I shook my head, my voice tight with pain. "More rest won't help until we've gotten food and water. But I will have glorious scars when this is over. As Mr. Charles Darwin says, *'Male stag-beetles sometimes bear wounds from the huge mandibles of other males.'* "

"You want to look like a beetle?" Brigitta scolded. "Oh, I wish I had some *sangitan*. Lean on me." She offered her shoulder, and I didn't protest, grateful for the help.

"Why? What's *sangitan*?"

"It can be used to relieve pain." She brushed her hair out of her eyes. "Although it does need to be boiled with water."

"I suppose it's just as well you don't have any, then."

"Banana could be used to treat the wounds."

"Stop telling me these things. It doesn't matter now."

The oranges, despite their awful taste, had helped. My mouth wasn't as dry as yesterday. My thirst was not as urgent.

We were weak, but the sun warmed our skin, giving us energy. "I never thought I would miss sunlight so much," Brigitta said.

"How could you not miss it?"

"I try to stay out of the midday sun. So I don't turn brown like the natives."

"I suppose I'm not in the sun much either. I'm usually in the jungle at midday. Or I was until . . . well, lately I've been at home."

She gazed at me questioningly.

"Anyway, the light in the forest is dim. Not much sunlight gets through. It's dappled and lovely." The sight of all the downed trees stabbed me through the heart. "I suppose that won't be true now." My voice broke.

"It will grow back," she said, reassuring me with a gentle squeeze. "No matter how many times my father cuts down plants, they always return." A bitter note filled her voice.

"What do you mean?"

She shrugged. "Plants. They grow back."

"No." I struggled to ask my question. "What did you mean about your father?"

"Oh." She sighed. "He thinks—thought—my interests in plants were unladylike."

"What? Tante Greet has a flower garden, and she is forever trying to get me to help her in it. I thought flower gardens were a woman's domain."

She adjusted my arms around her. "Gardening can be something for women to occupy their time. But I don't want to merely garden."

"What do you want?"

"To know plants' medicinal qualities. To help people. Kuwat assisted me. His mother practiced *jamu*—native medicine. I needed Kuwat's help with the plants and he taught me what he remembered about his mother's knowledge. But after Father caught us with the hibiscus cuttings from the Ousterhoudts, he threatened to fire Kuwat and ripped all the cuttings out of the soil."

Her words astonished me. "You do have an interest in botany." Even though I knew she was clever, I never thought of Brigitta as someone with a scientific mind.

"It's not botany. It's native remedies." A pink tint colored her cheeks. "But please don't tell anyone."

I arched my eyebrows. "Who would I tell?"

"I don't know, but I would prefer—"

"Your secret is safe with me."

"*Dank u.*" She smiled. "And don't worry about the jungle. It will grow back."

"I suppose." It would take years for the forest to return. "After all, '*Every one has heard that when an American forest is cut down, a very different vegetation springs up.*' "

"Why do you do that?" she asked, shifting me in her arms.

"Do what?"

"Say such odd things." Her face rumpled in confusion. "Are you quoting Darwin again?"

"Why wouldn't I quote him? Who else should I quote?"

"I don't know. The Bible?"

"Mr. Charles Darwin makes more sense to me."

She stumbled a bit, and I slipped along with her. "*Darwin* makes more sense than the word of the *Lord?*" She shifted me back into a firmer grip.

"Brigitta, if you think the word of the Lord makes such sense, why don't you quote Him?"

Shrugging, she said, "I don't know. I suppose I don't feel a need to. I don't need to quote the Bible to prove how well I know the book."

"To prove...?"

"You don't think you do that?" Her round eyes were wide with the question.

I pushed away from her and sank to the ground. Did I do that?

No. That was not what I did. I refused to believe that was what I did.

After Vader, Mr. Charles Darwin was the greatest man I knew. His words helped me make sense of the world.

Brigitta sat beside me. "Katrien, I would much rather hear what *you* have to say than what Charles Darwin does."

I blinked. "You would?"

She nodded.

"*You?*"

"*Ja,*" she said firmly. "In your own words."

I turned away from her, unsure what to think of this kinder, more interesting Brigitta. The only other person who ever wanted me to think and speak my own mind was Vader. I pushed Sister Hilde's spectacles up and forced myself off the ground. Brigitta grasped me under my arm and helped me to stand once more. "In my own words," I said, "I think we should keep going. Despite my swollen feet."

She squeezed my shoulder. "Then that is precisely what we'll do."

We walked in slow silence for a long time. Snails were probably passing us—if there were any snails left.

More bodies lay scattered around the forest, wedged under fallen trees, piled on top of each other. Like something out of a nightmare.

We kept going.

"I think I can walk on my own now," I said. I no longer felt the pain in my feet, and when Brigitta released me, I found I could stumble along with a clumsy, shifting gait. My puffy, tight toes left odd impressions in the mud. As long as I focused on moving forward,

I avoided thinking about all the dead around me—and the reality that I might just find Vader and Tante Greet or Indah and Slamet among them.

After hours of slow progress, at last, we passed what had been the edge of the jungle and beheld Anjer.

No amount of mental preparation would have ever been enough. Even the darkest, most insidious workings of my imagination could never have conjured the scene before us.

A new pain struck me as I gazed out over the remains of my home.

Chapter 42

I pushed Sister Hilde's spectacles up, hoping to wake from the nightmare in front of me, but Brigitta confirmed what I knew in my heart was the reality.

"Nothing's left," she whispered.

"*Ja.*"

I thought the first wave had been bad. But now, there truly was nothing. Not a single building, not a wall, not even fences stood. Only splinters remained where homes and offices once sat. Small bits of shredded bark and twigs were all that remained of trees. Even the huge stones of the Catholic church had been scattered like beach sand. There was nothing to indicate that a town had been here. That people had lived here.

Anjer had been annihilated.

I swayed, and Brigitta steadied me. My heart pounded in my ears.

Brigitta gasped and pointed. "Katrien, look. The lighthouse."

The sturdy Anjer lighthouse that once rested so proudly on its rocky spit of land was gone.

In its place was a piece of coral so large and heavy that it had obliterated the stone beacon. I never realized nature had that much power.

Brigitta squeezed my hand. "There are so many people, Katrien."

It was true. Bodies were strewn everywhere. What was, three days ago, a thriving, beautiful town full of thousands of vibrant, healthy people was now nothing but an open mass grave.

A numbness settled over me.

"We should see if anyone needs help," she said.

"Needs help?" I gestured to the devastation. "Is anyone even alive?"

She bit her lip. "Someone has to be. Don't they? We can't be the only survivors."

I wasn't sure about that, and I was suddenly gripped again with the dreadful fear that somewhere down there I might find Vader and Tante Greet.

As we wove around the dead, Brigitta called out the names of those she knew. She recognized so many. "There's Mrs. Van Tassel. And that's Mr. Bleeker. Over there is..." Her voice faded.

"Who?"

"Adriaan Vogel." She stared at the body about halfway between us.

I didn't say anything. I couldn't say anything.

"I hope he found his brother before...well...before..." She let out a watery breath.

I turned away. I had no interest in identifying bodies, only in finding my family. "Vader! Tante Greet!" My voice rang out across the desolation.

Behind me, Brigitta continued moving through the bodies. "Oh, no."

"What?" I made my clumsy way toward her. My swollen feet were acting like heavy clubs as I stepped gingerly through the carnage. "Is it Vader?"

"No." She shook her head. "It's old Mrs. Schoonhoven. She always called me 'Bibby' and never seemed to remember my real name."

"How can you tell that's her?" All that was visible was the back of a yellow blouse and gray hair.

"She always wore a yellow blouse. Did you not notice?"

"Oh." I didn't notice. For all my observational skills, I never paid much attention to details about other people. "I never realized it was always."

The thought weighed heavily upon me. I had lived here my whole life. Could I not name anyone in this mass of death? Perhaps if there was just one person lying before me, like Sister Hilde, or even a few at a time, then I could identify them. But the hundreds scattered around us now were too much.

I took a wobbling step over another body and then fell. Brigitta caught me before I crashed into the corpse. When I saw its face, I gasped. There was no mistaking its identity, and I immediately decided it had been easier not knowing.

"Is it your aunt? Or your father?" she asked, trying to steady me.

I shook my head. "It's Wilhemina De Graff."

"From the hotel?"

I nodded.

We knelt beside her. "She was so nice," I said. "She lent me a handkerchief to get home in the ash." As I spoke I realized that made two people whose kindness—and handkerchiefs—had helped me since the eruption. I wished I could tell Wilhemenia and Sister Hilde how grateful I was.

"She waved at me whenever she saw me," Brigitta said, brushing Wilhemina's hair out of her eyes.

"I used to think she was independent and adventurous."

"Why?"

"Because she had come here from the Netherlands all alone. But then she told me she was only trying to find a rich husband. That's why she came to Java." Disappointment filled my voice, and I instantly regretted it. Wilhemina had had a dream, and her dream didn't come true.

"That's ridiculous," Brigitta said.

Amazed that she and I agreed about something like husband-hunting, I said, "I thought so, too."

"She should have stayed in the Netherlands. I imagine you would find richer men in Amsterdam."

I smiled wryly as Brigitta helped me to my feet.

Picking our way past more and more friends and neighbors, we reached the shoreline. The tide was in and the coral was covered, and then our living nightmare became something far worse.

"My God," Brigitta murmured, and crossed herself.

Floating in the Sunda Strait were more bodies, as far as the eye could see. In every direction. Nothing but bodies.

"It looks like they go all the way to Sumatra," I whispered.

A mournful awe filled her voice. "So many people, Katrien. How could so many people die at one time?"

"The waves." They tore through Anjer and ravaged not just buildings, but people, too. They seemed to have taken every person they met. Except us.

And maybe, maybe my father and my aunt.

But I still could not find them. Turning my mind from darker thoughts, I shifted my gaze to Krakatau. A choked cry escaped my throat.

"What?" Brigitta clutched my arm. "What is it?"

"Krakatau." I squinted through Sister Hilde's spectacles. "It's gone!"

"Don't be silly. How can an island be gone?"

I pointed where the island used to stand.

"That's not poss—" She stopped when she saw.

Where Krakatau once stood, guarding the entrance to the Sunda Strait, there was now nothing. I scoured my memory to find an instance in history of a volcano erupting and disappearing. But I could think of nothing. "Vader would know," I muttered to myself.

But he was not here. Nor was Tante Greet.

My feet began hurting again, and I let the pain overwhelm me. At least this kind of agony I knew and understood. The gritty beach sand cut into the soles of my swollen feet like glass. I needed to get off them.

I found a small patch of beach and sat, extending my legs straight in front of me. My back slumped, and my mind went blank.

I had no idea what to do next.

Chapter 43

Brigitta found a space next to me, and we sat in silence.

The water lapped the shore with gentle waves and soothing sounds.

They were so different from the monstrous ones that had changed everything I knew.

My toes, red and sausagelike, were nearly unrecognizable. Somewhere along our journey I had lost Sister Hilde's handkerchief. I pulled my feet close and rubbed them. Pain shot through my legs and I hissed aloud. I stopped rubbing.

The sun crawled across the sky as the afternoon wore on. It warmed my skin and tickled my scalp.

Everything about the feeling of the beach was normal. The breeze cooled my face. The sand danced across my fingers.

I wished it were possible to imagine away all the destruction and loss of life. All the fear and misery.

Still Brigitta and I sat.

We didn't move.

We didn't speak.

I let the truth wash over me. Vader and Tante Greet were gone. I would never see them again. Vader would never again encourage me to use logic. Tante Greet would never again try to make me more ladylike.

I squeezed my eyes shut as memories flooded over me in a rush more powerful than any giant wave.

Vader. Taking me into the jungle for the first time. Pointing to the stars and telling me their names. Encouraging me to collect beetles. Giving me a copy of *On the Origin of Species*. Teaching me Latin.

Tante Greet. Arriving in Anjer. Digging in her flower garden. Correcting my posture and language. Lecturing me about judging people. Making me read books other than Mr. Charles Darwin's. Teaching me to cook.

Brigitta and I were, quite possibly, the only people alive in Anjer. Perhaps even the only people alive for kilometers.

The only people alive.

I broke down and great, gulping dry heaves wracked my body. But I shed no tears. I was so thirsty; my body had no water to spare.

Brigitta wrapped her arms around me and pulled me close. I sobbed and moaned for long moments, and she soothed me, rubbing my back and whispering a song.

"Full moon, full moon
are you a guard at night
high in the starry sky?
Full moon, full moon
I look at you and I'm
sure that you smile."

When I quit hiccupping, I sat up and wiped my eyes out of habit.

Somewhere, among those thousands of bodies surrounding us, were Vader and Tante Greet. I had to find them. "Help me find them." I clutched Brigitta's arm.

"Find who?" She, too, had no tears, but grief contorted her face.

"My father and my aunt."

She removed her arm from my grasp. "They're dead, Katrien. Surely you know that." Her voice, gentle and soothing, was not the harsh slap I expected.

"I do know, Brigitta. Why do you think I was crying?" My own tone was far harsher than hers. "But I want to find them. I want to bury them."

"Bury them? Have you lost your mind?" There was the Brigitta I remembered. "How do you propose to do that?"

"By digging a hole and placing them in it." Had the sun affected her brain? I thought she was clever. How else did she think I would bury them?

She rolled her eyes. "You don't have a shovel. Or a spade! Even if you could find them, you could never get them buried. Think, Katrien!"

I flinched as she echoed Vader's words. But I also thought. It was almost instinct. "Then I'll use my hands! Like I did with that baby."

She grabbed my shoulders and shook me. "They're much larger than that baby. You're not making sense. There are thousands of bodies here. It would take weeks to get all those bodies out of the ocean."

"I don't care! Mr. Charles Darwin says, *'Shells and bones decay and disappear when left on the bottom of the sea.'* We have to find them before that happens."

"Stop quoting Darwin! They're dead, Katrien. They're all dead. Whether you find them or not, they're not coming back. I saw my family. Nothing was left but a shell. All the life was gone."

In my delirium I seized on false hopes once more. "That's just it, Brigitta! I don't know they're gone. I haven't seen their bodies. Maybe...maybe...I don't know...maybe they survived!"

Brigitta stared at me with eyes full of pity. Pity! From Brigitta Burkart! "Katrien, do you truly think that's possible? Look around you."

I pushed Sister Hilde's spectacles up and reality set in again.

She was right. I would never find them. They were lost within this faceless mass of death along with everyone else.

And yet...there were survivors somewhere. There had to be. Which meant maybe help was out there, too. Not all of Java had been inundated by the waves. The forest around the clearing was still there. Raharjo was still in the jungle. The water hadn't destroyed everything.

Brigitta wrapped her arms around me again. "We're all each other has," she said, repeating my words to her from days ago.

"How can you be handling this so well? Why haven't you flown into hysterical fits?"

"I told you I was stronger than you knew. And this isn't the jungle anymore, Katrien." She gestured to the devastation. "This isn't bugs or animals that might eat me, or dangerous people. There is no threat here."

"No," I whispered, taking in the bodies around us. They blanketed the ground like a new layer of earth.

"Of course, now that we've reached Anjer, I don't know what to do. I admit, I wasn't expecting this."

"Nor I." I thought for a minute, as Vader taught me. "We still need food and water."

Brigitta nodded. "Where are we going to find anything?"

"We should head north." My instincts told me that was the way to go. I would trust my instincts, as any animal would.

"Why?" she said.

"Maybe we'll find something farther north. Farther from Krakatau."

"Merak," she suggested. "Maybe Merak is unharmed."

Merak was on the coast, too, about twenty kilometers from Anjer.

Twenty kilometers.

That never seemed far when Vader and Tante Greet and I took a wagon. But on foot, through this devastation, with no food or water—twenty kilometers may as well have been two thousand.

Chapter 44

As far as Merak was, we knew the journey was our only hope. The longer we sat exposed on this beach, the weaker we would become.

Brigitta stood. "Oh!" She swayed, and I grabbed the bottom of her shirt to keep her from pitching forward.

"Are you well?" I asked.

She pressed her palm to her forehead. "A bit dizzy. Give me a moment." She closed her eyes and took some calming breaths. "Now." She reached out a hand for me. "I'm better now."

Helping me to my feet, she held me while a wave of dizziness passed over me as well.

We made our way out of Anjer as best we could. The Great Post Road was destroyed. We had only our memories to guide us. But as long as we stayed close to the beach, we knew we should be able to find Merak.

We walked and we walked and we walked.

Brigitta led the way, wrapping my arm about her neck and shoulders. We said nothing, keeping our eyes on the ground. I didn't have the strength to lift my head. My feet dragged.

Had we passed the mosque yet?

"Mosque?" I croaked. My voice scratched my throat.

"Think...we...passed...," Brigitta wheezed. Her voice came from a distance.

I hadn't seen it. The mosque had always been visible from the ocean. Now it had vanished. It, too, was destroyed by the wave.

Which meant, if they had reached it...

Indah and Slamet were gone, too.

Indah and her struggle to prepare Dutch food. Her pride in her small successes. Her fierce love for Slamet.

Slamet. The Slamet I used to know. Climbing trees with me in the jungle. Racing on the beach to see who would reach the docks first. The boy who knew so much about the jungle's vegetation.

I wanted to weep for them, but somehow I couldn't. I couldn't feel much of anything at that moment.

Brigitta maneuvered us around more bodies and debris. It was going to take us days to reach Merak.

And we still hadn't found any food.

"Need...to rest...Katrien." She panted.

I sank to the ground with her, my legs wedged under me at an awkward angle. Brigitta—her kindness amazed me—dug a little channel with her hands. "Legs...out...now?"

"Dank u." I moaned as the sand cut into my feet when I stretched them in front of me.

The sun sat high over our head. The ugly sight of floating bodies blighted the beautiful sea.

Our breath came in short bursts, and my heart felt like it would surge out of my chest. My face crumpled, and now I would have cried if my body had let me.

She placed a gentle hand on my knee. "It's normal...to mourn." Her voice broke. "To grieve."

I wiped my face. "I know."

"We're both lucky, you know." As we rested and gathered what little energy we had, we could talk again.

"What makes you say that?"

Sadness filled her face, but she, too, had no tears. "We're not alone. We have each other. We both know what we've lost." Brigitta's hand sat on my knee, giving me a slight squeeze.

"How is it that you have the right words to say, Brigitta?"

"It's what my father said to us when my baby sister died."

"You had a baby sister? Why don't I remember her?"

Her voice turned wistful. "She didn't live even two days, but we all loved her. She was beautiful. Born with a full head of blond curls. Can you believe that? She looked just like my doll."

"How old were you?"

"Five."

I pushed Sister Hilde's spectacles up. "I was six when my mother died."

"I barely remember when that happened. How did she die? My parents never told me."

Shaking my head, I said, "I don't know. She was sick for a very long time."

"I'm sorry."

"No. I think that made it easier. She was in pain, and when she died, she wasn't in pain anymore. It made the grieving easier. Vader let me run a little wild after that."

"Just a little?" She smiled.

"Maybe more than a little." I let out a sound that was supposed to be a laugh though it came out more like a bark. "But then he decided I needed a woman's influence and sent for my aunt. She was still living in the Netherlands at the time."

"Where is your family from? In the Netherlands."

"Groningen. Vader and Oom Maarten both went to university there."

"Where is your uncle now?"

"He's in Batavia." A thought flickered through my mind. I had just enough strength to latch onto it. "*Ja!* Brigitta, Oom Maarten is in Batavia!"

She looked at me like I had grown another head. "You just said that."

"No, don't you see? We can go to Batavia! He has a little house."

Understanding lit her face. "Oh! A plan!" Her whole demeanor brightened.

"*Ja*," I said, nodding. "A wonderful plan."

But then she deflated. "Are you sure your uncle would let me stay?"

"Of course. Oom Maarten is a bit ridiculous but his heart is good."

She bit her lip and opened her mouth. Paused. Tried again.

"What is it, Brigitta?"

"Would...would *you* mind if I stayed with your uncle?" she asked in a tiny, hesitant voice.

There was a time I would have said, "*Ja*, I would mind." But that wasn't true anymore. We had survived a cataclysm of disasters and emerged on the other side, battered but alive. And together. I found I no longer felt hostile or tense in Brigitta's presence. Our world had changed. Perhaps our relationship was changing, too. I grinned. "I would mind if you didn't."

She choked on her emotion. "Do you know what I think, Katrien?"

"What?"

"I think we should have stayed friends. I'm sorry we ever fought."

"Why *did* we fight, Brigitta?"

"It was at my birthday party. Don't you remember?"

I nodded. "Of course I remember. But I still don't know why you got so angry."

"Oh." She played with the hem of her oversized shirt. "Well, first off, that bug terrified me."

"Insect."

"I still don't know how you can touch those things, especially pick one up." She shuddered. "They're hideous."

"That's it?" I asked, flabbergasted. "You were scared of the beetle?"

"No, Katrien, that's not it." She held my gaze. "I thought, by choosing to play with that bug instead of me, by suddenly wandering away from our game as if you had something more important to do, that you were insulting me in some way. Or even trying to get attention for yourself, waving it in everyone's face and making them cry like that. It was my birthday. My special day. I had been so nice to you. But, to me, it looked like you preferred bugs, and that made me mad."

"I guess we both let that fight ruin our friendship. Tante Greet always wanted me to renew it."

"Why don't we try now?" Brigitta asked.

I smiled and watched as the sun began its descent beyond Sumatra. "Have you ever been to the Netherlands?" I asked.

She shook her head. "My mother's parents are still in Amsterdam. Have you been?"

"No. Vader and Tante Greet thought I should visit next year. In fact, they were discussing that very thing before the eruption. At first, I didn't want to go, but now..." My voice faded, and I waved my hand at the devastation before us. "What about your father's family? I get the impression they aren't from Amsterdam."

"They lived in a small town east of Batavia." She lay down beside me.

"Your father is from Java?" Surprise filled my voice.

She nodded.

"How did he meet your mother?"

"At university. She wasn't a student, of course, but she attended some of the social events. Father didn't usually go to the dances, but some friends talked him into it. That's where he met Mother. They always said it was love at first sight."

"That's a nice story."

"How did your parents meet?"

"I... I don't know," I answered wistfully. The clouds above us changed shape from a rusa deer to the long catlike shape of a binturong. Why didn't I know more about my parents' lives? The truth was, I never asked. I suddenly wanted to change the subject. "Did your father always want to come back to Java?" I asked.

"*Ja.* It was his home. He found work with the government and proved himself worthy of every opportunity he was given." Pride rang through her entire being.

"I didn't know him very well, but I told you that Vader liked him, and that's the truth." I squeezed her hand. "I'm sorry he's gone."

Sensing her sadness, I tried to think of something more cheerful.

"Did you know, my tante Greet had the most difficult time adjusting to the weather here?" I said, smiling. "I remember when she first arrived, she had a lace fan that she waved back and forth, back and forth. She would say, 'I am sweating carrots,' and then whip that fan even faster. I asked if she was trying to create a typhoon."

Brigitta laughed. "What did she say?"

"She told me not to be impertinent. And Vader said I was being rude."

"Rude? How is that rude?"

I shrugged. "I'm not sure. I told him I was only having fun, but he didn't want me teasing people. He said life was too short not to be taken seriously." It felt wrong to talk about Vader in this way, as if I was betraying him. "I think I understand what he meant, now."

Brigitta patted my hand. Darkness fell, and we continued talking until exhaustion overtook us.

Chapter 45

The sun baked my skin as it rose the next morning, and an awful odor smothered me. I gagged and coughed.

"What is that smell?" Brigitta asked, sitting up.

The answer came to me as I caught my breath. "It must be all the bodies. They're beginning to..."

"To rot," she finished.

I nodded, managing to sit up beside her. I looked down at my legs and inspected my feet. They were still swollen and red, and small cuts and nicks covered the soles and tops. The truth of my predicament hit me hard. "Brigitta, I can't walk anymore."

She nodded.

"I know our plan was to get to Batavia, but I don't think I can make it." I pushed Sister Hilde's spectacles up. "I'm sorry."

"Whatever for?"

"For getting us in this mess. Perhaps it would have been better if the wave had washed us away. We would be out there." I pointed to the body-filled Sunda Strait. "We wouldn't be suffering now."

"Don't say that, Katrien. You have nothing to be sorry for." She pulled her shirt off and laid it over my bare legs.

"You should go on without me," I said dully. I could barely feel the cloth on my skin.

"Have you lost your mind? Definitely not."

I didn't respond. I couldn't respond. We had no food, no water and no way to get to Batavia. We were going to die here.

What would that be like? Letting go of life? Was it easy? I remembered my mother's last days. They hadn't seemed easy.

I thought about everything I would miss. The discoveries I would never make. New ideas I would never learn.

I would never prove Mr. Charles Darwin's theory of natural selection.

"When we reflect on this struggle we may console ourselves with the full belief that the war of nature is not incessant, that no fear is felt, that death is generally prompt."

The sun climbed into the sky, and the smell grew stronger. I covered my nose with my hand, but it did little to help.

The sunlight dancing on the water's surface and the waves rocking the bodies in a gentle rhythm hypnotized me. Brigitta sat by my side, her eyes half closed and her hand over her face, too.

No one was left.

Vader. Tante Greet. Indah. Slamet. Mr. and Mrs. Burkart. Little Jeroen. Sister Hilde. Wilhemina De Graff. The man whose shirt we took.

Even Krakatau itself was gone.

My head drooped, and I fell back against the hot sand, waiting for death to take me, too.

It was then that Brigitta shook me. "We can't stay here." Her voice was the barest whisper. I strained to hear it over the ocean's waves.

Unable to argue, I squinted at her in confusion. "Where are we going?" My own voice came out like the sigh of a butterfly.

She pointed to her left ear. "What?"

Struggling to sit up, I couldn't speak any louder. Using my finger, I scrawled my question into the sand, hoping she could read my dreadful writing.

She shook her head.

I swept over my words and tried again. Slower. Careful to form each letter. My eyes swam, and the letters danced under my finger.

Was I even writing Dutch? I couldn't read what I wrote. How could Brigitta?

She must have, though, because she pointed north.

"How?" I wrote and gestured to my feet. They were a violent shade of red now.

Crawling on her hands and knees, she beckoned me.

Through sheer force of will, I managed to copy her. The sand coated my damp palms and stuck in the wrinkles of my knees.

My neck prickled with heat, and I fought dizziness even though I wasn't standing. The beach tilted, and I stumbled to my elbows over and over again.

This was futile. We couldn't crawl to Batavia.

I collapsed. With my last bit of strength, I tossed a small piece of wood at Brigitta. She stopped and turned to me.

Shaking my head, I said, "I can't go on." No sound came out. My heart beat so fast I thought it would burst from my chest. I couldn't seem to get enough air, and I panted rapidly. The world tilted again, and I collapsed onto the sand.

Making her way back to me, Brigitta cradled my head in her lap. Her face was bright pink from the sun, and her cracked lips were white and flaky.

I tried to lick my own lips, but my tongue felt thick and useless, like a dry bit of meat stuck in my mouth.

Both of us were starving, thirsty, burned. Both of us so close to death I could feel the Reaper standing behind us.

Waiting.

And then Brigitta spoke.

"A boat." Her soft whisper floated in the breeze. "Katrien, a boat!"

Chapter 46

"Look, Katrien! Do you see? It's a boat!" I knew Brigitta was shouting as loudly as she could, but to me it sounded like the croaking of a far-off frog.

Somehow—I don't know where she drew the strength—she stood and waved her hands back and forth. "Here! We're over here! Please help us!" She rasped and motioned her arms for many long minutes until her voice gave out and exhaustion overtook her.

The boat didn't move.

Brigitta collapsed beside me.

A shadow passed over us. I knew what it was. "Death," I murmured. I could not even hear my own voice.

But it was not Death I saw when I looked up. It was a group of men who stood above us, staring. They were natives, though their clothing did not look like the sarongs and batik prints I saw on the men in Anjer.

I struggled to sit up, but my arms wouldn't work and I dropped back onto the sand. Beside me, Brigitta's breath came in short pants.

"Water?" No sound came out.

They gave me a quizzical look.

Lethargically, I mimed eating and drinking.

The man in front turned to his companions. They conversed in a loud, rapid language I did not know. The man, apparently the leader, waved at us and pointed.

Another ship, smaller than the one Brigitta had seen, was anchored not far off shore. How had we missed it?

He gestured to us, then to himself and then to the ship.

I nodded.

He said something I didn't understand and motioned toward the ship again.

Brigitta squeezed my fingers. I tried once more to sit up, but I could not manage it.

The leader whispered to two of his men. In one swift motion, they bent down and scooped us up as if we each weighed no more than a mouse.

The boat was moored in the water, and the men had to walk through it to reach the side. Bodies swirled around us as we splashed to the vessel. The saltwater stung every sore on my feet. It felt like fire burning my toes. I cried out but no noises escaped my throat.

The men either didn't know or didn't care about my pain. Time slowed on our slog. The man carrying me tripped over a body and nearly dropped me. One of my feet submerged completely before he righted himself. Boiling oil would have been less painful. I knew I would never recover from this agony.

Finally we reached the boat. They hauled us onboard and set us down on the deck. The pain in my feet was unbearable. Was this rescue? My vision blurred. I couldn't focus.

An old man greeted us in Dutch. "So good to see some more faces." He smiled. "I was beginning to wonder if anyone was left besides us." He pointed to a woman holding a baby.

The woman had skin like polished wood and was the darkest person I had ever seen. She was beautiful.

The baby was wrapped in a bundle of cloth like a sack of rags.

The old man introduced himself. "I'm Brecht Roemer, this is Kagiso and the baby is Pim."

My manners. Where were my manners? I must have left them

on the beach. Did I leave anything else on the beach? What about *On the Origin of Species*? And my *Hexarthrius rhinoceros rhinoceros* collection?

Oh, *ja*.

They were gone.

What was I thinking?

Manners. *Ja*. This man had said something. I told him my name and Brigitta's, but it was pointless. He couldn't hear me. No one could hear me. My voice was gone.

Brigitta let out a terrible noise—like a heavy chair being dragged across a quiet room. It took me a moment to realize she was telling this man our names.

"Where are you from?" the man—what was his name?—asked.

"Anjer," said Brigitta in that awful rasp.

I mouthed a request but no one heard me.

"Anjer," he said. "Anything left there?"

Brigitta shook her head.

He nodded. "Nothing in Merak either. That's where we're from—Merak. Well, truth be told, I've been living there for forty years. Originally, I'm from Rotterdam. But an old seaman like me has got to live near the shore. And Kagiso here, well, I'm not really sure where she's from."

"Africa." Her accent sounded clipped. "I work for the Steenbergen family. I am the nanny of Pim." She handed the bundle to the man and began rummaging in a crate that sat near the boat's stern.

My eyes would not focus. I didn't even have the strength to push up Sister Hilde's spectacles.

"If you don't mind my saying, you two look like you've been through Hell." He gave us an apologetic look.

I rolled my head, trying to nod. That was precisely where we had been.

"Escaped to jungle. Been walking. Want get Batavia." Brigitta's croak was getting weaker with every word.

He blinked a few times. "I climbed a palm tree, and I didn't let go. That wasn't easy, but I climbed ship rigging all my life."

Kagiso returned with two small bowls. "This will help." She scooped some sort of white mush and held it out to me. "Eat."

I tried to lift my hands, but they wouldn't move. I tried to open my mouth, but I couldn't. My head rested against the side of the ship, and I didn't even have the strength to lift it. I closed my eyes. So tired. So . . .

A slight sting on my cheek roused me and I heard my name being bellowed like a far-off crack of thunder. "Katrien!" the voice yelled. My mouth was forced open. Something soft and cool was shoved inside. I managed to close my mouth on my own and I chewed the white mush. Swallowing took such an effort. I coughed and fought to keep from spitting the food out.

"More," the voice said. Another mouthful was stuffed between my lips.

I chewed again. A bit easier this time.

"And another." That same voice again.

A bowl was placed in my hands. "Eat it all."

I eased my eyes open and saw Kagiso turn from me to Brigitta. I watched as she forced Brigitta to eat three mouthsful before giving her the bowl. Brigitta grabbed at it eagerly.

Staring at the bowl in my hands, I wondered, *Am I supposed to eat this?* My arms and hands seemed useless.

Kagiso scooped some of the white stuff from my bowl again. "Eat."

I ate, but Kagiso hand-fed me every bite.

When the bowls were emptied, she took them from us.

"More?" Brigitta asked.

Kagiso shook her head. "Too much is dangerous."

"*Dank u,*" I said. My voice sounded old and unused, but at least I heard myself.

Kagiso smiled. Brigitta reached over and took my hand. My eyes closed again, and I slumped against the side of the boat.

Part Three

Batavia, Java, Dutch East Indies

Chapter 47

The room around me glowed white. Soft sheets enveloped me, and I tried to focus on the constellations above my head.

Only they weren't there. Had Vader painted over them? Why would he do that?

"The stars," I mumbled.

"Katrien?" a soft voice beside me said. "You're awake!"

"'Course." My tongue was thick and heavy in my throat.

Another voice said, "Oh, thank goodness."

A familiar face hovered by my bed. I must be dreaming. "Brigitta?" Why on Earth was she here?

A warm hand clasped mine, and I turned to see who it was. "Oom Maarten?" What was going on?

Brigitta grabbed my other hand. "Do you know where you are, Katrien? Do you remember what happened?"

I gazed at her pink face and struggled to think. "The last thing I remember is a boat."

"Ja." She smiled and nodded. "Some men rescued us. Mr. Roemer helped us to the hospital."

"Mr. Roemer?" I had no idea who she was talking about.

"He was in the boat. And he also helped notify your uncle."

Oom Maarten squeezed my hand. "When I learned where you were, I rushed here as fast as I could."

A pain in my feet—a pain I hadn't felt before—struck me then and I cried out. "Aaahh!"

The sheet no longer felt soft and comfortable. Now it was coarse, rubbing my feet like sandpaper, and I yanked it off so I could inspect my lower limbs. I thought I saw bandages, but I couldn't be sure. I reached to push Sister Hilde's spectacles up, but I wasn't wearing them.

Brigitta handed them to me.

I put them on and instantly everything came into focus. I stared at my feet. They looked misshapen and foreign. They had no connection to me at all.

Except for the pain.

That was connected to me.

Brigitta clutched my hand. Tears filled her eyes. Why was she crying?

I tried to sit up, but Oom Maarten held me down. "Rest, Katrien. You need to rest."

"Why aren't you in a hospital bed?" I asked Brigitta.

She gave a short laugh. "I was, for about two days."

"Two days? How long have I been—?"

Oom Maarten patted my hand. "You've been in and out of consciousness for five days."

"What?" It didn't feel like five days.

He felt my forehead. "I think your fever has finally broken."

"Fever?"

"We were worried about you. The doctor didn't think you would make it." He drew in a ragged breath. "But I knew you would pull through."

I moaned and shifted in the bed.

"Shhh." Brigitta rubbed a wet cloth over my forehead. It was cool and heavenly.

A blond man with a haggard face walked up to the bed, and Oom Maarten stood to speak with him.

Brigitta squeezed my hand so hard I moaned again.

"Sorry," she whispered, loosening her grasp. She kept her right ear angled toward the men.

Oom Maarten glanced at me and nodded toward the other man. With an exhausted sigh, the man said, "I see you've decided to wake up."

I nodded.

"I'm Dr. Akkerman." He held out his hand for me to take, which I did. "I need to take a look at your feet."

He peeled the bandages off, and the sight turned my world upside down.

Black stitches crisscrossed the tips of my feet where my toes had once been.

Gone! My toes were gone!

I didn't say a word. I just stared in disbelief at my feet that no longer looked like feet.

"I'm sorry, Miss Courtlandt," the doctor said, not sounding apologetic at all. "We didn't have a choice. We had to act or the infection would have spread, and you would have lost both feet or even your legs. With more injured people arriving daily from the catastrophe, our supply of chloroform is dwindling. If we didn't remove your toes when you arrived, you might have required far greater surgery, possibly with no anesthetic. I don't know if you would have survived the stress."

"No." I shook my head. "They could have gotten better."

"They wouldn't have." He spoke with no feeling at all, almost casually.

Oom Maarten stepped beside me and grasped my other hand. "Katrien, I'm so, so sorry." His voice broke on the words. He looked so much like Vader and yet they were so different. Vader never cried. He didn't even cry when my mother died.

My own eyes remained dry. No tears. No hysterics.

Brigitta gripped my hand even tighter. "It had to happen, Katrien." Then she whispered in my ear, "I was here beside you the whole time. I didn't leave."

Oom Maarten's sniffles sounded like a foraging animal.

"And I'll help you recover," Brigitta said. "I promise."

I watched Dr. Akkerman wrap new bandages around my feet. The black stitches stood out in stark contrast to the soft white linen. The strange new shape of my foot looked more like a duck's than a human's.

Mr. Charles Darwin's words popped into my head. *"Whilst this planet has gone cycling on according to the fixed law of gravity, from so simple a beginning endless forms most beautiful and most wonderful have been, and are being, evolved."* My relationship with Brigitta had evolved. We had saved each other's lives.

Trusting her, I nodded.

Oom Maarten sobbed and hugged me while Brigitta patted my hand.

Chapter 48

When I next awoke, a nurse was leaning over the patient in the bed beside mine. Although the nurse's clothes were wrinkled and stained from treating patients, her manner was chirpy and pleasant. "How are you today, Mrs. Brinckerhoff?" she asked.

I gasped. The ravaged face and arms of my aunt's dear friend, who had apparently been beside me this whole time, were bright pink with sores and covered in gauze. The sores oozed and the gauze was a horrible shade of yellowish green. I nearly gagged at the sight. Poor Mrs. Brinckerhoff. I hadn't even recognized her.

Her voice, which I always thought of as haughty, sounded raspy and strangely soothing. "I am suffering, but not as badly as others." She lifted her hand a slight distance from her side but let it drop.

"Shhh," the nurse said, "calm yourself. You need to rest to get better. I'll get someone to help me change your dressings."

She moved to the foot of the bed, but Mrs. Brinckerhoff asked, "What of my husband? My children?"

"They are here. In the hospital. They are being cared for as best we can." She added quietly, "You are all being cared for as best we can."

Coming to me, the nurse pried the bandages away from my feet. I winced but did not cry out.

"Your feet appear to be healing nicely." She smiled and spoke over me to Mrs. Brinckerhoff while replacing my bandages. "Katrien here is another person who was injured by the volcano. She lost her toes." The nurse draped the sheet back over me before coming to feel my forehead. "Still warm, but I think that has more to do with the time you were in the sun than any illness. We'll keep checking." She bent down and whispered, "Try to help Mrs. Brinckerhoff. She's having a terrible time, but she won't really talk to anyone."

I nodded.

Her request reminded me of Tante Greet trying to get me to visit old Mrs. Schoonhoven. How many times had she urged me to be less judgmental? To make friends? Now, Brigitta and I were friends. My aunt would be so pleased.

Wait.

"Where is Brigitta?" I asked the nurse.

"Who? Oh. Your friend. Your uncle insisted on taking her home for some rest. They should be back this afternoon." She bustled off.

The pain hit me again, and I pulled the sheet off my legs. The fabric dragging over the bandages felt like skin pulling off a sore. I bit my lip.

Mrs. Brinckerhoff lay on her back, eyes closed. What should I say? I had never had much luck chatting with her. A simple 'How are you?' was out of the question. I knew how she was. Terrible. We all were. I pushed Sister Hilde's spectacles up and blurted, "How did you survive, Mrs. Brinckerhoff?"

A horrible stained piece of gauze covered one eye and part of her face. "Katrien Courtlandt? Is that you?"

"*Ja*, Mrs. Brinckerhoff, it is."

"Is your aunt with you?"

"No," I whispered. "She—she didn't make it."

"Oh, my dear girl, I'm so sorry." She paused, and I thought she might not wish to speak anymore. But she did.

"Greet was a good friend." Her voice cracked. "A good friend. I shall miss her. You were lucky to have her in your life. You must think about that, Katrien. Remember the good times and do not dwell on the bad."

I nodded. Her words soothed in a way I didn't expect, especially not from Mrs. Brinckerhoff. "What about your family?" I asked.

"All but my youngest survived. And he made it through the explosion and the terrible rain of fire. It was the days without water that were too much for his little body to bear."

"The rain of fire only lasted a short while, but it set buildings ablaze and caused an explosion at the docks." I realized now that Vader may have perished at that time, and a knife of pain stabbed my heart. I hoped that wasn't true. Better to have been washed to sea by the waves than burn. "Ash fell for days and days and the giant waves hit us."

"The waves." Her voice sounded distant, as if she were reliving the nightmare of Krakatau's eruption. "We managed to escape the waves. We ran to our cabin in the hills. Hundreds of natives joined us and slept around the cabin. I think they hoped we could protect them in some way. As if we had any more control over that blasted volcano. It was awful. I didn't sleep. I made sure my children were safe, and all night I was terrified the cabin would burst into flames."

"Vader went to his office on the waterfront after the first eruption. To send telegraph messages to Batavia." I swallowed. "I never saw him again. He's gone, too."

"Niels and Greet are both gone?" Her voice rose in shock. "You poor thing." She tried waving her hand but sobbed in pain. "When we get out of this hospital you are welcome to join us. I'm going to try to convince Willem to return to the Netherlands. I no longer want to live here. I want no part of rebuilding any of the East Indies. I want to leave."

Did she just ask me to return to the Netherlands with her? Mrs. Brinckerhoff? She had never shown much kindness toward me before. "Why would you offer to help me?" I asked. The question sounded so rude—even to my ears—that I bit my lip and covered my mouth.

She did not notice. "As I said, your aunt was a dear friend. Friends care for each other—and, by extension, we care for each other's families. It's what friends are for, isn't it?"

I thought about everything Brigitta and I had been through. At that moment, I would do anything for her. She had gotten us rescued. She had saved us. I may have kept us from getting killed by giant waves, but ultimately it was she who had saved our lives.

"Yes. It is what friends do for each other, Mrs. Brinckerhoff," I answered. "And I appreciate your kindness. However, my uncle Maarten is caring for me now. I don't know what we'll do when I get out of the hospital, but I would like to hear from you when you get settled in the Netherlands."

"It's good you still have family here, Katrien. Family is important."

"*Ja*. So are friends."

"Friends are walking miracles given to us by God."

I pushed Sister Hilde's spectacles up. Dragging Brigitta into the jungle had been the best decision of my life. I forced her to climb trees and trudge kilometers from Anjer and sleep on the ground. If I hadn't done that, I would be dead now. That Brigitta and I had survived the eruption, the waves and the lack of food and water without killing each other was unexpected. But the fact that we had emerged from that nightmare as friends was miraculous.

I was still pondering this when Brigitta approached my bed that afternoon. Her face was still pink from the sun, but her smile was cheerful and bright. I used to think it was smug. Getting to know someone could change your entire perspective. Tante Greet had tried to teach me that.

"You are right," I called to Mrs. Brinckerhoff. "Friends are special. I wouldn't be here now without mine."

I thought I saw her smile. "However cruel nature may be, Katrien, and however mysterious God's ways, He did save us. His name be praised."

"Amen," Brigitta said, taking her seat beside me.

Chapter 49

Nine days later, Oom Maarten carried me from a carriage into his small parlor with its new wallpaper. Green vines covered the walls, reminding me of the jungle before its destruction.

He and Brigitta had transformed the space. Instead of the furniture that normally filled the room, I saw they had moved the bed down from the spare room upstairs—the bed Tante Greet and I had always shared when we visited. Tables stood on either side, topped with simple candle lanterns.

And there, in the center of the room, was a wooden wheeled chair. Torben sat in the seat and bounded off when he saw us. His sharp yips echoed around the room.

"Oh, Torben," Brigitta said. "Shhh. You don't need to be so loud. Katrien can see you."

Oom Maarten chuckled. "She almost didn't. He disappeared about two days before the disaster. I searched for him but couldn't find him anywhere. Then I heard you were in the hospital. I honestly quit looking for him after that." He shifted me in his arms. "Do you know what I found when I came home from the hospital that night?"

"Torben?" I guessed.

"Torben!" A huge grin lit his face. "Sitting in front of the door looking at me like *he* wondered where *I* had been!"

"People do say that animals can sense danger," Brigitta said. "Maybe he fled and only returned when he knew it was safe."

Her words struck me, and I thought about our escape into the jungle. Was that why we didn't see any animals? Had they sensed the impending eruption and fled?

For the first time since the catastrophe, I felt a spark of curiosity illuminate my brain, and I couldn't help smiling. My feet as I knew them were gone, but my mind, at least for a moment, had felt familiar again. Perhaps I'd explore this theory further someday.

Oom Maarten placed me into the seat of the wheeled chair with great care. "I bought it from a man at work. His father used it in the last years of his life. But now it's yours." He smiled at me and turned to Brigitta, who carried a pair of wooden crutches into the room. "I always thought it would be neat to be in a wheeled chair. Maybe you'll let me borrow it, Katrien?"

"Maybe," I said in as light a tone as I could muster. My heart ached as I stared at the crutches. I had tried using them at the hospital, but I fell with a loud yelp and woke all the sleeping patients. The staff refused to let me practice again.

Now, in the comfort of my uncle's home, I vowed I would not spend the rest of my life tied to this blasted chair. I was determined to use the crutches.

Oom Maarten picked Torben up and smiled again. "I'll leave you two girls alone. This is your room now. Make it yours. If you want to decorate it, I will be only too happy to assist." At the door, he turned serious. "I am sorry for the circumstances that brought you here." Tears filled his eyes, and I realized for the first time that he had lost a brother and sister in the catastrophe. "But," he continued, more controlled now, "I'm so glad I'm here to help." Then he closed the door and left us alone.

Brigitta leaned the crutches against the wall. "I hope you don't mind sharing the room."

"Of course not."

"Let me know when you're prepared to practice with these."

"Now. Let's begin now."

She startled. "Now?"

"*Ja.*" I nodded.

"Don't you wish to rest a bit first?" She gestured to the bed.

I shook my head. "No. Why would I want to wait?"

She shrugged. "I thought you might be tired."

"No." I waved at the crutches. "I want to get started."

She sighed and set them on the floor in front of my chair. "No time like the present."

Smiling, I grabbed the handles. "No time indeed." I tried pushing myself out of the chair, but it rolled backward. "Homo sapiens."

Brigitta gasped.

I tried again, but the chair moved once more. "Terra firma."

Brigitta edged around to the back of the chair. "Would you like assistance?"

"Just hold the chair still."

She braced her foot against one of the wheels and grasped the handles.

Pushing again, I used all the strength in my arms to heave myself up. Then, one of the crutches slipped on the varnished floor and clattered to the ground. For once, my Latin failed me. "Oh, damn and blast!" I flung the other crutch across the room. Torben barked in the hall.

"Katrien! Don't do that," Brigitta scolded.

"Why not?" I cried. "I'll never learn to walk with the blasted things! I may as well give up now."

She picked up both crutches and stood them in front of my chair, appraising me.

I avoided her gaze.

She didn't say a word, but I could imagine the vitriol she wanted to spew.

Then I silently berated myself. Brigitta had been nothing like her old self since the disaster. She had changed. Or maybe I had. Maybe she had always been caring. Maybe she had been right in the jungle. Maybe I was detestable.

Unable to bear the silence, I blurted, "What?"

"It's just that I never thought of you as a quitter before."

That stung. "I've never had to relearn a skill I mastered by the age of two before." I slapped the arms of the chair.

She sat on the edge of the bed. "Do you truly want to stay in that chair?"

"No."

"Then stand up."

"Brigitta." I slumped. "I can't."

"I'll help you."

I pushed Sister Hilde's spectacles up. "But I need to be able to do it on my own."

"Not at first, you don't." She came over and took my hand, kneeling by my feet. "Katrien, learning to walk is not an overnight process—it wasn't even when you were a baby. It's going to take time. Believe me, I helped little Jeroen, and I intend to help you. You'll get there."

"Do you really believe that?"

Her eyes grew intense. "I *know* that. You're tough and brave and capable."

"Let's get to work then." I smiled. "Together."

She grinned. "It will be my pleasure."

Helping me out of the chair, she gave me the crutches for balance, and I took my first wobbly step into my new life.

Chapter 50

After weeks of work, I had made progress walking with crutches. I could even get out of bed on my own. Brigitta laughed until she cried the first time she saw me roll onto my belly, drop my legs over the side and push off with my arms. The method worked, comical or not.

Getting in and out of chairs was still a difficult maneuver. I never realized how much I used my toes to sit and stand.

Brigitta divided her time between helping me and running Oom Maarten's home. He tried to stop her, claiming he was a confirmed bachelor set in his ways, but she smiled and told him it was her way of thanking him.

One morning, I woke to the sound of a heavy downpour falling on the tamarind trees that were planted in a neat row along the street. "It's raining pipe stems!" I cried. Even if it stopped, the ground would be muddy. "No chance of practicing outside." I sighed. I didn't have many opportunities left to walk with Brigitta.

My friend would leave for the Netherlands next week. Her grandparents—to whom she had sent a telegram when I came home from the hospital—had mailed her a note filled with loving words, money and a ticket to Amsterdam the moment they heard from her. As glad as I was that Brigitta had a caring family to go to, I was dreading her departure.

An ache formed in the pit of my stomach as I listened to the rain. "What will I do without her?" I whispered, rubbing Torben's belly.

Brigitta's voice carried down the hall from the kitchen. She was singing again.

"On a giant mushroom
red with many white dots
Spindle-shank the little gnome
was wobbling back and forward."

Although I wasn't hungry, I snatched up Sister Hilde's spectacles and wriggled off the bed. Grabbing my crutches, I walked in my slow, halting manner down the hall. Torben trotted in front of me, his nails clicking on the wooden floor.

I held onto the table's edge and eased myself into a chair. Brigitta was nowhere to be seen, but her voice came from the pantry. "Do you want jam or cheese with your bread?" Torben followed the sound.

"Jam." I hadn't eaten cheese since that last night with Tante Greet. "Where's Oom Maarten?" I asked.

"He left early, before the rain began. Sit, Torben. I think he was going to arrange a carriage for us next week."

"Oh," I whispered.

"Here." She set the jam jar on the table. "Can you cut the bread?"

"Of course."

She grabbed the bread out of the bread box and set it in front of me, along with a knife. "Then get to it. Do you think you're crippled or something?" she teased. A bit of Oom Maarten's silliness had rubbed off on Brigitta. She was more carefree than I remembered. But perhaps that was because the low opinion I had held for her colored my memories of the past.

Her gentle teasing reassured me, and I smiled in spite of my dreary mood. "Are we having tea or coffee this morning?"

"Tea." She set plates on a tray. "Would you like some butter?"

I shook my head and added the slices of bread to the plates. She popped the loaf back into the bread box.

"I need to make the bed," she muttered, leaving the kitchen for our room. "Come on, Torben. Help me." He trotted behind her.

The silence she left behind filled the room like a scream, and a wave of melancholy hit me. "When she leaves, I'll have no one to talk to," I whispered to myself. "Oom Maarten can never understand what we've been through." My eyes unfocused and tears streamed down my cheeks.

The idea of Brigitta leaving truly hurt. She was my last connection with Anjer. Oom Maarten checked every day, but the only other survivors from Anjer were the lighthouse keeper and a retired ship captain neither Brigitta nor I knew.

I placed my hands on the varnished table. The smooth, polished surface felt wrong. Our table in Anjer had been rough and plain and stained with use. *A table in a kitchen shouldn't be smooth*, I thought. *There should be nicks and cuts and marks and* damage.

But Oom Maarten's kitchen was immaculate. It always had been. Even Brigitta—who had grown up with a housekeeper and a cook and knew the way things ought to be—did not have to do much to keep the room pristine. Except for the dishes now sitting on the tray, everything was in its place. The fruit sat in a wooden bowl, the bread hid in the bread box, the staples resided in the pantry.

With a frustrated growl, I hurled the jam jar against the wall. It shattered with a satisfying crash, and the jam made a wet splashing sound when it hit the floor.

"What was that for?" Brigitta asked, returning to the kitchen just in time to witness my fit of pique.

I shrugged. "No reason."

She put her hands on her hips. "So we're not having jam for breakfast, I gather."

I shook my head.

Torben walked over to the mess, sniffing. "No, Torben," Brigitta ordered. He backed off and looked at her expectantly. "What else is there to eat with bread?"

"There may be some honey in the pantry." I traced the pattern in the grain.

She moved to the stove; Torben followed. "Why don't you check?"

"You know I need help getting out of chairs." I hated relying on other people for assistance. And I hated the whine in my voice.

"I thought you wanted to do things on your own."

"I do." A rumble of thunder echoed outside. The rain wasn't stopping anytime soon.

"Then do it," she said. "You can get out of that chair by yourself, Katrien. I know you can."

"No, I can't."

She walked over to the table, her expression touched with amusement. "You are acting like a child right now. I don't know why, but I wish you would stop. You aren't a child, Katrien. You can get out of that chair. Anyone who has been through volcanoes, and giant waves and nearly died of thirst can certainly stand up from a seated position." She crossed her arms and gave me an indulgent smile.

I pushed up Sister Hilde's spectacles and glared at Brigitta. "You forgot amputation."

"No, I didn't." She brushed some crumbs off the table. "I was hoping you would. You can stand up on your own, Katrien." She squeezed my shoulder and moved back to the stove. "What would Darwin say?"

The answer came automatically. " 'Battle within battle must be ever recurring with varying success.' "

"Why don't you follow his advice, then?"

"Fine!" Slapping the table, I pushed myself up. But my arms wobbled, and I dropped back in the chair. "I told you I couldn't do it."

She set the silverware on the tray. "Do you think Darwin would have given up so easily? Try again," she said, patting my hand and returning to the stove.

Taking a fortifying breath, I curled my fingers around the table's edge and clung to the wood like I had clung to the trees during the waves. My knuckles were as white as pearls. The tendons in my arms were taut like ropes. Bit by slow bit, I managed to pull myself erect.

"I did it!" I was astonished.

Brigitta handed me my crutches. "I knew you could." Her face glowed with pride. "Now, go look for honey."

I stumbled with my crutches over to the pantry and found a pot of sticky gold. "There is some here, but I can't carry it and work the crutches. I need a third hand." My voice was no longer whining, but tinged with suppressed laughter.

"I'll get it as soon as I clean up this mess." She bent down to the floor and scooped the jam and broken jar into a rag, which I noticed was made from the shirt I had forced her to wear in the jungle. "Why don't we have some *belimbing* with breakfast, too? And I'll get the tea. We're going to eat in the dining room. I think we need a good start to the day."

After taking out the rubbish, she carried breakfast into the dining room on the tray. Bread and honey and *belimbing* and tea. The juicy star fruit sparkled in the dreary light.

"There," she said, placing my plate in front of me and pouring a cup of tea. "Doesn't that look nice? It's so much better to eat in a beautiful dining room than around the kitchen table."

Tears blurred my vision, but I managed a steady reply. "You're a good cook."

"*Dank u.*" She smiled. "My mother taught me."

"You're an even better friend," I added.

She gave a small laugh. "You're a good friend, too."

Torben barked at us, and I slipped him a piece of bread.

Chapter 51

The carriage lurched to a stop. We were at the docks. Brigitta squeezed my hand, and I clenched my jaw.

This was it.

She was leaving today.

My friend was going to her grandparents'.

Oom Maarten climbed out first, and I passed him my crutches. With Brigitta's help I made it to the door of the carriage, and Oom Maarten lifted me to the ground. After that I was on my own. "What we'll do at home, without Brigitta, I don't know," I whispered.

The two of them joined me where I stood, and we watched the porters haul Brigitta's small trunk onto the ship. Part of the money her grandparents had sent her was meant for new clothes. She had generously split it between the two of us, and she still had enough left over to buy herself four blouses, three skirts, new undergarments and the trunk.

I leaned on my crutches, and they cut into my underarms. Tante Greet's voice popped into my head. "Stand up straight, Katrien." So I did, my feet wobbling on the wet docks.

"Ah," said Oom Martin with satisfaction. His attention had turned from the porters to a large group of families preparing to board the ship. "You will have good company for your voyage, Brigitta," he said. There was a hint of relief in his voice.

The three of us made our way toward the group, which had begun boarding. But in front of the gangplank, Brigitta hesitated. "Katrien, I do not want to go." She clutched her reticule. "Not by myself. How will I manage an entire ocean voyage all alone? I cannot even hear out of my left ear."

Oom Maarten still stood nearby, and I crutched a few steps farther away, motioning for her to follow. By the time she joined me, I had my speech prepared. "Brigitta Burkart," I said sternly. "You escaped giant waves. You marched for days in the jungle. You survived on oranges and hope." I smiled at her. "You can certainly handle a simple sea voyage of a few weeks."

"That lecture sounds vaguely familiar," she said, arching an eyebrow.

"It should. I heard it from a trusted source." I wavered a bit on the crutches, and she steadied me.

She bit her lip. "I'm still scared."

"I know. I would be, too. But you're brave and strong. You can do it."

"It's not the voyage. Not entirely."

I searched her face. "Then what is it?"

She took a deep breath. "I've never been to the Netherlands before. I've never met my grandparents." Her voice turned thin, like a mouse's squeak. "I know they've been very kind to me, sending me that letter and offering to take me in, but what if they decide they hate me? What if they blame me for surviving?"

I placed my hands on her shoulders and looked her full in the eyes. "Brigitta, you have done nothing wrong by surviving. Do you understand that? You can't blame yourself for that. That has nothing to do with strength or weakness or any biological characteristic."

She grinned at me.

"You survived," I continued. "I survived. Both of us survived for no reason except coincidence. We're not stronger than those who died. We're not better examples of our species. We're just lucky. I know you don't want to hear it, but Mr. Charles Darwin said it best, that *species are produced and exterminated by slowly acting and still existing causes, and not by miraculous acts of creation and by catastro-phes.'* Do you see? Catastrophic disaster can wreak havoc with natu-ral selection, but it doesn't destroy the process. We're still here. You are going to be fine."

She nodded, tears streaming down her face.

"And if you find you cannot tolerate Amsterdam or the Nether-lands or your family, you can always come to us. Oom Maarten and I will welcome you back with open arms."

"Would you? Truly?"

"Of course."

And at that moment, I knew at last what Tante Greet had tried so hard to make me understand.

"You wouldn't even have to knock," I said, choking on the words. "Because that's what friends do."

"*Ja,* we are friends now, aren't we?" she said, using a handker-chief to wipe her eyes.

"The very best," I agreed.

Oom Maarten walked over to us. "They're asking everyone to board, *lieve.* We will miss you terribly. Torben most of all."

"I'll miss you, too, sir."

"None of that 'sir' nonsense." He engulfed her in his arms and kissed her cheeks.

I hugged her, too. "Don't forget to write when you arrive."

"I'll write more often than that."

Smiling, I said, "You had better."

"*Dank u,* Katrien."

"Whatever for?" I asked, pushing Sister Hilde's spectacles up.

"For saving my life. For being my friend."

"You would have done the same for me." I rocked back onto my crutches.

"Would I?" She shrugged. "I'm not so sure."

I laughed. "It's done. And I don't regret my decision." I leaned over and whispered in her good ear. "*You're* the one who saved us. You helped me on the beach. You spotted the boat. And even after we were rescued, you saved me."

She gave me a puzzled look.

"You taught me to walk on these." I lifted the crutches. "If I was still in that chair, I don't know what I would do. But you..."

She squeezed my hand.

"I can never repay you for that," I said.

"Nevertheless, *dank u*." She kissed me on the cheeks—right, left, right.

We hugged each other again, said our last good-byes, and she walked up the gangplank. When she got on board the ship, she waved.

Tears fell down my face as I waved back. Oom Maarten squeezed my shoulders. I kept waving until the boat was a speck on the horizon.

Chapter 52

By the end of October, I was able to stand a bit easier with my crutches and I even managed to visit the market a few times. One Sunday, Oom Maarten suggested we attend mass. Since I no longer thought of myself as housebound, I agreed.

"I'm glad you're willing to come," my uncle said softly, taking my hand. "You should know, though, that today's mass will honor the people we lost in the disaster."

I took a moment to digest this. I wondered if I would be better off staying home. Oom Maarten could go alone, and when he returned, we could talk about it together. But when I looked up and saw the love and kindness in my uncle's eyes, my hesitation dissolved. I gave his hand a squeeze and, with a few wobbles, stood up. "I'll get ready, Oom Maarten."

Hundreds of people filled the pews in the Catholic church that morning. I'd forgotten that the church in Batavia was about twice the size of the one in Anjer. I hadn't been inside this church since my trip last May with Vader and Tante Greet. Had that only been five months ago? How could so much happen in such a short amount of time?

Oom Maarten and I took our seats near the back. My crutches slipped from my hand as I laid them at my feet. The clatter reverberated around the nave, much louder than the whispers of the crowd. Some people glanced at me with irritated looks.

I glared back. I didn't drop them on purpose!

An awkward silence descended as the last people to arrive settled into seats. Then, above us, the choir sang. The congregation stood, and Oom Maarten helped me to my feet. The priest, in black mourning vestments, led the procession solemnly up the aisle. Their lumbering pace reminded me of the heavy footsteps of a Javan rhinoceros.

The choir sang the same song that was sung at my mother's funeral. She had died so long ago, I thought the pain from her loss had gone away. It hadn't. It still hurt. And now that hurt was compounded many times over.

Oom Maarten placed his arm around me, and I leaned against him.

The priest reached the altar, and the choir ended their hymn. While he began the rituals, memories of Vader and Tante Greet filled my mind.

I could feel Vader's hand around mine as he tried to improve my penmanship. I could hear Tante Greet's soothing voice in my ear as I tried to chop vegetables. Each of them, in their own ways, tried to make me a better person.

The congregation sat, and I focused on the service.

The reader stepped up to the lectern. His deep voice resonated throughout the building. "A reading from the book of Wisdom. Chapter three, verses one through nine. 'The souls of the virtuous are in the hands of God, no torment shall ever touch them. In the eyes of the unwise, they did appear to die, their going looked like a disaster, their leaving us, like annihilation; but they are in peace.

" 'If they experienced punishment as people see it, their hope was rich with immortality; slight was their affliction, great will their blessing be. God has put them to the test and proved them worthy to be with him; God has tested them like gold in a furnace, and accepted them as a holocaust. When the time comes for his visitation, they will shine out; as sparks run through the stubble, so will they. They shall judge nations, rule over peoples, and the Lord will be their king forever. They who trust in him will understand the truth, those who are faithful will live with Him in love; for grace and mercy await those He has chosen.' The word of the Lord."

"Thanks be to God," the congregation replied.

Tears ran down my cheeks, and I couldn't stop them. Oom Maarten wrapped his arms around me and held me in a strong hug. His chest muffled my sobs.

I cried and cried.

I cried for my beloved Anjer.

I cried for all those lost whom I would never know.

I cried for people I didn't even like—Adriaan Vogel, Maud, Rika and Inge.

I cried for the jungle.

I cried for my *Hexarthrius rhinoceros rhinoceros* collection.

I cried for my books.

But, mostly, I cried for those I loved.

I cried for Vader.

I cried for Tante Greet.

I cried for Brigitta and her family.

I cried for Indah and Slamet.

I didn't stop crying until people began to leave. The service was over, and I missed it. Oom Maarten retrieved my crutches and helped me out of the pew.

We left the church without saying a word, and he led me to a bench underneath an enormous fig tree. He took my hand and gave it a gentle squeeze. Tears stained his cheeks, too, and I wondered if he had cried as long as I.

"Katrien, I have no idea what you went through," he said. His voice sounded like it would shatter into pieces at any moment. "But I know the loss of your family—" He stopped for a moment, swallowed and took a deep breath. "The loss of your friends."

A cynical laugh left my throat. "Friends."

He nodded and squeezed my hand again. "I am so, so sorry."

I shook my head. "Oom Maarten, I only ever had one real friend in Anjer. And we fought before the eruption. I'm not even sure we were friends. In the end." It was true.

"But what about Brigitta?"

"Brigitta and I despised each other. I told you about her."

He leaned against the bench, stunned. *"That's* the girl you wrote me about? The one you hated for so long? The one who always bothered you? You seem so close."

"We are. Now. It took nearly dying to realize how much we had in common." I sighed. "I miss her."

"I do, too." He smiled. "We should get home. I need to change out of these wet clothes before I catch my death."

"Wet clothes...?"

He pointed to his shirt. The front was soaked from my tears.

"Apologies, Oom Maarten. It won't happen again." Vader would have been shocked at my lack of composure in public. He would have been disappointed. "Truly. I'm very sorry."

"Katrien," my uncle said, helping me stand, "you have nothing to apologize for."

Chapter 53

We returned home and I went to my room to rest. Torben jumped up on the bed beside me and licked my face. I closed my eyes and imagined I was in my old room in Anjer. Vader was writing a report in the study; Tante Greet was pulling weeds in the flower garden; Indah was humming a little tune in the kitchen; and Slamet would run inside at any moment to help his mother.

A knock on the door pulled me out of my reverie. Torben flew off the bed, barking excitedly. By the time I reached the entry hall, Oom Maarten had already welcomed Mrs. Brinckerhoff and her husband inside. I didn't even know she knew how to knock.

After shutting Torben in my room, Oom Maarten said, "I hope you don't mind if we go to the kitchen. We've had to do a little rearranging, and my niece has taken over the parlor. Stairs are her Waterloo."

I shook my head as I followed them.

While they settled down at the table, I set the kettle on the stove to boil. Tante Greet would be pleased I could make tea. It wasn't much, but it was a step toward domestic skill.

"I recall Greet mentioning your name, Mrs. Brinckerhoff," Oom Maarten said.

"Please," she said, "call me Johanna."

The three of them chatted about nothing in particular while I poured the tea and added it to the tray, along with some pastries Oom Maarten had bought yesterday. "Oom Maarten?" I pointed to the tray. "Will you..."

"Of course, *lieve*." He rose from his chair, but Mrs. Brinckerhoff stopped him. She retrieved the tray instead, and I had my first good look at her since the hospital.

A scar blotted her right cheek. Her blouse had long sleeves, and I suspected those were covering more disfigurements. She smiled at me, and the skin around her scar twisted.

After we both sat down, Oom Maarten poured the tea. "Katrien and I just returned from mass. The priest held a sort-of funeral for those who were lost."

"What a beautiful gesture," Mrs. Brinckerhoff said, taking a sip of the steaming tea.

"Are your children out of the hospital?" I asked.

Mr. Brinckerhoff answered, "*Ja*. We're together again."

"And I wanted to make sure you were settled, Katrien," Mrs. Brinckerhoff said. "I remembered you mentioning your uncle, and of course Greet talked about you, Maarten."

He gave her a melancholy smile, and I wondered how he must feel. Rather like Brigitta did about her loss of little Jeroen?

"We wanted to make sure you were safe," Mrs. Brinckerhoff said. Her eyes filled with warmth, and I realized that I had always been wrong about her. She did have my best interests at heart, just as Tante Greet said. I wished I could tell my aunt how sorry I was. "*Dank u*, Mrs. Brinckerhoff."

Her husband leaned forward and refilled his cup. "What are your plans for the future, Maarten?"

Oom Maarten paused with his drink halfway to his lips. "What do you mean?"

"Do you plan to stay in Batavia?"

He swallowed the last of his tea. "I haven't decided."

I froze, and my cup slipped from my fingers. It clattered onto the table with such force that a crack began to run up the side. Tea seeped from the crack and formed a large brown puddle on the table.

Mrs. Brinckerhoff snatched a napkin from the tray and draped it over the liquid. Then she patted my hand before mopping up the rest of the tea.

"What do you mean you haven't decided?" I asked.

"Just that." He bit into a pastry.

"But this is my home."

Mrs. Brinckerhoff returned to her seat. "Willem and I thought that, too. We believed we would never leave. Our children had many friends. We had a pleasant life. There was no reason to doubt it would go on."

"But we were mistaken," Mr. Brinckerhoff said. "Nothing will be the same."

I leaned back in my chair. What were they saying? Mrs. Brinckerhoff had told me in the hospital that she wanted to leave, but I didn't think she would get her way.

"You don't plan to rebuild?" asked Oom Maarten.

"No," Mr. Brinckerhoff said, a wistfulness in his voice. "There are too many memories in Ketimbang."

"But, surely, you could stay in the East Indies?" I asked. "You could go to Yogyakarta or somewhere in the east."

They shook their heads. A defeated look crossed Mr. Brinckerhoff's face. "We're going to the Netherlands."

"I don't understand."

Mrs. Brinckerhoff reached across the table to take my hand. "Would you want to return to Anjer?"

"There's nothing left," I whispered.

She squeezed my fingers gently. "There's nothing left in Ketimbang either, but even if there were, we would not return. It would be too hard, too painful."

"But I still don't see why you have to leave entirely."

Oom Maarten rubbed my back. "If we stay, we'll be forced to confront memories. Sometimes confronting memories can be a good thing, but not if you get caught up in them to the point where you can't move forward. That's not a way to heal."

"Memories such as . . . ?" I didn't understand. I couldn't think how any memory could make my heart hurt worse than it already did.

"Arguments, rude behavior, our own sorrows and regrets toward those we loved—being reminded of those kinds of things every day can lead to disaster. Personal disaster, at least. And that can be avoided."

I tore off a piece of pastry. Oom Maarten's words struck me. I did have regrets about my behavior. I wanted desperately to apologize to Vader and Tante Greet for all the rude things I said and did. I had never felt that way about my mother, but I was only six when she died. How many terrible offenses can a person commit by age six?

At thirteen, I could fill a steamship with my misdeeds—small and large. Would leaving Java mean leaving those memories behind? I didn't think so, but Oom Maarten and the Brinckerhoffs seemed to believe it would. Or maybe what they meant was that leaving would give us all a proper distance.

But what if I didn't want distance? What if I wanted to see Java recover?

"When do you sail?" Oom Maarten asked.

"March," Mr. Brinckerhoff answered.

"We would need to find a place to live," Oom Maarten said thoughtfully. "I'll begin making inquiries at once."

Epilogue
Groningen, The Netherlands
JANUARY 1885

"Katrien, we need to leave soon," Oom Maarten said, popping his head into the kitchen.

"Homo sapiens!" I cried. Then I slapped my hand over my mouth. "Apologies, Oom."

"Whatever for?"

I stood at the stove with a slotted spoon in my hand and blinked at him. "For—for—my poor language."

He raised an eyebrow. "Good grief, *lieve*, if you want poor language, I'll teach you better words to use."

I blushed. "That won't be necessary."

"Fine, but hurry." Torben followed him through the door.

I dipped the spoon into the steaming water. The last of the *Rhagonycha fulva* beetles I had collected in the fall floated on the surface. I would have to work on this later. I scooped the beetles out of the water and placed them on a wooden cutting board to dry. Oom Maarten was not as picky as Tante Greet had been. He didn't mind my using kitchen utensils to create my new beetle displays. But I still only used specific items and kept them separate from the ones used for cooking.

The little insects—no bigger than peas—rested on the

cutting board. They were much smaller and less intimidating than my *Hexarthrius rhinoceros rhinoceros*. I let out a short sigh, and my breath made them skitter across the board.

"Come along, Katrien," Oom Maarten called from the front hall. Torben scratched at the door. "Torben, stay."

My cane leaned against the table. I grabbed it and hobbled to join him.

Once I'd mastered walking with the crutches, I had moved to two canes. Now I was down to one. I still walked with an odd, shuffling gate and needed the cane for balance, but I could stand up from chairs and climb stairs without too much trouble and with no assistance from anyone.

I could not, however, climb any more trees.

Not that it mattered. Most of the trees were in parks here, and people weren't allowed to climb them. We had only one weeping beech in our small outdoor space beside the canal. It was a good place to read in the summer. At the bookshop, I discovered *The Descent of Man* by Mr. Charles Darwin and was busy committing new passages to memory—when I wasn't buried in my other studies.

The University of Groningen accepted female students, and Oom Maarten thought I should apply when I graduated from school. "Your father would have wanted you to," he said.

Two of the girls in my class—Inge and Paulien—had befriended me. Although neither of them had an interest in science, they both wanted to help me get accepted to the university. They had plans of attending themselves—though they intended to study literature—and said another friend would be welcome indeed. Inge was even helping me improve my penmanship. I looked forward to introducing them to Brigitta.

Outside, the snow crunched beneath my heavy shoes and cold seeped up my legs as I struggled toward the train station.

"The world is glorious today, isn't it?" Oom Maarten said as he walked slowly beside me. "Though it is colder than I remember."

"All those years in Java made you forget," I chided.

He laughed. "Fifteen years in the tropics will do that." He stamped his feet. "But I truly don't recall it ever being this cold." Puffs of steam shot out of his mouth as he spoke. "What about you, Katrien? What do you think of Old Man Winter?"

"He's a force to be reckoned with," I said with a wry smile.

My first winter was certainly a new experience. The snow, the ice, the roaring fires blazing in the fireplace, the heavy clothes, and the oppressive, unyielding cold...I did not like any of it, but I would never say so to Oom Maarten.

I recalled that when we arrived in the Netherlands, the weather had been warm, the countryside green, the trees dripping with new leaves. It had not been as hot as Java, but it was nice. I thought I could learn to love it.

That had all changed with the first winter storm.

I decided at once that I did not like snow. It fell in silence, piling and drifting, very much like ash. And it stuck to the ground and never seemed to leave either. It transformed everything familiar into an eerie world of strange white shapes.

When the wind blew, icy air crawled into the sleeves and under the hem of my heavy wool coat. Even my gloves and boots were not enough to keep it at bay.

My feet ached in the cold, too. They were completely healed, but the frigid temperatures brought all the original pain screaming back.

No, I did not like winter one bit. I longed for the sticky heat of Anjer. The salty breezes from the Sunda Strait. The gentle rains and raging thunderstorms of the wet season.

The Netherlands was so very different from what I'd known before.

Oom Maarten's decision to move here had shocked me at first, especially his seriousness. I had never seen him so serious as he was while trying to find a place for us to live. He must have spent a fortune in telegraph fees before he found our little house, but he refused to accept any place that couldn't accommodate my needs—such as no room on the ground floor that could be used as a bedroom.

I loved him for that. He had taken me in and cared for me as if I were his own daughter, and I knew if I had ever asked him, he would have stayed in Batavia for me. At one point I considered taking advantage of his kindness. When I saw how determined he was to move, I thought about telling him I wouldn't go—that I would get by on my own. But the truth was, I still needed help then. I couldn't have managed. And he would never have left me in Batavia alone, so he would have stayed, too.

I was glad I hadn't forced him to make that choice, but now, so many months later, as the dark winter enveloped Groningen, there were still days when I wished we could return to Java. Part of me wanted to know that Anjer was being rebuilt, even though I knew it would take years to complete the job and that the town would never be the same as it was. I imagined there would be some comfort in seeing its reconstruction with my own eyes. And of course, I knew for a fact that I would find comfort in the climate. I wouldn't be cold anymore, and my feet wouldn't hurt.

But my heart would. Of that I was certain. Here, in the Netherlands, I was far more removed from the loss I had suffered. Oom Maarten had been right when he said that part of healing was moving ahead, avoiding getting caught up in remorse and regret. In Groningen, I had far less fear of coming around a corner and stopping cold, remembering an incident with Vader or Tante Greet. There were no kampongs surrounding me here or smells of native cooking to regularly remind me of my arguments with Slamet.

I still thought of my loved ones all the time. But here, at a distance, I knew I could get through my days and plan for my future without constant reminders of my loss.

This knowledge was both welcome and unwelcome.

Oom Maarten often asked me how I was faring. But how could I explain all this without sounding ungrateful? For my uncle, I wished only to concentrate on the positives, for I *was* happy here. Vader had been correct. I did find much to study and observe and see.

Now, in the throes of winter, I mostly observed the slippery ground, though sometimes my watchfulness did me no good. As I pushed my spectacles up and hurried alongside Oom Maarten, I hit a patch of ice and skidded. My legs flailed under me, my arms spun like windmills, and I dropped my cane.

"Oops!" Oom Maarten righted me before retrieving the silver-handled cane. "Here you are, *lieve*."

I laughed and thanked him. Despite the dreary weather and my near fall, my spirits now flew like sparrows. Brigitta was arriving for a visit, and I could not wait to see her.

"What time did she say her train would arrive?" Oom Maarten asked, glancing at his pocket watch.

"Around three."

His eyebrows twitched in concern. "We should hurry. I don't want to leave your friend waiting. Come along, my little cripple." He laughed and picked up speed.

His nickname gave me a soft chuckle, and I tried to move a bit faster, though it was difficult in wet snow with heavy boots and bad feet. "Wait, Oom!"

He immediately turned and rejoined me.

Just then, a flash of sunlight shot through the gloomy

sky and lit up the trees. The sight of the snow piled on the leafless branches stopped me in my tracks.

"What are you looking at?" Oom Maarten asked.

"The ash."

"The what?"

I shook my head. "The snow. I meant the snow. It reminds me of the ash."

He turned grave. "If you ever need to talk, *lieve*, you know I'm here for you."

Smiling, I took his hand. "I know that, Oom Maarten. You are my hero."

His eyes twinkled again, and he blushed. "At least I'm someone's hero." He squeezed my hand. "Now, come on. We'll be late." He winked.

We walked into the huge redbrick train station, even larger than our church in Anjer. People streamed in and out of the doorways to the platforms.

I pushed my spectacles up. How would we ever find Brigitta in this mass of humanity?

Oom Maarten and I stood near the main entrance staring in every direction. People jostled us as they hurried past. I gripped my cane tighter. Oom Maarten took about three steps toward one doorway and then another before stopping and rejoining me. "This is madness. We'll never find her."

Then, a tap on my shoulder caused me to turn, and Brigitta stood before me, smiling. Her golden hair was styled into neat braids. My own mess of hair lay hidden beneath a wooly hat.

She spread her arms and kissed me. "It's so good to see you, Katrien!"

"You, too!" I exclaimed, embracing her back.

"What?"

I was against her bad ear. "Sorry." Pulling back, I said, "I'm glad to see you, too."

She reached her hand out to take Oom Maarten's.

He shook his head. "No, no, no. I won't have a simple handshake." He wrapped his arms around her, kissing her cheeks.

Brigitta gave a little squeak, but she smiled.

"Where's your trunk?" he asked when he released her.

"The porter has it." She handed the ticket to Oom Maarten.

He nodded. "I'll get the trunk, and we'll take a cab back home. Torben can't wait to see you."

We watched him scurry off before facing each other. Brigitta grinned and pointed to my cane. "The crutches are gone, I see."

I showed her the cane and then tilted the handle toward her.

"Is that—"

"A *Hexarthrius rhinoceros rhinoceros*. Oom Maarten had it made for me as a gift."

A bark of laughter escaped her lips. "Only you would have a monstrous bug as a handle on a cane."

More than surviving the eruption of Krakatau, more than surviving multiple giant waves, more than learning to walk again, more than moving to the Netherlands, more than everything I had so recently accomplished and overcome, I thought my friendship with Brigitta would be the thing Vader and Tante Greet would be most proud of.

My personal evolution astonished even me. *"He has great power of adapting his habits to new conditions of life,"* Mr. Charles Darwin wrote in *The Descent of Man*, but until recently, I never thought I was capable of much changing. I didn't think it necessary. I thought I knew everything I needed to get by in the world.

Vader had been right, though. I did need people. I needed Brigitta in the jungle. I needed complete strangers at the hospital. I needed Oom Maarten, period.

Tante Greet had been right, too. Brigitta and I hadn't seen each other in more than a year, but there was no awkwardness between us. We picked up right where we left off.

I linked arms with my friend, and we shuffled after Oom Maarten. "I have so much to tell you."

Author's Note

Like many works of historical fiction, this story was inspired by true events. In this case, Krakatau, a volcanic island located in the Sunda Strait between Java and Sumatra, really did erupt on August 26 and 27 in 1883. If you have heard of this event at all, you may be more familiar with the name Krakatoa, which is how the name was misspelled in telegraphs in the aftermath of the disaster. Krakatau is the Indonesian name of the island.

Most of the characters in this story are entirely creations of my own imagination. However, a few are based on historical figures.

A man named Mr. C. Schuit ran the Hotel Anjer and was the inspiration for Mr. Caspar Schuyler. In addition to running the hotel, Mr. Schuit was also an agent for Lloyd's of London, an insurance company, and reported information of potential interest back to the home office in London.

Thomas Burkart, Brigitta's father, is inspired by Thomas Buijs who was in fact the Assistant Resident of Anjer and lived in a fine brick house on the water. Although the Burkart family in the story is fictional, the real Thomas Buijs did die in the catastrophe.

The Brinckerhoff family is based upon the Beyerinck family, who lived in Ketimbang and lost their youngest child in the disaster. Although I have been unable to determine if the Beyerincks left the

Dutch East Indies or not, the last sentence Mrs. Brinckerhoff says to Katrien in the hospital ("However cruel nature may be, Katrien, and however mysterious God's ways, He did save us. His name be praised.") is paraphrased from the real Mrs. Beyerinck's diary. During the course of my research, a translated, abridged version was available online. Unfortunately, it has since been taken down.

While the real Mrs. Beyerinck's account of Krakatau's eruption greatly informed my writing, the relationships I created between the Brinckerhoffs and the Courtlandt family, and all related dialogue, are entirely fiction.

Mr. Charles Darwin, whose words fill Katrien's thoughts and permeate her dialogue, was very much a real person. His book *On the Origin of Species; Or the Preservation of Favoured Races in the Struggle for Life*, published in 1859, revolutionized science. His theory of natural selection—the idea that all life around us evolved from a few simple organisms over millions of years—was, and still is, controversial. His suggestion that the world was much older than religious scholars, preachers and most ordinary people believed, and that life was not created by God, caused tremendous upheaval throughout society. When Darwin published *The Descent of Man* in 1871, he postulated that humans evolved from apes. This theory has proved to be even more controversial and problematic and continues to be a lightning rod to this day.

The Dutch had a physical presence in what is now Indonesia since 1602. That was the year the United East India Company (known as the VOC) was granted a twenty-one-year monopoly in the spice trade. In addition to trading in spices, the VOC had the authority to wage war, treat convicts as it saw fit, negotiate treaties, coin money and even establish other colonies.

Its first permanent trading post was established in Banten, Java, in 1603. Over time, the VOC expanded its influence in the region by establishing additional trading posts throughout Java and defeating both the British and the Portuguese, who also had economic interests there, in various battles in the region.

The VOC eventually went bankrupt, and the Dutch government took over the colony in 1800. With few exceptions, much of Indonesia remained under Dutch control until World War II when Japanese forces invaded Java in 1942. When the war ended, the Dutch tried to reestablish their domination of the colony. However, Indonesians had long wanted to control their own country and seized this opportunity to do so. In the story, Raharjo makes it clear to Katrien that the Dutch should not control the destinies of the native population. Katrien, herself, has had an inkling of unrest since the time she was small and first overheard adults discussing fighting in Aceh, a region in Sumatra, where war between the Sultanate and the Netherlands went on for decades.

Indonesia proclaimed its independence in August 1945 after the end of World War II. Fighting between pro-Indonesian and pro-Dutch forces continued for four years until the Dutch finally acknowledged Indonesia's independence in 1949. However, many reminders of Dutch influence remain. Buildings erected by the Dutch still stand. Even some of the language remains—Slamet's word *ya* is the Indonesian version of the Dutch *ja*.

The history of the Dutch presence and influence in Indonesia is long, complicated and tempestuous. I have not even scratched the surface in this description, but I hope it provides a little more context. I have suggested further reading about it in the Resources section of this author's note.

Finally, the eruption of Krakatau marks one of the first natural disasters to receive worldwide media coverage relatively soon after the event transpired. The fast coverage was possible thanks to the invention and spread of the telegraph.

In the 1860s, engineers began connecting the world via underwater telegraph cables. Eventually Java joined the rest of Asia and Europe through underwater wires. These were connected to the United States and other countries. Messages from Java, which used to take weeks or months by ship to reach the Netherlands, could now be relayed to Europe in a matter of a few days. That was close to instantaneous in 1883. When Katrien marvels at this technology, she does so with good reason: the telegraph was revolutionizing communication worldwide.

Accounts of the eruption itself differ among survivors. Some described the smoke coming from Krakatau as black; others swore it was white. The final blast from Krakatau on the morning of August 27 was heard 3,000 miles away on the island of Rodrigues in the Indian Ocean. People there thought it was cannon fire from a nearby ship. Although it seems incredible, given how loud the sound was elsewhere, not everyone near the center of the eruption heard the explosion. This is most likely due to the pressure wave generated by the blast. The pressure wave traveled at 675 miles per hour and hit many people's ears silently. In several instances, sailors on ships nearest the explosion in the Sunda Strait had their eardrums ruptured. Barograph readings from all over the world showed that the pressure wave circled the globe seven times before dissipating.

Krakatau was an uninhabited island. Tourists from Batavia did go there throughout the summer before the eruption in late August, along with several scientists and geologists. The last boat left the island on August 12, just two weeks before the disaster.

Unlike the stereotypical image of a volcano, Krakatau did not erupt with a river of lava moving down the side of the mountain. The actual eruption was similar to that of Mount St. Helens in Washington State in 1980, with a blast of ash shooting into the sky. It is estimated that the blast from Krakatau went almost thirty miles into the air. After that, a fiery rain of ash fell in Ketimbang, where the Brinckerhoff/Beyerinck family lived, killing about one thousand people. These were the only direct victims of the explosion itself. Although I describe fire falling in Anjer in this story, this phenomenon did not actually occur there. It is a bit of authorial manipulation of the facts to bring even more drama to the tale.

Official Dutch records put the death toll at 36,417. However, some historians believe that almost 120,000 people died in the disaster. While the precise number may never be known, it is clear that most were killed by the tsunamis, which are estimated to have been between 95 and 150 feet high. The towns of Anjer and Merak were completely destroyed, and it is true that a giant piece of coral did obliterate the Anjer lighthouse, as Katrien and Brigitta saw. Although the lighthouse keeper survived, his family did not.

The tsunamis traveled far, too, growing weaker the farther they went. Small waves were even noted in the English Channel. For up to a year after the eruption, there were reports of bodies floating in the ocean and washing up on the coasts of Africa.

Parts of Java were never repopulated after the eruption of Krakatau, including the area south of Anjer. This region is now the Ujung Kulon National Park, and it is the only place on Earth where the critically endangered Javan rhinoceros can be found. As of this writing, there may be only forty of these creatures left in the world. None are in captivity.

The force of the explosions destroyed most of the island of Krakatau, obliterating the volcanic mountain and creating the dust and ash that fell over the region. Underwater, however, eruptions continued. In 1927, a new island broke the surface of the water in the footprint of what vanished that August morning more than forty years before. This island is called Anak Krakatau, which means "child of Krakatau." It continues to grow, and perhaps one day will rival its parent in size and power.

Sara K Joiner
May 2015

RESOURCES

How do you write a book about a place you've never been and a time that has long since passed?

Research!

Fortunately, I'm a librarian, so I knew just how to find information about the topics I needed. I relied on lots of books and Internet sites, plus one movie.

The movie was *The Impossible*, directed by J. A. Bayona (2012), and it is based on one family's experience during the 2004 tsunami in Southeast Asia. The astounding Hollywood effects helped me visualize a tsunami more clearly in my head.

Here are some of the best print resources I used in the almost five years it took to write this book. Although some of these titles are older and do not deal directly with the eruption of Krakatau, I used them to better understand how conditions would have been in Anjer during and after the eruption and tsunamis. Books written specifically for younger readers are marked with an asterisk.

*Adamson, Thomas K. *Tsunamis*. Mankato, MN: Capstone Press, 2006.

*Aylesworth, Thomas G., and Virginia L. Aylesworth. *The Mount St. Helens Disaster*. Danbury, CT: Franklin Watts, 1983.

Beers, Susan-Jane. *Jamu: The Ancient Indonesian Art of Herbal Healing*. Riverside, NJ: Tuttle Publishing, 2012.

*Benoit, Peter. *The Krakatau Eruption*. New York: Children's Press, 2011.

*Bredeson, Carmen. *Fiery Volcano: The Eruption of Mount St. Helens*. Berkeley Heights, NJ: Enslow Publishers, 2012.

Bullard, Fred M. *Volcanoes of the Earth*. Austin: University of Texas Press, 1984, second revised edition.

*Fradin, Judy, and Dennis Fradin. *Volcanoes: Witness to Disaster*. Washington, DC: National Geographic, 2007.

*Matthews, Rupert. *The Eruption of Krakatoa*. New York: The Bookwright Press, 1989.

McGuire, Bill, and Christopher Kilburn. *Volcanoes of the World*. San Diego, CA: Thunder Bay Press, 1997.

Merrilees, Scott. *Batavia in Nineteenth-Century Photographs.* Brooklyn, NY: Archipelago Press. 2000.

*Morris, Ann, and Heidi Larson. *Tsunami: Helping Each Other.* Minneapolis, MN: Millbrook Press, 2005.

*Nardo, Don. *Krakatoa.* San Diego, CA: Lucent Books, 1990.

*Orr, Tamra. *Indonesia.* New York: Children's Press, 2005.

Sanna, Ellyn. *Nature's Wrath: Surviving Natural Disasters.* Broomall, PA: Mason Crest, 2009.

*Stewart, Gail B. *Catastophe in Southern Asia: The Tsunami of 2004.* Detroit, MI: Thomson Gale, 2005.

*Winchester, Simon. *The Day the World Exploded: The Earthshaking Catastrophe at Krakatoa.* New York: HarperCollins, 2008.

Winchester, Simon. *Krakatoa: The Day the World Exploded: August 27, 1883.* New York: HarperCollins, 2003.

In addition to the print resources, I also found helpful information on the Internet. Some of the most useful sites I found are listed below (all links were active as of this writing).

ARKive
www.arkive.org

The Dutch East Indies in Photographs, 1860–1940—Collections—Memory of the Netherlands
www.geheugenvannederland.nl/?/en/collecties/nederlands-indie_in_fotos,_1860-1940

Max Havelaar 150 jaar: An Album on Flickr
www.flickr.com/photos/nationaalarchief/sets/721576239207
74561/

Project Gutenberg: *Holland: The History of the Netherlands* by
Thomas Colley Grattan
www.gutenberg.org/cache/epub/10583/pg10583.html

Project Gutenberg: *The Descent of Man* by Charles Darwin
www.gutenberg.org/cache/epub/2300/pg2300.html

Project Gutenberg: *On the Origin of Species* by Charles Darwin
www.gutenberg.org/files/1228/1228-h/1228-h.htm

Tropenmuseum: Search for Anjer
collectie.tropenmuseum.nl/default.aspx?idx=ALL&field
=*&search=anjer

You Tube: Tsunami Coming Japan 2011
www.youtube.com/watch?v=LbscSyy0Oic